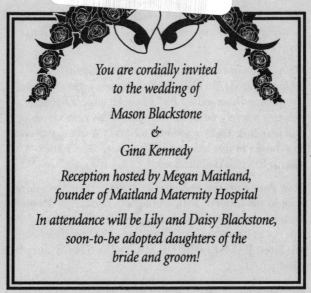

You are cordially invited
to the wedding of

Mason Blackstone
&
Gina Kennedy

Reception hosted by Megan Maitland,
founder of Maitland Maternity Hospital

In attendance will be Lily and Daisy Blackstone,
soon-to-be adopted daughters of the
bride and groom!

Harlequin American Romance's
MAITLAND MATERNITY series continues with
Jacqueline Diamond's delightful *I Do! I Do!*

Dear Reader,

Welcome to another joy-filled month of heart, home and happiness from Harlequin American Romance! We're pleased to bring you four new stories filled with people you'll always remember and romance you'll never forget.

We've got more excitement for you this month as MAITLAND MATERNITY continues with Jacqueline Diamond's *I Do! I Do!* An elusive bachelor marries a lovely nurse for the sake of his twin nieces— will love turn their house into a home? Watch for twelve new books in this heartwarming series, starting next month from Harlequin Books!

How does a proper preacher's daughter tame the wildest man in the county? With a little help from a few Montana matchmakers determined to repopulate their town! Sparks are sure to fly in *The Playboy's Own Miss Prim*, the latest BACHELORS OF SHOTGUN RIDGE story by Mindy Neff!

An expectant mother, blinded from an accident, learns that the heart recognizes what the eye cannot see in Lisa Bingham's touching novel *Man Behind the Voice*. And when a little boy refuses to leave his ranch home, his mother must make a deal with the brooding, sexy new owner. Don't miss Carol Grace's delightful *Family Tree*.

Spice up your summer days with the best of Harlequin American Romance!

Warm wishes,

Melissa Jeglinski
Associate Senior Editor

I Do! I Do!

JACQUELINE DIAMOND

HARLEQUIN®

TORONTO • NEW YORK • LONDON
AMSTERDAM • PARIS • SYDNEY • HAMBURG
STOCKHOLM • ATHENS • TOKYO • MILAN • MADRID
PRAGUE • WARSAW • BUDAPEST • AUCKLAND

Special thanks and acknowledgment are given
to Jacqueline Diamond for her contribution to the
Maitland Maternity series.

With special thanks to Marcia Holman

ISBN 0-373-16833-0

I DO! I DO!

Visit us at www.eHarlequin.com

Printed in U.S.A.

ABOUT THE AUTHOR

Jacqueline Diamond was born in Menard, Texas, a small town in the region in which the fictional Blackstone Bar Ranch is located. Her father, Maurice, was the town's doctor and made house calls to ranches.

In October 2000, Harlequin Duets will publish her book *Designer Genes*. It's set in the fictional town of Nowhere Junction, in the same area of Texas.

Jackie now makes her home in Southern California and likes to hear from readers at P.O. Box 1315, Brea, CA 92822.

Books by Jacqueline Diamond

HARLEQUIN AMERICAN ROMANCE

79—THE DREAM NEVER DIES
196—AN UNEXPECTED MAN
218—UNLIKELY PARTNERS
239—THE CINDERELLA DARE
270—CAPERS AND RAINBOWS
279—A GHOST OF A CHANCE
315—FLIGHT OF MAGIC
351—BY LEAPS AND BOUNDS
406—OLD DREAMS, NEW DREAMS
446—THE TROUBLE WITH TERRY
491—A DANGEROUS GUY
583—THE RUNAWAY BRIDE
615—YOURS, MINE AND OURS
631—THE COWBOY AND THE HEIRESS

642—ONE HUSBAND TOO MANY
645—DEAR LONELY IN L.A....
674—MILLION-DOLLAR MOMMY
687—DADDY WARLOCK
716—A REAL-LIVE SHEIKH
734—THE COWBOY & THE SHOTGUN BRIDE
763—LET'S MAKE A BABY!
791—ASSIGNMENT: GROOM!
804—MISTLETOE DADDY
833—I DO! I DO!

HARLEQUIN INTRIGUE

435—AND THE BRIDE VANISHES
512—HIS SECRET SON
550—CAPTURED BY A SHEIKH

CAST OF CHARACTERS

Mason Blackstone—A rancher doesn't go from herding cows to changing diapers overnight—not without the right woman by his side.

Gina Kennedy—The virginal nurse had a crush on the sexy rancher. She'd do anything to be his wife—including agree to a temporary marriage.

Daisy and Lily Blackstone—Orphaned newborn twins, they found a good home with their uncle Mason. But would they be able to grow up in his loving care?

Margaret and Stuart Waldman—Mason's sister and brother-in-law wanted to adopt the baby girls for the wrong reasons.

Megan Maitland—The founder of Maitland Maternity opened up her family's home to host a very special wedding....

Chapter One

When she got to the clinic, he might be waiting. Or on his way, driving from his ranch in the pickup truck.

Gina Kennedy's step quickened as she hurried down Mayfair Avenue in the early morning quiet. Her shift in the intermediate-care nursery didn't start for half an hour. What was her hurry?

His dark eyes would warm when he came in. The other nurses would sneak glances at him, but his smile would be for Gina alone.

On a humid July day like this, Austin, Texas, felt more like the Old South than the Wild West. Gina could feel her hair wilting, even though the full heat wouldn't hit for hours yet.

She glanced at her reflection in a shop window. The straight, light-blond hair that brushed the tops of her shoulders was a bit damp, but holding its own thanks to a heavy dose of mousse.

Critically, she examined the way the nurse's uniform clung to her figure. Gina knew that some of her friends envied her narrow waistline and well-proportioned bust, but she'd always wished she were taller. Tall enough to measure up to a big, brooding man.

He exuded power. It wasn't only the intensity of his gaze, but the way he dwarfed everyone around him.

Yet he handled those tiny babies with such incredible tenderness that she couldn't help wondering what kind of lover he would be.

Gina gripped her purse strap. Why on earth was she daydreaming about Mason Blackstone? This was the first time in her twenty-nine years that she'd fantasized about a man. Why did it have to be someone beyond her reach?

From the Austin Eats Diner, the smell of bacon, pancakes and maple syrup wafted toward her. Gina smiled. She would like to see Mason tackle a meal like that. No doubt he'd make short work of it.

To maintain her trim figure, she stuck to cereal or whole-wheat toast for breakfast. Still, she liked to see a man eat, a man who earned his Texas-size appetite through old-fashioned hard work.

Mason's ranch was a two-hour drive northwest of here, he'd told her. Most nights during the past two months, he'd made the trip back there to ensure that everything was functioning properly.

Once in a while, though, he stayed over at a hotel in Austin. He'd never suggested that they get together after hours, which, Gina told herself, was a good thing. The two of them were wildly ill-suited. Besides, it would be inappropriate as long as she was caring for his premature twin nieces.

She would like to see him polish off a steak and potatoes just once, though. The possibility that he might choose her for dessert sent a small thrill down her spine.

Foolish make-believe, that's what she was indulging in. A rough-and-ready guy like Mason needed a sturdy ranch woman who knew one end of a horse from the other. Once he took the little orphaned girls home, he would have nothing in common with a sheltered, daydreaming neo-natal nurse whose brief relationships with men always ended when she refused to hop into bed with them.

Gina walked alongside the sweeping front driveway that led to the Maitland Maternity Clinic. After graduating from nursing school at the University of Texas here in Austin, she was lucky to have landed a job at the modern, family-run facility that served rich and poor women alike.

In her half-dozen years on the staff, she'd come to think of the clinic as home. She always looked forward to coming to work each day, more than ever in the two months since Mason and his little nieces had become fixtures in the nursery.

He hadn't arrived yet this morning, she saw. Usually, his extended pickup truck with a covered bed loomed over the other vehicles in the parking lot. Still, he might pull in at any minute.

Heading for the employee entrance, she hurried inside to tuck her purse into her locker. In the corridor, she was about to dodge by Ford Carrington, the clinic's pediatric surgeon, when he said, "Miss Kennedy? Could I speak with you a moment?"

Although he was handsome, with a reputation as a play-boy, Gina knew him as a dedicated doctor, one who rarely had occasion to speak to her. "Yes, Doctor?" she said.

"I wanted to say I think you've done a superb job with the Blackstone twins." Ford paused as if mentally review-ing the case. "Daisy's made a much faster recovery from her hernia operation than I expected. From what Katie Toper says, your TLC has helped compensate for the tragic loss of their mother."

"Their uncle's the one who deserves the credit." Gina didn't believe she deserved praise for doing what came naturally, although she appreciated the good word from

Katie, a fellow nurse who often assisted Dr. Carrington. "Besides, there's something special about those girls."

"Don't sell yourself short, Gina," he said. "You've helped give those little girls a fine start in life."

"Thanks, Dr. Carrington." It was almost seven, and after he turned away, she had to hurry to reach the nursery on time. It was worth it, though, to receive praise from a man she respected so highly.

For the last three years, Gina had been assigned to the intensive and intermediate-care nurseries. Due to the low staff-to-patient ratio, she had time to grow attached to her little charges, but none had affected her as much as Daisy and her twin sister, Lily.

Maybe it was the fact that their father had died in a car crash before they were born, and their mother had succumbed to her injuries less than a day after giving birth. Maybe it was because the little girls, struggling for life despite their fragility, reminded Gina in some ways of herself.

They seemed like the daughters she'd hoped someday to have but perhaps never would. Her future was a growing concern as she neared her thirtieth birthday, less than a month away, without a boyfriend in sight.

Gina pushed aside personal concerns as she entered the staff area of the nursery. Katie was already there, updating charts from the night shift.

"How is everything?" Gina asked.

"Quiet." Her friend smiled. "Thank goodness. The Lopez girl is going home today and the Simmons boy's temperature is back to normal."

"By the way, thanks for putting in the good word with Dr. Carrington," Gina said when Katie finished.

"He spoke to you?" The other nurse waited, as if hoping for more.

"He complimented me on showing affection to Daisy and Lily. It would have been hard not to!"

"How did he look?" Katie probed. "He didn't get enough sleep night before last. Did you notice any dark circles under his eyes?"

"He looked perfect. As always."

Katie sighed. It was well known among the nurses that she had a long-standing crush on the surgeon. His chosen companions, however, were stunning model types, not down-to-earth nurses.

Gina couldn't help but sympathize. Not that she had a crush on Mason Blackstone. She was too practical, she told herself firmly.

Besides being her opposite in many ways, he'd never even hinted at wanting a relationship. So soon after the deaths of his brother and sister-in-law, it was unlikely he thought of her as anything more than a caretaker for his nieces.

After she pinned back her hair, scrubbed and put on a sterile gown, Gina went into the nursery. She was assigned to four patients, including Lily and Daisy.

"Good morning." She smiled down at Daisy. "Let's check those bandages and weigh you, shall we?"

The next half hour passed quickly, taken up with checking medications, weighing, feeding and changing all four babies. Matters were complicated by the fact that, before being handled, they had to be detached from monitors that warned if their respiration or heartbeat ran too low or too high.

As she fed Lily, Gina regarded a small bare patch on the baby's crown, where, like Daisy, she'd been fed intravenously during her first few weeks. It seemed a shame that the girls' earliest photos would be marred. Still, it was a minor flaw, and the hair would grow out quickly.

"You won't even remember it by prom night," she assured the baby.

"What won't she remember by prom night?"

The baritone voice startled her out of her reverie. How had Mason heard her, all the way across the room?

"I was teasing her about her bald spot." Gina tried to sound normal, although, as usual, Mason made her breath come faster.

Against the pastel decor of the nursery, he loomed large. The brawny chest and shoulders were developed as only a cowboy's could be, strong enough to rope a calf or dig a post hole. As he reached to put on a sterile gown, she glimpsed a yoked shirt tucked into jeans, a leather belt dominated by a Mexican silver buckle, and a pair of polished dress boots.

He removed his Stetson and set it aside, crown side down. Thick black hair, a testament to his Native American heritage, sprang up defiantly.

Gina drank in every inch of his appearance. Soon, he and these precious babies would vanish from her life. Not too soon, though, she hoped.

"You're already planning their senior prom?" Mason gave her a rueful smile as he crossed the nursery. "I can hardly think beyond how often to feed them and how many diapers to buy!"

She finished feeding Lily, noted how many ounces she had taken, then rolled the baby onto her stomach to burp her. At scarcely four and a half pounds each, the babies were still a bit fragile to hold against the shoulder.

"You'll do fine," she said. "Also, didn't you say your housekeeper has experience with babies?"

"Bonita can manage, but she isn't an expert like you." He offered a finger to his niece, who gummed it happily. "May I take her?"

"Of course." As Gina guided the tiny baby into his grasp, their hands touched. The brief contact sent heat flaring through her.

She struggled not to show how profoundly this man affected her. It would only embarrass them both. Maybe it was a good thing he didn't feel the same way.

Gina had vowed long ago to save herself for the man she would someday marry. As the prospect of marriage grew more and more remote, she sometimes doubted her resolve. What she didn't need was a man like Mason tempting her.

Lily nestled into her uncle's arms and stared up at him. Although the baby hadn't started smiling yet, Gina knew her well enough to read the alert interest that indicated the infant was emotionally engaged. That was a technical way of saying she loved her uncle.

As for Mason, his emotions were written across his tanned, high-boned face as he returned his niece's gaze. There was enough warmth shining there to light the dark corners of the universe.

Gina snapped back to duty as the nursery door opened and Dr. Ephraim Rogers entered. The graying pediatrician scrubbed, donned a sterile gown and came into the main nursery.

By then, she had the charts ready for him. They discussed each of the other two babies, agreed on some minor changes in their care, and then moved to Lily and Daisy.

"You certainly are a devoted uncle, Mr. Blackstone." The doctor shook hands with him. "These girls are doing well. Have you given any thought to who will care for them when they're released?"

"I will," he said. "With the help of my housekeeper."

The doctor nodded. "She should come into the hospital

to learn infant CPR.'' Mason had already undergone his training. ''Also, we'd like to show her how to use the apnea monitors we'll be sending home with the babies.''

''Monitors?'' His forehead creased. ''No one mentioned this before.''

''It's a precaution,'' Dr. Rogers said. ''It's much simpler than these devices they use in the hospital. Just a belt that wraps around their chest. I can understand your concern, Mr. Blackstone, and I know you live out on a ranch. Aren't there any female relatives who could take these girls?''

Mason drew himself up to his full height, which gave him the advantage over the doctor. ''I can take care of them. My late sister-in-law's parents aren't in good health, and besides, I consider Lily and Daisy to be my own daughters. I'll bring my housekeeper here for training.''

''In that case, I'm going to write a release order for tomorrow,'' the doctor said. ''Congratulations, Mr. Blackstone. It's time to take your daughters home.''

With another handshake, he departed. Mason stood staring after him.

Gina was grateful that the girls had been pronounced well enough to leave. And devastated that she would never see them, or their uncle, again.

HE'D BEEN AWAITING this good news eagerly for weeks. Now that it had come, Mason felt a shock of dismay.

How would he sustain these tiny girls without the assistance of trained medical staff? He knew his own skills and capabilities as a rancher, whether it came to managing finance, tending an injured calf or repairing anything from a bridle to a pickup truck.

But babies? What if something went wrong? He could never forgive himself.

It also meant that, after tomorrow, he would never see Gina Kennedy again. Of course, he knew she was too delicate for ranch life. And that he wasn't husband material.

Yet he'd grown to depend on the quiet strength revealed in her blue eyes. Each day, he felt he knew her a little better, until it seemed that she had been a part of his life forever.

It made no sense. Her upbringing, as she'd described it one day while they were chatting, was so different from his that she might as well have come from another planet. He was a down-home Texas man, through and through. She had an air of sophistication that had developed as her engineer father moved the family to Kuwait, Alaska and Japan before settling in Austin.

Mason ought to be glad he was free to take the girls home. Instead, he kept longing to spend more time with Gina, to touch her soft hair, to grip that tiny waist and lift her onto his lap, to kiss her until time stood still.

She replaced Lily in her bassinet. "That's wonderful news."

"Is it?" he asked.

"What do you mean?" Some emotion he couldn't identify fleeted across her face and vanished almost immediately. "If you're worried, you could arrange for a private nurse. There must be someone in the town near your ranch. What's it called—Horseshoe Bend?"

"I wouldn't need to go that far for help. The girls will have a ready-made family on the ranch," Mason said, to reassure himself as much as her. "Some of my cousins live there."

She gave him a fleeting smile. "Does your housekeeper have children?"

"Actually, no," he admitted. "She never married. But

she raised one of her nephews, and she takes care of her mother. Nana lives with her in the village.''

''In Horseshoe Bend?''

Mason shook his head. ''The village is a cluster of houses on my property, just down the way from the big house. My cousin Ed—he's the foreman—and his family have their own house. So do a couple of ranch hands, and Bonita and her mother.''

''Aren't there other children?'' she asked. ''For the girls to play with when they get older?''

He hadn't thought beyond their infancy. Certainly playmates hadn't entered his mind. ''Not at the moment,'' he admitted. ''I can look for a family man though. I'll need to hire someone to take my brother's place.''

A wave of pain hit him, one that hurt no less for having become familiar during the past two months. No one could replace his brother, not in any sense of the word.

Gina dragged him back from his dark thoughts. ''Get plenty of sleep tonight.'' She took out a clean crib sheet, frowned at what appeared to be a freshly changed bassinet, and put the sheet back in the cabinet. ''You'll need it.''

She was, he realized, avoiding eye contact. He wished he knew what was upsetting her.

''I can manage without sleep if I have to,'' he said. ''I've done it before.''

''Not with two premature infants to take care of, you haven't!''

Mason caught her shoulders. It was the only way to hold her still so he could address her. ''Don't tell me that you doubt me, Gina. Not you of all people.''

Trapped, she raised her face toward his. He'd never seen the blue of her eyes so brilliant and glittery. It was, he realized, the effect of tears.

"You're going to miss them, aren't you?" he asked gruffly.

She swallowed hard and nodded.

"You could…come and visit." Even as he said it, he knew it wasn't feasible. "Besides, a beautiful woman like you will have babies of your own. I'm surprised you don't already."

"Haven't met the right man yet, I guess." She ducked away.

At least he understood what was bothering her. It was Lily and Daisy. She'd grown to love them, just as he had.

Did she react this way when all of her patients left? He wished he could read her moods better.

"Mr. Blackstone?" One of the other nurses signaled to him. "Eleanor Maitland wants to talk to you."

"Much obliged." Through the glass window of the nursery, he saw the hospital administrator waving from the corridor.

A daughter of Maitland Maternity founder Megan Maitland, Miss Elly—as he'd heard her teasingly called in a reference to the TV series *Dallas*—was only twenty-five, the same age as the hospital. She wore glasses and tailored suits that made her look a bit older than her age, but not by much.

"Maybe she has some words of advice about the girls," Gina said. "After all, she's a twin herself."

"I guess I'll find out." Regretfully, he turned away. He wished Gina could come into the hall with him. Heck, he wished she could come all the way to the ranch with him.

There was no point in deluding himself. Mason couldn't picture the doll-like blonde living on the Blackstone Bar Ranch. And why would a pretty girl like her want to tear herself away from Austin's music clubs and, no doubt, her many admirers?

On the way out of the nursery, he shrugged off his gown and dropped it in the laundry container, then collected his hat. Elly Maitland met him at the door.

"Congratulations," she said. "Dr. Rogers tells me the girls are going home."

"Yes, ma'am." Mason gripped the hat in both hands. Give him a stray heifer to rope any day over the need to carry on polite chitchat.

"You know, there's a good chance the press will be here tomorrow when they're released," she said. "There's been a lot of interest in the twins."

The deaths of both parents, orphaning the little girls, had stirred the public's curiosity. Also, there'd been interest in the fact that two sets of twins had been delivered at the clinic on the same day.

Despite his absorption with his family's double tragedy and his nieces' medical progress, Mason had noticed the Winston boys, Henry and Hayden, and how their mother hovered over them. He hadn't seen the father, though, and hoped matters had improved between the couple since the boys had gone home.

Elly seemed to be waiting for a response, so he said, "I'm aware of the media interest, ma'am."

"If you like, we can arrange for you to leave by a rear entrance," she said.

He shrugged. "I figure I can weather a few gabby reporters."

"That's fine, then." She cleared her throat. "There is one other thing, Mr. Blackstone."

"If it's about the bill—"

"No, no," she said. "The paperwork's gone through fine."

He was glad to hear it. Every spare minute of the past

two months had been spent on one form of paperwork or another.

Through the glass, he could see some other parents arriving in the nursery, asking questions of Gina. She answered them in the same kind, steady manner she used with Mason himself.

After tomorrow, he and the girls would be gone. But for Gina, everything would continue, undisturbed. For some reason, that prospect irked him.

"Mr. Blackstone?" Elly said. "Are you all right?"

"What?"

"You seem distracted."

"I'm a mite tired." That was the truth. "It's a long drive between here and my ranch."

"Well, that's about to end, isn't it?" she said. "One way or another."

"Excuse me?" He didn't like the sound of that phrase.

"I just received a phone call from Stuart Waldman," she said. "That's what I needed to talk to you about."

"My brother-in-law called you?" The Dallas attorney was married to Mason's older sister, Margaret.

After Rance and Amy's funerals in Horseshoe Bend, Stuart had offered his legal services to deal with the couple's estate. Neither of the Waldmans had visited Austin to see their nieces, however.

"Apparently someone notified him, as the attorney to your brother's estate, that Lily and Daisy are being released," she said. "He and your sister will be here tomorrow."

"Why?" Mason hoped he didn't sound as irritable as he felt. Eight years his senior, Marge still regarded him as her kid brother. Furthermore, since childhood she'd had a way of hogging the limelight, performing a small amount of work and expecting a large amount of credit.

"He said your sister intends to raise the babies herself."

Mason's gut tightened. He'd gone through so much with these little girls. What the heck did Marge think she was doing?

If she loved them even a tenth as much as he did, she'd have come to Austin long ago. She'd have camped out, as he had, unable to bear missing a single day with them.

"My sister has no right to these children," he said.

"According to your brother-in-law, she believes she could provide them with the best home," Elly said mildly.

"The best home is the one where they're loved." He couldn't keep an edge from his voice.

"I won't disagree with you," the administrator said.

"Did Stuart happen to mention why they never brought this up until now?"

"According to him, your sister needed time to 'clear the decks' of other involvements," she said. "Still that wouldn't prevent her from picking up a telephone and calling you, would it?"

Mason knew quite well why his sister hadn't contacted him directly—because she didn't want to give him a chance to speak bluntly. Acknowledging painful truths had never been Margaret's favorite activity.

"She wants to take charge and be the center of attention," he said. "In a few months, she'll get tired of playing nursemaid and turn them over to a series of nannies. That may sound uncharitable on my part, Miss Maitland, but I've known my sister for a long time."

"You understand that, no matter where my sympathies lie, I can't get involved." She tapped a pen against her clipboard. "Mr. Waldman asked me to delay the girls' release for another day, to give them more time to get here. However, there's no medical reason to hold them, so I declined.''

"Much obliged," Mason said.

"It was the least I could do."

As the administrator departed, the full impact of this development hit him. He might lose the girls. If Margaret was determined to take Lily and Daisy, she would have the odds stacked in her favor.

A lawyer for a husband. An elegant home in Dallas. Three nearly grown kids of her own as proof that she knew how to raise children. A judge wouldn't understand that, to Margaret, the baby girls were ornaments to show off, while Mason loved them with all his heart.

He must have been scowling when he returned to the nursery, because several people scooted out of his way. Gina didn't budge. "What's wrong?"

He became aware of the other nurses and parents around them. It was too personal a subject to discuss here.

"There's a problem I'd like to discuss with you," he said. "But not here. Could I take you out to dinner after your shift?"

Mason caught his breath, realizing that he'd just asked her on a date. Of course, she would refuse—politely and sweetly, but firmly. Why should she agree to spend time with him?

"Something's wrong that affects the girls? Of course," she said.

Suddenly it wasn't a date, just a conference about the twins. He wished he didn't feel so disappointed.

Chapter Two

Across one of the plank-style tables at Lone Star's, a steak house down the street from Maitland Maternity, Gina studied Mason.

She hadn't been able to finish her barbecued chicken, although it was excellent. The huge portions, however, didn't prevent him from making short work of a platter of steak and fries, along with a salad. He ate exactly the way she'd imagined he would.

He also managed to tell her quite a bit about himself, and especially his relationship with his sister. Until now, Gina had known Mason primarily as Lily and Daisy's uncle. It was intriguing to glimpse the larger scope of his life and his family.

Margaret, he'd explained, was eight years older than him and had already married and left the Blackstone Bar ranch when their mother died. Mason, who'd been twelve at the time, had helped raise Rance, five years his junior, and had assisted their father on the ranch.

In Dallas, Marge kept a busy schedule. She headed several social committees and ran a charity art gallery and craft shop.

"Why do you suppose she wants to go back to changing diapers and staying up half the night for two babies she's never met?'' Gina asked. ''She'd have to give up most of her other activities. And it doesn't get any easier when they're toddlers, or teenagers, either! This is a twenty-year commitment.''

She stopped, surprised by her outburst. She didn't usually state her opinions so boldly.

Mason spread his hands in a gesture of frustration. ''Maybe because she knows she can win. What would I say to a judge? 'Your honor, my brother and I were so close, he and his wife meant everything to me. Their children were going to be my children, too. Now that they're gone, these girls are all I have left.' That's not a strong argument.''

''It ought to be!'' Gina said.

''She'll say she's better suited in every way to raise the girls, and the judge will agree,'' he concluded. ''I have to come up with a counterargument. That's where I could use your advice.''

''I can testify that they never visited the nursery,'' she said. ''You were there every day.''

''It might not be enough,'' he said. ''Before I knew for certain that Amy's parents didn't want the children, I talked to a lawyer about custody issues. He told me judges have a hard time weighing intangibles like bonding, so they take a by-the-numbers approach. Margaret can list a lot more advantages than I can.''

''Can't you reason with her?'' she asked. ''The direct approach is sometimes the best one.''

The waitress stopped to take their dessert order, apple pie for him, sherbet for Gina. When they were alone again, he said, ''Reason with her? I tried that this afternoon, on the phone. Margaret didn't even hear what I was saying. To her, I'm still her kid brother.''

It was hard to imagine how anyone could see Mason

as a kid. From across the booth, Gina could feel the heat of the man and smell the leathery fragrance he exuded.

"I wish I could help," she said. "With all their activities, the Waldmans don't sound like ideal parents for two medically fragile infants."

"Medically fragile?" he repeated.

She hadn't meant to alarm him. "I don't mean that they're in imminent danger. But they need extra care."

"Like attaching the monitors." He spoke to himself more than to her.

"Yes. Someone will need to check their weight gains, and take their temperatures, and log how much they're eating," she explained. "It's not the sort of thing a person can do easily in between running a store and organizing a charity event."

"It's not the sort of thing a person can do while running a ranch, either." He shook his head. "From a judge's point of view, this looks hopeless."

To Gina, the difference was clear. "You've got a full-time housekeeper, someone you've known for years, who's dedicated to you. And you won't get tired of the girls after a few months. You've shown you're willing to sacrifice for them."

Their dessert came. Mason stared at his apple pie. "You know what I want them to have?" he said.

"Love?" Gina guessed.

"Of course." He gave her a weary smile. "Also, a sense of belonging. Memories, traditions. The kind of thing you get on a ranch or in a small community."

She toyed with her sherbet spoon. "I wish I'd had that experience. The places we lived were fascinating, but I never truly belonged in any of them."

"You must have been close to your parents, though," he said.

A hollow sensation ran through her. She'd first become aware of it at her parents' funeral, when she realized that in essential ways they'd remained strangers to her.

"We all kept so busy," she said. "Dad worked long hours, Mom worked part-time and volunteered at church. I sang in the choir and took honors classes, and was a candy-striper in a nursing home. We hardly ever discussed anything except schedules."

"Are they still living?" he asked.

"They died four years ago," she said. "Their boat turned over on Lake Travis. A witness said Mom got trapped and Dad tried to save her." Tears threatened Gina's composure, but she held them back. "There are so many things we never discussed, so many ways I never knew them. I'd hate for Lily and Daisy to grow up like that."

He studied her with an expression she couldn't read. The silence stretched out before he asked, "How much would you hate it?"

"Hate what?" Lost in a swirl of memories, she could barely remember what they'd been talking about.

"How much would you hate for the twins to grow up without a sense of belonging?" he said. "How much would you hate for them to grow up as cute playthings for a couple who'll barely have time for them?"

"I'd adopt them myself if I could, that's how much I care," Gina answered frankly. "Assuming, of course, that you weren't in the picture."

He flinched, and she realized he'd misunderstood. "I meant that of course you have the first claim on them," she added hurriedly. "Not that I wouldn't want you around. I mean..." To her chagrin, heat crept across her cheeks.

Mason smiled. "Good. Because I've got the most out-rageous idea I'm ever likely to have. Want to hear it?"

"Sure," she said, eager for a distraction from her embarrassment.

"Let's get married," he said.

MASON COULD HARDLY believe what he'd proposed. Or rather, *that* he'd proposed.

The last thing he'd had in mind when he asked Gina to dinner was marriage. Not because he wouldn't want her. A man would be incredibly lucky to walk an angel like her down the aisle.

He simply wasn't cut out for marriage. He belonged in the saddle or behind the wheel of a pickup. When he got into one of his black moods, he needed the open range to vent.

Three years ago, he'd fallen in love with Francine Lee, a pretty blond accountant who'd been visiting her brother, the veterinarian in Horseshoe Bend. They'd dated intensely, and she'd prolonged her stay for several weeks.

One night at the ranch, they'd cooked dinner together after giving Bonita the evening off. Mason had planned to pop the question, until Rance hurried in to tell him that a cowhand had ridden one of their horses without permission and treated it so badly the horse had suffered permanent damage.

The man had created problems before, although never anything so serious. He'd been tolerated because he was a friend of their late father's.

At the news, something had snapped inside Mason. With Francine and Rance watching, he'd hauled the drunken cowboy out of the barn where he was cowering and punched him so hard the man flew across the yard.

Mason didn't remember much else, except that he'd fired the man amid a string of profanities.

Francine had been shocked. "You lost control of yourself!" she'd said. "How do I know you won't do that again? Maybe next time, I'll be the one you take it out on!"

She'd refused to listen to his protests, and demanded that he drive her to her brother's, which he did. The next day, she'd returned to Houston, and hadn't answered his letter of apology.

Mason knew that emotions could still run away with him under certain circumstances. There was a wildness to him that was part of his nature. He could usually keep it under control, but not always.

Over the years, he'd met rough-and-tumble women who could stand up to him, but none of them had come close to winning his heart. He had to accept the plain fact that he wasn't suited for marriage to the kind of gracious, tenderhearted woman who appealed to him.

When Rance wed his high school sweetheart, Amy, and she became pregnant with twins, it had seemed like the answer to Mason's prayers. The future of the ranch would be assured. He didn't need to marry, as long as he had his brother's family.

Yet here he was proposing to Gina Kennedy, a woman who was even more delicate than Francine. Was he out of his mind? He was doing it for the twins, though, not for himself.

"It makes perfect sense," Mason said to the stunned nurse sitting across from him. "If I hired you to take care of the girls, even assuming you were available, it wouldn't be enough to persuade a judge in my favor. But as my wife, you'd be unbeatable!"

She blinked a couple of times. "Mason, what are you talking about?"

"Didn't I make myself clear?" he said. "I'm asking you to marry me."

She swallowed hard before continuing. "So you can trump your sister and keep the twins?"

"And you can keep them, too," he pointed out. "That's what you said you wanted."

Those blue eyes regarded him levelly. "I'm going to do us both a favor, Mason. I'm going to assume you've suffered temporary insanity. Do you think you might wake up if I count to three and snap my fingers?"

At least she wasn't stomping out of the restaurant. "Surely you can see the logic of it," he persisted.

"People don't marry just to get custody of children," she said.

"People used to marry for all sorts of practical reasons," he argued. "As I recall, the divorce rate back then wasn't nearly as high as it is today."

"That's because people died young," she said, then turned pale. "I didn't mean...I guess that was kind of insensitive, under the circumstances."

"No offense taken." His sorrow over Rance and Amy's premature deaths didn't mean he couldn't see her point. "I'll tell you what, Gina. How about a compromise?"

"How does one compromise about getting married?" she asked.

Now that he'd had a few minutes to think about it, Mason could see that a marriage for the children's sake, while it might suit him, wasn't going to be enough for Gina. Sooner or later, she would weary of the grueling ranch life. Or worse, she'd become disgusted with his temper and walk out.

To make Gina unhappy and watch her lose respect for

him would be agony. There was no need to put them both through such an experience.

"Let's at least do what we can for the girls," he said. "We could marry long enough for me to adopt them, then quietly divorce."

"You're kidding, right?" she said.

He ought to stop, but Mason couldn't. If he did, he knew with sickening certainty that he would lose his nieces.

Without them he couldn't face going back to the ranch. There would be no future, nothing to hope for. He needed a reason to go on living.

"Do this for Lily and Daisy, and for me," he said. "Please. They could use your care for the first few months, anyway. You know that would be the safest thing for them."

"I suppose so," she conceded.

"I know it would be a sacrifice," he said. "I can't tell you how much it would mean—"

A thickness in his throat cut off the words. For a man who hated to display emotions, Mason had revealed more than he intended.

"I—I wish I could, Mason...."

He could hear the "no" in her tone. She might change her mind, though. "Don't give me an answer yet. Of course, in the divorce settlement, I'll compensate you for lost income and arrange for regular visitation with the girls. Please, at least give it some thought."

"It won't make..." She stopped. "I would enjoy taking care of the girls, but..."

He didn't want to discuss this any further tonight. He might easily say too much. About how he ached to touch the spun-gold of her hair, for instance, and to tip her chin upward and explore her mouth with his own.

That would scare her off for certain. "Sleep on it, all right?" he said.

She nodded in reluctant agreement.

WHY HADN'T SHE just said no? Gina wondered as she parted with Mason outside the restaurant. Politely refusing his offer to escort her home, she chose to walk alone and clear her head.

To devote a few more months to the twins would help ensure them a safe start. Maybe she owed them that much. And what about herself? She might never again get a chance at motherhood.

Gina deliberately chose a roundabout route back to Mrs. Parker's Inn. Although it was dinnertime, lingering July sunlight lured quite a few window-shoppers to browse along Mayfair Avenue. She tried to focus on the mix of tourists and casually dressed students, and on the city's pleasing mixture of modern, Victorian and classic Southern architecture.

If she didn't care for Mason, it would have been easy to refuse him, she acknowledged. But now…

Her thirtieth birthday was next month, in mid-August. Although these days women often married and had children late, to Gina that anniversary loomed like a deadline.

Now that she'd met a man she might actually want to marry, how could she refuse him? Yet how could she agree to spend months with him and then walk away? Her marriage of convenience would surely end in heartbreak.

Gina's footsteps carried her toward the Oh, Baby! shop on Kings Avenue. Popular with the Maitland Maternity staff and clients, it featured baby clothes, toys and accessories. From half a block away, she thought she could detect the scent of baby powder.

It wouldn't hurt to buy a going-away gift for the girls,

she decided. At least they'd have something to remember her by.

In the ribbon-bedecked window, she spotted two yellow gowns trimmed with white lace and dotted with red hearts. They'd be perfect for Lily and Daisy to wear tomorrow when they were released. What were the chances that Mason would remember to buy going-home outfits?

Inside, Gina found the shop nearly empty at this hour and quickly made her purchases. When she emerged, she saw two friends from the clinic staring at the window display, and wondered what they were doing here. Neither Katie Toper nor Hope Logan, who ran the hospital's gift shop, had children.

Of course, they might be wondering the same thing about her. "I was picking out something for the twins." Gina indicated her packaged gift. "They're going home tomorrow."

"How sweet!" Katie said. "I know you'll miss them."

Wistfully, Hope spared one more glance into the window. "I've got to be getting home myself. I just…well, I'll see you both later." With a small wave, she hurried away.

It didn't take a detective to note the distressed undercurrents. "What's going on?" Gina asked as she and Katie fell into step.

"Hope and her husband can't agree about having children," her friend said. "Kids are so precious, it's hard to imagine anyone not wanting them."

"Some people want them for the wrong reasons," Gina muttered.

Her friend cocked an eyebrow. "You mean Mason's sister? I heard she's trying to claim the girls. She isn't going to go through with it, is she? I mean, she hasn't even seen them!"

"Yes, she is, and Mason thinks she might succeed." If she didn't open up to someone, Gina might explode, so she plunged on. "He's got this crazy idea that we ought to get married until he can persuade a judge to let him adopt Lily and Daisy! Have you ever heard of such a thing?"

"Marriage isn't something to be taken lightly," the other nurse said.

"You're not kidding!"

They wandered past a French bakery and were enveloped by tantalizing aromas. From a nearby club drifted the rolling beat of country music.

How could she consider leaving Austin? Gina wondered. She'd never lived outside a city, and, since her early teen years, had rarely traveled far from this one. It had so much to offer.

Including loneliness, when Mason wasn't there.

"The scary part is that I keep thinking of reasons why I ought to do it," she admitted. "For the girls' sake. And because it might be my only chance to experience marriage and motherhood."

"Experience marriage?" Katie asked. "As in experience Europe on your summer vacation?"

"I didn't mean it that way!" she protested.

"Is this supposed to be a real marriage or a platonic relationship?" her friend demanded.

Mason hadn't specified, Gina conceded. "I assume it's a marriage in name only. I mean, he's never…well, tried to get physical."

"He's a man, isn't he? He can't spend that much time with you and not eventually want more!" Katie halted, then made a clucking sound. "Would you listen to me? Ford Carrington's a man, too, but no matter how long I've worked with him, he considers me a robot in a nurse's uniform. It's a lost cause.''

Gina hoped her friend was wrong. To her, the doctor and the nurse seemed ideally suited. ''He might wake up one of these days....''

A couple of passing men broke stride to speak to them. Judging by their brand-new jeans, fake-looking buckles and stiff cowboy hats, the pair were tourists pretending to be Texans. The impression was confirmed when one of them said, ''Howdy, ladies. Could y'all use some company?'' It sounded like a line from a movie.

''Get real,'' said Katie, and the two of them hurried on. They waited at least half a block before indulging in giggles.

''There are worse things than being alone!'' Gina teased.

''Name three,'' Katie said. ''And you can't count getting 'lassoed' by a couple of fake 'cowpokes.'''

''Getting married, falling in love with your husband and then having to say goodbye,'' she replied, sobering. ''That's three things in one.''

''A lot can happen in a few months, though,'' her friend pointed out. ''Isolated on a ranch, with nothing to do on those long, summer nights...''

''I don't know what Mason has in mind,'' Gina admitted. ''But he didn't make it sound like he's in love with me. He wasn't the least bit romantic.''

Katie's expression grew thoughtful as the twilight lowered around them. ''You'd have the satisfaction of knowing you tried. That you got off the bench and into the game at least once.''

It wasn't the first time the two women had discussed their similar problems. Both were twenty-nine-year-old virgins, and they both longed for marriage and children.

Until now, the main difference had been that Katie knew *who* she wanted, while Gina didn't. Now Gina knew, too, but she wasn't sure she dared accept his offer.

"It's such a risk," she told her friend. "I wish I were braver."

"You're plenty brave," said the other nurse. "I've seen you give your heart to babies that you knew weren't likely to survive. That takes courage."

"I couldn't help it," she said. "I don't deserve any credit for that."

"And remember that tough-talking young couple who wouldn't take their son's medication schedule seriously? When he was released, you stood up to them and laid out every terrible thing that could happen if they got careless. The father—he had a snake tattooed on his neck, remember?—at first I thought he was going to rough you up. Then he started blubbering. I'll never forget the way he hugged that baby and said he couldn't bear it if anything went wrong."

"They came to see me on their son's first birthday," Gina recalled. "He's doing well. I guess my horror stories worked."

"So don't tell me you're a coward," Katie finished. "Hey, look at the time! I promised to meet some friends at a club in ten minutes. Want to come along? There's a bluegrass band tonight."

"No, thanks. I've got some heavy thinking to do." She gave her friend a pat on the arm. "Thanks for your support."

"Any time."

Operating on automatic pilot, Gina strolled back to her boardinghouse and went upstairs. Entering her room was like returning to the home where she'd lived with her parents until four years ago. Her mother's china figurines filled a display case. Dainty lace curtains hung at the window, and Victorian-style furniture gave a sense of stepping into the past. It was a refuge from disappointments, from stress, from the modern era.

Gina got a chill when she tried to picture how she would feel, returning to this room or one like it after months as Mason's temporary wife. How could she expect to fit back into her old life?

If she didn't care so much, perhaps she might regard the temporary marriage as an extended vacation. But she did care. She cared too much.

She wasn't willing to chance a heartbreak that would cut so deeply. Better to live with might-have-beens than to lie here aching, night after night, for something she'd briefly possessed and could never have again.

For her own self-preservation, her answer had to be no.

Chapter Three

Was he being selfish? Mason had never asked himself that question before. He asked it a lot that night at the ranch, and the next morning on the two-hour drive to Austin.

All his life, until now, the future and his place in it had spread before him as neatly as the procession of the seasons. He and Rance would grow up to take over the ranch. They would run it together, expand their operations and leave a rich heritage for the next generation.

For years, they'd kept on course. After their father's death, when Mason was twenty-three and Rance eighteen, the younger brother had taken over the horse-training operation while the elder focused on cattle and oil. Although both preferred working with animals, their finances depended on the pumps that worked with steady efficiency around the range.

Mason didn't have to question why he did what he did. It was simply there, a force of nature. He was a rancher, he was his father's son and he was Rance's brother.

Two months ago, when he received the phone call telling him Rance was dead, he'd desperately turned his attention to saving Amy. Then she, too, had slipped away.

Now he had Daisy and Lily. He needed them more

than anything. A man could only rebuild his future if there was a purpose to it.

Was he being fair in asking Gina to come to the ranch with him? For all her skill in the nursery, she looked as delicate as an orchid. How would she cope with a hardened man like him, one who might be gone all day and return exhausted and covered with dirt?

Nevertheless, Gina attracted him more than any woman he'd ever met. He hoped she would say yes, and he didn't care if he was being selfish.

If she agreed even to a short-term union, there was hope she'd want to stay. Maybe he could win her, despite logic and everything he knew about himself.

Mason wasn't a man to give up easily. Not with his daughters, and not with the woman he wanted.

At Maitland Maternity, he parked in the visitors' lot and went inside. The place seemed different—something about the light. Or the dimensions. Or the fact that, after today, he would no longer be a part of its daily goings-on.

"Darn." He stopped in the lobby. "I forgot to get going-home clothes." When a grandmotherly woman smiled at him, he realized he'd spoken aloud.

"Try the gift shop," she said.

"Much obliged."

He checked inside. There was a refrigerated case full of flowers, along with shelves of paperback books, magazines and stuffed animals, almost as many as he'd already bought for the girls' room at home. In one corner, he found baby rattles, booties, diapers and some clothing, but if the store carried little dresses, they must be sold out.

He was willing to bet Margaret would arrive with an

armload of gowns and bonnets. No doubt she would count it as evidence of her superior parental fitness.

Had she and Stuart already landed in town? Mason hoped not. He wanted to complete the paperwork and whisk the girls back to the ranch before his sister could complicate the situation.

Possession might not be nine-tenths of the law when it came to children, but it would give him an edge. He intended to take any advantage he could find.

It was after eight. Gina would be on duty, fresh and bright as always. Mason speeded his footsteps.

He saw her through the nursery window, feeding one of the girls. The way she bent over the baby on her lap, he couldn't see her expression.

Then she glanced toward one of the other nurses, and he noted the puffiness under her eyes. She'd been crying.

Chagrin filled him. A woman about to marry the man she adored wouldn't be crying about it. Gina must have decided to give up the girls, rather than spend even a few months with him.

Mason squared his shoulders. He couldn't make her love him, but he didn't intend to take no for an answer. For his daughters' sake, he had to give it his best shot.

Surely Gina wouldn't really mind spending time at the ranch, as long as he left her strictly alone. She'd said herself that she loved the girls enough to want to adopt them.

Moving away from the window, he allowed himself a couple of deep breaths. So far, she hadn't noticed him.

Suppressing his doubts, he assumed a confident air. Before he could talk to her, though, he needed to prepare by handling a few details at the administration office.

Once he cajoled her consent, he didn't want anything to delay their departure.

GINA HAD SAID GOODBYE to hundreds of babies. Off they would go in their mothers' arms, and she'd miss them for a few hours, until another newborn arrived. She'd cherish it for a few days or weeks, and then she would say goodbye to it, too.

As she changed the dressing on Daisy's rapidly healing surgical wound, she wished she could detach herself as readily from the twins as from so many others. "What is it about you that makes you special?" she asked.

Daisy gripped her thumb and gazed intently into Gina's eyes. A vise squeezed her heart.

How could she let them go? These girls felt like her daughters.

Their first steps. Daisy would clutch Gina's hand and step out cautiously, her tiny feet making no sound on the floor.

Lily would tear herself from Mason's loving grasp and plunk forward, arms waving, knees wobbling, until she plopped onto all fours. A second later, she'd be on her feet again, flinging herself into life with joyous abandon.

Before Gina could finish the daydream, a change in the air told her Mason had come into the nursery. Scarcely daring to trust her composure, she peeked at him from beneath lowered lashes.

He wore a gray three-piece suit. Sunday best, she thought. It emphasized the tan richness of his skin and the dark penetration of his gaze.

"Mason…" Her throat caught.

"For you." He held out a bouquet of red roses. "I'm not sure if they're allowed in here, so I sneaked them in."

"Oh!" When she held them to her nose, their summery scent invaded her bloodstream. "They're beautiful."

"You should be surrounded by flowers," he said. "My

mother planted a rose garden at the ranch. I'll make sure you have fresh flowers every day.''

But she wasn't going to live on the ranch. If there were flowers, they'd be for someone else.

"We need to talk." She hoped he couldn't hear the quaver in her voice.

"Sure thing." His expression warmed as he touched her hair lightly. The brush of his hand warmed Gina's scalp. Did he have to make it so hard to say no?

"I don't think there's anyone in the parents' lounge. We could talk there." She was about to lead the way when, through the glass, she spotted Elly Maitland in the corridor. The administrator pointed at Mason and held up a sheaf of papers. "I wonder why she's in such a hurry about the paperwork."

He shrugged. "I guess she knows I want to hit the road before my sister shows up."

"You're in a hurry?" she asked. "Oh, dear. I have to make some final preparations for the girls." Remembering her gift, she added, "And I brought a going-away present for them." From a table, she produced a wrapped package.

He studied it with a bemused expression. "This wouldn't be something for the girls to wear home, would it?"

"As a matter of fact, yes," she said. "I thought you might forget."

His rueful grin made her head whirl. How could the man be so endearing?

"I did forget," he acknowledged, and opened the package. "Gina, these are precious."

"Thanks. But before you go see Miss Maitland, could we have that talk?"

Elly tapped on the glass and gestured to Mason more urgently. "What *is* the big deal?" Gina asked.

"I did tell her that I needed to get out as soon as possible. It appears she took me at my word. I'll come back as fast as I can, okay?" Mason caught her hand. The pressure of his blunt fingers against her palm made her even more light-headed. "Would you put the new dresses on the girls? They'll be knockouts."

"Of course." Gina stood stock-still as he strode from the room. His warmth, his obvious expectation that she would accept, and his gentle caress had made it hard to keep her resolve.

But he wasn't offering a real marriage. And she could accept nothing less.

MASON WONDERED IF HE'D pushed her too far. Gina didn't seem to mind when he touched her. It wasn't part of his plan; he simply hadn't been able to resist.

As for the flowers, and arranging for Elly Maitland to interrupt, they'd been attempts to forestall Gina from giving him a negative answer. So far, they'd worked.

From here on, he'd have to wing it. He would play on her devotion to the twins, which shouldn't be too difficult. Her caring shone in her eyes every time she gazed at those babies.

A twinge of guilt threw Mason off stride as he accompanied Elly. It was wrong to manipulate a person who meant so much to him.

But a few months on a ranch wouldn't harm Gina, and could mean all the difference for Daisy and Lily's futures. "Any word from my brother-in-law?" he asked.

"He called about six o'clock last evening." The administrator had a reputation for working fourteen-hour days, so that probably didn't seem late to her. "When I told him we were releasing the girls today, he sounded more disappointed than angry. He said he and his wife would be here.''

''He didn't specify a time?''

''No.''

It was almost nine-thirty, by Mason's watch. If his sister and Stuart had caught an early morning flight, they might arrive soon.

No sense in worrying about it. The best he could do was take care of business as quickly as possible and depart, preferably with Gina.

At the office, an assistant went through a sheaf of papers with him, methodically explaining what each one was for. A hospital survey, and insurance records, and obtaining social security numbers, and on and on.

His restlessness made it hard to concentrate. Only after a while did Mason put his finger on what was bothering him.

It wasn't just Margaret and Stuart's impending arrival. It was the observation that Gina had been crying.

She must love those girls almost as much as he did. The situation was tearing her apart.

It tore at him, too. The last thing he wanted was to hurt Gina. Couldn't she put up with him, even for a few months? She would gain not only more time with Lily and Daisy, but, as he'd promised, regular visitation afterward.

Of course, while they were married, he would keep his distance, especially now that he'd seen from her expression that she had no desire to become his wife. He would respect her reticence completely.

While Mason might be unpolished compared to the doctors at the clinic or to his brother-in-law, Stuart, he possessed an old-fashioned sense of honor. If Gina didn't already know that, he would simply have to prove it to her.

He was finishing the last document when Elly Maitland returned from an errand. "As I suspected, some of the press has gathered," she said. "There are a couple of newspaper reporters, and Chelsea Markum from *Tattle Today* brought a camera crew."

"This could be awkward." He'd almost forgotten that the media would be on hand. "I'm not used to giving press conferences."

"If you like, I'll ask Dr. Abby to speak to them. With your permission, she could answer questions about the babies' medical condition." Abigail Maitland, Elly's older sister, was chief of obstetrics and gynecology at the clinic and had delivered Lily and Daisy.

"That would be fine," Mason said distractedly. He'd intended to spend more time with Gina. How was he going to win her over and cope with reporters at the same time?

"I'll get a couple of volunteers to escort the babies when they're released," Elly added.

"Excuse me?"

"We have a policy of not allowing the babies to be carried outside. Just imagine if a parent tripped and dropped one!" she explained. "We arrange for a volunteer to wheel the bassinet out front and wait until the parents bring the car around. Also, we can lend a car seat if they don't have one."

He didn't want a volunteer to assist him. He wanted Gina. "Would you mind if Miss Kennedy was the one who escorted them?" Mason asked. "It would mean a lot to me."

"What a lovely idea!" the administrator said. "That way, someone's sure to take her picture with the babies.

I know she's grown fond of them these past few months. I'm sure she'd like to have a souvenir clipping.''

Mason wished he'd come up with the idea of photographing Gina with his daughters. He'd have to make sure he got a copy of whatever ran in the newspaper.

But then, he intended to have plenty of pictures taken. At their wedding.

I'M SORRY. I've thought your offer over carefully, but I can't accept. I do love Lily and Daisy, and I want what's best for them. But becoming their mother, then having to give them up—well, I'm not sure I could handle it.

No, she didn't dare give him wiggle room. *I can't handle spending months as Lily and Daisy's mother, and then leaving and only seeing them on rare occasions. Please, let's not argue about it. Let's stay friends.*

Gina sighed. She'd been going over and over in her mind what she was going to say to Mason. If only he would hurry back so she could stop torturing herself!

Freshly changed and cute as kittens in their springlike dresses, the two little girls were ready to go. Each was accompanied by an apnea monitor slightly smaller than a VCR.

The Velcro chest belts didn't need to be attached while the girls were awake, although they should be put in place for the long ride home. Mason had been instructed in their use yesterday afternoon and, unlike some parents, had mastered the correct degree of tautness right away.

As for Bonita, the housekeeper, he'd called her yesterday and she'd promised to come in for CPR training next week. Gina hoped there wouldn't be any need for emergency resuscitation before then—or ever.

Katie stopped by, holding one of her charges. ''What

did you decide to do about Mason? I saw the roses on the counter, by the way. They're gorgeous!''

On the verge of answering, Gina decided it wouldn't be right to disclose her decision to someone else before she informed Mason. ''I'd like to tell him first.''

''You always do things so discreetly!'' Katie said. ''You're what people call a real lady. I aspire to be like you, Gina, although I'm not sure I'll ever make it.''

''Please don't use me as a shining example of anything!'' she protested. At the moment, she felt more like a squashed cabbage leaf than a lady.

Eleanor Maitland's assistant poked her head into the room. ''Nurse Kennedy? They'd like you to wheel the Blackstone babies to the lobby, please.''

Gina froze. The girls were being released already? But Mason hadn't returned to talk to her!

''She'll need someone to push the second bassinet,'' Katie pointed out. ''Oh, good, Susan's here!'' Susan, a nurse assigned to the intermediate nursery, had been delayed by a flat tire. ''I'm supposed to assist Dr. Carrington in half an hour, so I can spare the time to push the other one.''

''Thanks.'' The assistant ducked out, then stuck her head in again. ''By the way, there's press all over the front steps, and Abby and Megan Maitland are out there, too, so make sure you've got lipstick on.''

Press? And Megan Maitland, the family matriarch who had founded Maitland Maternity nearly twenty-five years ago and still served as its CEO? This was getting more and more complicated.

Gina needed help. ''Katie, I don't know what I'm going to do. I need to talk to Mason.''

She was on the brink of confiding her decision to turn down his proposal when Susan bustled over. ''So these cuties are leaving us, huh? We're all going to miss them, not to mention that heartthrob uncle of theirs. How'd you let him slip through your fingers, Gina?''

She didn't know how to answer, even though the question was meant in jest. Fortunately, Katie intervened. "Don't make assumptions, Sue!"

"Just stating the obvious." The nurse bustled off to take care of her own charges.

The possibility of having a private conversation with Katie had vanished, Gina saw, when Elly Maitland appeared outside the glass partition and waved to them to hurry. She would have to figure out what to say to Mason by herself.

Was it possible he assumed he already knew her answer? Last night, Gina recalled, he'd brushed away her objections and insisted that a sham marriage made perfect sense. Perhaps, overnight, he'd convinced himself that his logic was so irrefutable that she couldn't possibly say no.

The last thing she wanted was a painful public confrontation with Mason. She preferred quiet discussions that preserved everyone's self-respect. They simply had to find a moment together.

WALKING THROUGH THE LOBBY toward the hospital's front entrance, Mason saw Dr. Abby standing outside talking to half a dozen reporters and a camera crew. Beside her, beaming, stood the proud figure of Dr. Abby's mother, Megan, head of Maitland Maternity.

The press gathered around them weren't nearly as numerous as he'd expected. He hoped they wouldn't be as obnoxious as he'd feared, either.

"...demonstrate one of the reasons I established this clinic," Megan was saying. At a well-publicized sixty-two years, she had a vigor and presence that dominated the scene. "Getting babies off to a healthy start is the most important job in the world."

"Here's Mr. Blackstone now," Abby said. "He can tell us about the twins from his perspective."

The moment he reached Dr. Abby's side, an attractive woman thrust a microphone toward Mason. He didn't watch much television, so it took a moment to place her as Chelsea Markum, a local reporter who specialized in gossip and human interest stories.

"Mr. Blackstone, who's going to take care of the twins while you're working on the ranch all day?" she demanded.

Did she have to ask *that* question right off the bat? "I've made arrangements for them to be well cared for, and I'll be spending every possible moment with them," he said.

"Taken care of by whom?" she asked.

"I'm not at liberty to…"

From the corner of his eye, he noticed a taxi pulling to the curb. The instant the wheels stopped, the doors flew open and two people hurried out.

Even if she hadn't been his sister, his attention would have gone first to Margaret. She was a striking woman, tall, with vivid dark coloring. Stuart, stockier and blander, could have been cast as a lawyer in the movies, as in real life.

"Just in time!" Marge called, striding toward him. "Where are my little darlings?"

The camera swung toward her. Chelsea Markum frowned. "Who's this?"

"I'm Margaret Blackstone Waldman, the babies' aunt." The knot of reporters parted and his sister marched through their center. Her husband, who had stopped to pay the cabbie, rushed to catch up. "Stuart and I will be taking them home with us to Dallas."

Mason struggled against a flare of anger. He loved his sister, but right now he could cheerfully have stuffed her into a box and mailed her to Siberia.

Leaning forward, he spoke into Chelsea's microphone. "I'm afraid you've caught us in the middle of a family disagreement. My sister and I are both offering our homes to Lily and Daisy. But as you may be aware, I've been the one who's been supervising their care and bonding with them."

Margaret snatched the microphone from Chelsea's hand. Mason could have taken it back, but he was loathe to stage a tug-of-war in public. This entire situation was undignified enough already.

"I'll give my brother credit for good intentions," she said. "But babies need a mother as well as a father. Stuart and I can provide both. Not to mention our experience in raising three children of our own."

A stir among the press and the crunch of small wheels behind him told Mason that the babies had arrived. Turning, he saw Gina standing behind one of the bassinets, staring at Margaret and Stuart. She must have guessed who they were, even if she hadn't heard their comments.

Her lips parted in dismay. In the sunlight, the translucent clarity of her skin made her look even younger than she was. He wanted her so much, he nearly forgot where they were.

"Mr. Blackstone?" Chelsea pressed, having reclaimed her microphone. "How do you respond to your sister's points? She tells us she has parenting experience, which I understand you don't. Furthermore, you never answered my question about who was going to care for the girls while you're working on the ranch."

"I'll tell you who." Marge, who had worked herself up into what Rance used to call a "bossy fit," seized the mike again. "He's got a housekeeper, a perfectly competent woman. She never had children of her own, though, and she's certainly not the twins' mother. That's who's going to take care of these girls if my brother has his way. Is that the mark of a man who loves his nieces? I'd say he was thinking more of himself than of them."

The unfairness of this remark brought gasps from several people, including Dr. Abby, who had witnessed Mason's devotion over the past two months. Megan Maitland glowered. But what could she or anyone else say?

"That's not true."

Gina's sweet voice carried over the crowd with surprising strength. Before anyone else could react, and no doubt before Margaret even figured out who had spoken, Chelsea snatched back her microphone and hurried over. "What makes you say that, Nurse?"

"I'm the one who's going to take care of Daisy and Lily," Gina announced. "Mason and I are getting married."

Chapter Four

She hadn't meant to say that. Until a minute ago, Gina had had every intention of declining his offer.

However, as Katie had pointed out yesterday, she couldn't help flying to the defense of people she cared about. And after hearing for herself how ruthless Mason's sister was, Gina had made the only move that could preserve his right to the girls.

On Mason's face she saw relief. If only he would put his arms around her and tell her that he cared about her, she would feel so much better. However, she reminded herself, he had proposed a practical arrangement, and she'd just agreed to it for practical reasons.

Her statement rang in her ears, through the buzz of congratulations from Katie and Abby and Megan Maitland. It took a moment to realize that Chelsea Markum was asking another question.

"When did this come about?" the reporter said.

"Very recently. We weren't going to announce it quite yet." Gina wasn't exactly lying. "Mason and I got to know each other over the past two months. I've been the primary-care nurse for Lily and Daisy."

She could hear reporters' pens scratching, and besides, the camera had captured every word. There would be no going back. She swallowed hard, a little afraid of the events she'd impulsively set into motion.

"Well!" Even the imposing Margaret, who looked as if she normally brooked no opposition, seemed at a loss for words, "This is a surprise!"

"I wish someone had told us sooner," her husband grumbled. "I'm missing an entire day's work."

"Stuart!" his wife reproved. "Just because—that is— we don't know anything about this young lady. Or how qualified she is to take care of *our* nieces."

"You're doubting the qualifications of a neonatal-care nurse?" Chelsea Markum asked. "Mrs. Waldman, how much experience do you have with premature babies?"

"That isn't the point!" Margaret blustered, and stopped, unable to define exactly what the point was.

"I'd like to know more about the upcoming nuptials," said one of the print reporters, finally getting a word in edgewise. "When and where are you two going to be married?"

Oh, help. "We hadn't discussed…"

Margaret butted in headfirst when Gina hesitated. "Exactly my point! Who's going to care for the girls in the meantime? Obviously, my kid brother hasn't thought far enough ahead to plan his wedding. Why, it could take months!"

"We don't need anything formal. I don't have any immediate family," Gina said wistfully. She'd always dreamed of a big wedding, with lace and flowers and lots of friends and relatives. It was hardly appropriate under the circumstances, though.

"Nonsense!" When Megan Maitland spoke, everyone else hushed. "Since there's no time to arrange for a facility, they'll be married at my mansion. The grounds are beautiful, and it's high time we used them for such a joyful purpose!''

The Maitland mansion, ten blocks from the clinic, was a stately white structure out of Gina's dreams. She'd often strolled past the four-story house, sneaking peaks at the Southern-style building and luxurious gardens.

The prospect of having a wedding there filled her with excitement. But what about Mason? Wouldn't he be upset, since he intended to stay married only long enough to adopt his nieces? Their marriage would be enough of a sham, without dragging so many other people into it.

He was smiling broadly, she saw through the crowd. Probably the implications of having a big splashy wedding hadn't dawned on him. Well, he appeared to have won at least the first round against his sister, and that was reason enough for elation.

MASON WAS ALMOST GRATEFUL to Marge. If she'd spoken with more diplomacy, Gina might not have felt compelled to declare that she was marrying him.

He didn't harbor any illusions about her being in love with him. It was the girls she cared about, and that was fair enough.

"So," he said to the press, "where does a guy rent a tux around here?"

"I'll tell you if you promise to invite me!" Chelsea Markum said.

He shook his head ruefully. "This isn't a media circus, it's a wedding. However, I'm happy to invite as many private guests as Mrs. Maitland is willing to accommodate. Including the staff of Maitland Maternity."

"Most of them will be working, but I think we can make a few exceptions," Megan said. "Starting with Gina, who is on paid vacation as of this moment."

"When is this event going to take place?" his sister asked suspiciously. "Despite your generous offer, Mrs. Maitland, it could be weeks!"

"Would tomorrow be soon enough?" asked the CEO. "It's all right with me if it's all right with our happy couple."

Mason heard Gina's sharp intake of breath. Was she regretting her decision, or simply worrying over logistics? As for him, the sooner the better. It gave her less time to change her mind.

"Suits me," he said. "How about you, Gina?"

His bride-to-be had gone pale, or perhaps it was the effect of bright sunshine on her ivory skin. "I don't know. I've never been married before. I mean...don't we need a license? And I'll have to buy a dress. Not to mention arranging for a minister and flowers."

"I'll put my staff on it immediately." Megan Maitland beamed at the prospect. "Don't you worry about the details. Just get the papers and the gown, and we can even assist with that if you like."

"Can I be your maid of honor?" Katie asked.

"Of course! I was just about to ask you!"

Mason had to admit he hadn't considered how complicated weddings were. His cousin Ed, the ranch foreman, and his wife, Linda, had gotten married on the Blackstone spread twenty years ago, when Mason was fourteen. All he remembered was a lot of music and colorful clothing.

Marge, who had been unaccustomedly silent, found one more tiny point to seize on. "And where are my precious nieces going to sleep tonight?" she cried. "In some hotel room where they won't even have proper cribs?"

Her concern might have been more touching, Mason reflected, had she gone over to see Lily and Daisy instead of remaining rooted in place. She hadn't even held them in her arms once, or gazed into their eyes, or touched their cheeks.

"They'll stay at my house," Megan declared. "We've got plenty of baby supplies and furniture, and I'll hire a special duty nurse for tonight. The bridal couple need to get ready!"

Suddenly the impact of what was happening flooded over Mason. These important people, virtual strangers to him, were opening their hearts to help Lily and Daisy and, of course, Gina and him.

Realizing the TV camera was still rolling, he said, "People talk about city folks as if they were cold and uncaring. I guess we can all see that in Austin, that isn't true."

"Certainly not! It isn't true of Dallas, either!" Margaret was determined to squabble whether anyone wanted to argue with her or not. "Which reminds me, brother. Do you intend to invite our relatives from the ranch, or have you forgotten about them?"

"I'll call them right away." As soon as he could get rid of these reporters, he wanted to add. Not to mention Marge and Stuart.

What he really wanted to do was be alone with Gina, to reassure her that she'd made the right decision. But it might be awhile before he got the chance.

"A WEDDING! How wonderful!" Mrs. Parker, Gina's landlady for the past three years, clapped her hands. "I hate to lose such a good boarder, but it couldn't be for a better reason."

Gina felt herself blushing. She couldn't tell anyone but Katie the truth about this marriage, and even her friend seemed to have forgotten that this was to be a union in name only.

Gina herself was still in shock. Events had taken on a momentum of their own, carrying her relentlessly forward. All she could do was tread water to keep from drowning.

She wasn't sure what she would say to Mason when they had a private moment. In any case, his sister and brother-in-law had dragged him off for lunch, while Megan Maitland had asked Gina to get the twins settled at her mansion. She'd waited until the private duty nurse showed up, then shopped until her feet ached. She hadn't yet found a dress.

Even amid all the activity, Gina missed Mason. She missed their leisurely conversations in the nursery, and their casual contact. She missed watching his face as he studied the babies in a haze of love.

If only her parents were here to advise her, she might be able to figure out whether she'd made the right decision. Instead, she felt off center and a little dizzy.

"And tomorrow, so soon!" her landlady continued. "Have you found a gown yet?"

"No," she admitted. "Nothing seemed quite special enough." Quickly, she added, "I hope you'll come! The ceremony's at five o'clock."

"Thank you, yes!" said the landlady. "Now, don't you worry about packing, except for your personal needs. You have so many pretty things from your mother that need to be wrapped carefully. I'll handle the china pieces myself."

Yet another task Gina hadn't considered! "I'd be grateful," she said. "As for the furniture, would you mind putting it in storage?"

That way, she wouldn't have to ship it all back when the marriage broke up, Gina reflected.

"Certainly, but there's no hurry," her landlady continued. "I can't find new boarders in July, not until classes at the university start this fall, so I'll leave your room as it is for a while. But listen, Gina! I have a special request!''

''I'd be glad to do whatever I can.''

''Come with me.'' The landlady led her through the overstuffed sitting room to her cheery bedroom. From one of the closets, she reverently produced a garment bag and, after hanging it on the back of the door, unzipped it with care.

''What's this?'' Gina came closer. ''Oh!''

Encased in clear plastic was a ballerina-style wedding dress. Above the layered, gauzy skirt, the elegant bodice rose to a square-cut neckline and short, lacy sleeves. From a separate case, Mrs. Parker produced a white cloche hat with an attached veil.

''It was my wedding dress, in the early sixties.'' The landlady wore a wistful expression. ''Such a happy time! It was inspired by Jacqueline Kennedy, who always wore such elegant clothes. I hoped to see my daughter walk down the aisle in it, but she said it was too simple for her. Would you possibly consider wearing it? I think it's just your size.''

Of course Gina would wear the dress! She loved the design, but more importantly, the gown had special meaning. Her own parents had eloped, so there'd been no heirloom wedding dress. Now, at last, she had one.

''It's beautiful. Thank you!'' she said.

''My dry cleaner can have it pressed and freshened by tomorrow morning,'' Mrs. Parker said. ''I'll take care of that. It will be my wedding present.''

Gina hugged the matronly woman. ''That's so kind of you!'' She hoped her generous landlady would never find out that the marriage hadn't been intended to last.

But since this might be the only wedding Gina would

ever have, she might as well pretend, just for a while, that it was real.

THE NEXT MORNING, Mason arranged to meet his bride-to-be at the courthouse so they could fill out the appropriate forms. She gave him a quick, nervous smile, but otherwise kept her attention on business.

If he was seeking a clue to her state of mind, he couldn't find it. To Mason, she seemed as even tempered as ever.

"How's your sister taking the prospect of our wedding?" she asked as they waited for the clerk to issue their marriage license. "Is she angry?"

"I think her pride is hurt more than anything else," he said. "I can't figure out why she's so determined to adopt the girls, unless it's sheer competitiveness with me."

"Yesterday, she scarcely seemed to notice them." Gina had clipped her hair behind her ears with barrettes, and wore hardly any makeup. To Mason, she looked perfect. "Has she shown any interest in them since then?"

"She and Stuart dropped by the mansion last night," he said. "They stayed about ten minutes, long enough to pat the girls on the head and try to figure out how to tell them apart. When I suggested Margaret hold them, she said she wasn't dressed for it."

Gina shook her head. "She's totally wrong for them."

"We haven't heard the last of her," Mason remarked. "My sister's like a bulldog. Once she sinks her teeth into something, she doesn't let go."

"She may have to," said his wife-to-be.

A few minutes later, they left the courthouse with the license in hand. At the afternoon ceremony, Gina's family's longtime pastor would officiate. Their witnesses, they'd agreed, would be the maid of honor and best man:

Katie Toper and Mason's cousin Ed, who would arrive from the ranch in early afternoon.

They'd handled an amazing number of practical details. The only matters they hadn't dealt with were the ones that really mattered.

"Gina, could we talk for a few minutes?" Mason asked as they left the courthouse. "Let's have coffee."

She checked her watch. "I'm having my hair and makeup done in an hour.... Oh, of course we can talk! I'm so flustered, I hardly know what I'm saying."

The confusion in her blue eyes brought out a fierce protective instinct that he had never felt toward anyone except his nieces. Catching Gina's elbow, he guided her toward a nearby café. Built of red brick, it had trendy bright green trim and lots of windows.

A waitress guided them to a table by a window. When she started to hand them menus, Mason waved them away. "Black coffee, please."

"I'll have hot tea," Gina said.

The woman returned with their mugs, a coffee carafe, hot water and a basket filled with tea bags. Mason hadn't realized the beverage came in so many flavors.

"I don't really know much about you," he said. "I didn't even know you drank tea."

"That's because you've seen me drinking coffee at work. I need it to keep alert," she explained as she selected something called Peppermint Delight. "This is a strange situation, isn't it, having a marriage without a courtship?"

"Thanks for what you did yesterday." He'd been wanting to say that for hours. "Until you announced our engagement, Margaret was scoring all the points with the media."

"As for my, er, announcement..." Gina hesitated.

"Mason, I—I think we should be honest with each other."

He didn't want to let her confess that she hadn't intended to marry him. Even at this late date, she might remember all the reasons for her decision and back down. "You hadn't given me an answer yet, so I assumed you were still making up your mind."

"You could put it that way," she conceded. "Until I blurted it out, I wasn't sure…I mean, Mason, the idea of a temporary marriage goes against everything I believe."

"But so does abandoning the people who need you," he added quickly.

"Yes." She nodded. "It does."

Reaching across the table, he cupped his hands over hers. "What you did for the girls was wonderful. Honey, I appreciate it more than I can say. I hope it's not too much of a sacrifice."

Her lips clamped together. After a moment, she said, "It's as much a sacrifice for you as for me. Isn't it?"

"Not at all," he said.

"Oh?" She brightened a little.

"I'm not the one who has to give up my job and my home," he explained. "I want you to know, Gina, that I'll do everything possible to make your stay comfortable. Anything you need, just ask."

A long, slow breath escaped her. "I see. Is that all?"

What had he left out? "You're welcome to invite your friends to visit. Also, if there's anything you've been wanting to do on a ranch—ride horses, whatever—it can be arranged."

"Thanks." She didn't look happy, though.

Mason wished he understood women better. Or, more particularly, that he understood Gina. He hoped she wasn't concerned about his taking advantage of the situation. "We'll have separate bedrooms, in case you were worried about that."

"That's—a good idea," she said. "How long do you think it will take?"

"The adoption?" he asked. "It depends on Margaret and Stuart. Once they stop seeking custody, it could be finalized quickly."

She rested her chin in her palm. "What do you think it will take to discourage your sister?"

"An act of God?" he teased.

"If only we understood her motives," Gina said. "Obviously, she hasn't bonded with the babies. I don't get the impression she needs to solidify a shaky marriage, either. Maybe she's trying to ease the empty-nest syndrome, since her kids are getting older."

It hadn't occurred to Mason that determining his sister's motive might help them find a way to dissuade her. "We'll have another chance to scope her out," he said. "They've promised to visit as soon as we get settled."

"I'll look forward to that."

He cocked an eyebrow dubiously.

"No, really!" Gina said.

"Why on earth?"

"Because they're going to be the twins' aunt and uncle for the rest of their lives." She fiddled with the napkin in her lap. "It will be good for Lily and Daisy to have a warm relationship with Margaret, especially after I'm gone. You've got other female relatives on the ranch, too, didn't you say? So Lily and Daisy won't grow up motherless."

"You can stay as long as you want, of course." He scarcely dared to breathe while he awaited her answer. *Stay forever. That would suit me fine.*

She toyed with her mug. "No, I'll…need to get on with

my life, Mason. We made a bargain, and I'll keep my end of it. As long as you—as long as that suits you.''

Darn it, was she hinting at something or was he being obtuse? ''Of course it suits me!'' he said.

''Good.'' Finally, she sipped the tea. Judging by her expression, it must have gone cold.

Chapter Five

The four-story white house on Maitland Avenue had served generations of Maitlands, long before the former Megan Kelly married into the family. From the time Gina and her family moved to Austin when she was thirteen, she'd viewed the house more as a movie set than as a real home where real people lived.

She'd heard the romantic stories about how Megan's father had been a groundskeeper on the estate. Megan herself had worked there as a maid until she fell in love and married her employer, William Maitland.

That had been nearly forty years ago. To Gina, it was the stuff of Cinderella legends.

As she gazed over the grounds from the third-floor bedroom provided for her bridal transformation, she couldn't believe that she was going to be married here. Below, staff members swarmed about the gazebo and lawn, setting up chairs and floral displays. Beyond, near the tennis courts, a long table was being hastily covered with a cloth and set with serving dishes for the buffet supper.

Everything had happened with impossible speed. Gina felt as if she wouldn't catch up with herself for at least a week.

She'd arrived early, to spend some time with the twins.

They'd nestled in her arms, gurgling and cooing like tur-tledoves. The harried private nurse who had taken over the day shift told her the girls had been fussy until she showed up.

"They missed you," the woman said. "You're not going to leave them while you take a honeymoon, are you?" She sounded alarmed at the prospect.

Gina's cheeks had heated at the suggestion. She certainly hoped none of their acquaintances were going to offer them tickets to Hawaii in a misguided fit of generosity. "No, we're…" What *were* they doing after the ceremony? They hadn't even talked about it. "We're going to keep them with us," she'd finished lamely.

Gina was roused from her reverie by the rustling sound of Katie slipping the wedding dress from its plastic cover. "This is gorgeous," the other nurse said. "Do you suppose if I move into Mrs. Parker's Inn, she might loan it to me one of these days?"

"I wouldn't be surprised."

"As if I'm likely to need it!" Katie plucked a stray thread from her lavender cocktail dress. "Is Ford—I mean, Dr. Carrington—here yet?"

"I haven't seen him." At a loss for someone to walk her down the aisle, Gina had asked the pediatric surgeon to serve as a representative of the Maitland staff. He'd always spoken kindly to her and, besides, he was the only man she knew who owned a tuxedo.

A tap on the door made them both start. "Who could that be?" Gina asked, clutching her dressing robe.

Katie peeked out. "We're not ready yet," she told someone in the hall. "Give us ten minutes, okay?"

"What's going on?" Gina asked. The ceremony wouldn't start for nearly an hour and, besides, people didn't usually pay their respects to the bride in advance.

"It's the photographer." Returning, Katie unzipped Mrs. Parker's gown.

"I wonder how they got somebody on such short notice?" Gina set aside the robe. She wore a long slip and glittery stockings that, in the full-length mirror, made her look like a dance-hall girl.

"He's the same one who'll be shooting the Maitland Maternity twenty-fifth anniversary party next March." Katie eyed the gown and Gina's newly coiffed hair. "Elly said he does all the shooting for the Maitlands, so he agreed to work you in."

"Oh, the party! I'd almost forgotten!" Gina stared at her friend in dismay. "Everyone's been talking about it for so long that I feel as if I should be there."

"I'm sure you and Mason can arrange it." Katie angled the gown so Gina could step into it. "The Maitlands won't forget to invite you. Not after today!"

"They're so kind. I'm sure you're right." *I'll probably be back here full-time by then.* A lump clogged her throat, and she forced herself to concentrate on wiggling into the dress without rumpling the silky fabric.

How could a person's world turn upside down in less than forty-eight hours? It had been two days ago that Mason first proposed. Until then, Gina had had no inkling that her life was about to change.

Not that she minded change. She'd been dreading the departure of Mason and the twins from the hospital. If only this wedding were real, she wouldn't mind the abrupt transition at all.

Katie chatted away about the upcoming festivities as she fixed the cloche hat in place and tilted the veil upward. "Now let's add a little powder to take off the shine, and you'll be ready for your close-up."

A wave of panic hit Gina. How could she perpetrate a

fraud in front of everyone she knew, and Mason's family as well? What would her parents have said if they'd known she was wedding a man who didn't love her, and planned to call the whole thing off in a few months as if it were a business arrangement?

"I can't go through with it," she blurted.

"You can and you will," her friend said calmly.

Katie obviously didn't understand. "Do you remember what I told you, night before last? About what Mason said when he proposed? That it was only—"

"I've seen the way he looks at you," her friend responded. "That's all I need to know. Now quit talking and let me powder your nose."

What did Katie mean, that she'd seen the way Mason looked at her? Gina searched her mind, wondering if she'd missed something. He doted on the twins, of course; maybe Katie had mistaken the object of his warm expression.

The scary part was that Gina's knees got quivery every time Mason touched her. He'd done that several times in the past few days, and she liked it. She liked it too much.

Living with him would be torment. Better to call it off now, before most of the guests arrived. She had to find Mason and tell him the bad news.

At a knock on the door, Gina started. That might be him now.

Gathering her courage, she went to answer it.

"YOU CAN'T SEE the bride before the wedding!" Beth Maitland, Elly's twin sister, stopped Mason at the foot of the main staircase.

"I was going to see the twins." It was half-true. He meant to visit Lily and Daisy, but he also hoped for a moment with his bride.

Mason couldn't explain, even to himself, this urgent need to stay close to Gina. He kept fearing that she might disappear into thin air and he'd never see her again. Perhaps because he knew he couldn't keep her for more than a few months, he wanted every moment he could snare with her.

When he was with her, he discovered a part of himself that he'd forgotten existed, the tender side that had all but disappeared after his mother died so many years ago. He wanted to experience more of it, and of Gina.

At the top of the stairs, Megan Maitland appeared. The matriarch wore a sophisticated blue suit that, Mason figured, had probably come from a New York designer and cost as much as a good horse. "I wanted to see the girls," he said.

"They're doing fine." A shadow crossed her face.

"Is something wrong?"

"Oh, no!" She gave him a tremulous half smile. "I was only thinking, well, it's for babies like them that I founded Maitland Maternity. Before that, there wasn't adequate care for many women. So many children were lost."

"No one can save them all," Mason said.

"I suppose not." Her mouth trembled. Then she squared her shoulders and became the imposing society leader once more. "In any case, Mr. Blackstone, I'll ask you to respect tradition and not intrude on the bride's final moments as Miss Kennedy."

How could he argue? "Well, ma'am, I know when I'm licked." With what he hoped was a gallant bow, he offered his arm to escort Megan Maitland outside.

A SHORT, CHUBBY MAN sporting an oversize camera around his neck beamed at Gina like a cheery gnome.

"You must be the bride! How can I tell? It's the dress!"

Behind her, Katie laughed. "Come on in. We're ready."

Gina felt foolish for having forgotten about the photographer. "I was hoping to see my...fiancé."

"In less than an hour, you'll be seeing as much of him as you want." Katie steered her toward the dressing table.

"Let's take a picture of the bride with her best friend!" chortled the gnome. "Miss Happily Ever After, you sit right there. Miss Catch the Bouquet, why don't you lean down as if you're adjusting her hat?"

The man rapped out orders with such good humor that Gina found it easier to comply than to argue. A quarter of an hour later, he'd finished and was on his way downstairs.

"That wasn't so bad, was it?" Katie asked.

Another knock interrupted them. It was the florist, bringing a bouquet of roses and baby's breath for Gina and a smaller bouquet for Katie. He was followed by Ford Carrington.

"I'm not exactly au courant on this walking down the aisle business," he said. "Would someone mind explaining it to me?"

"Certainly, Doctor, but you needn't worry." Despite a flare of color in her cheeks, Katie spoke with her usual brisk professionalism. "Since we didn't have time to stage a rehearsal last night, we're all playing it by ear."

Ford ran his hand through his thick hair. "Speaking of last night, I shouldn't have stayed out so late. But never mind. At least I didn't have any surgeries today."

Gina could see her friend's dismay at the implication that he'd spent the previous evening with one of his new flames. To spare Katie the need to carry on any further conversation with him, she hurried to explain his duties at the ceremony.

"It's going to be a simple procession," Gina said, drawing on her not-so-vast experience in having served as a bridesmaid twice during her years in nursing school. "Katie's my only attendant, so she'll go first. Then I'll take your arm and we'll walk slowly down the aisle…."

When she finished, Ford went downstairs to wait for her. Before she could send Katie to find Mason, however, the minister stopped in to explain a few details. Elly dropped by next, to assure them that everything was proceeding without a hitch.

"I can't thank you and your family enough," Gina said.

"It's been fun." The administrator smiled wryly. "Everybody loves a wedding, don't they? Well, I'll see you there!" She departed, still wearing a wistful expression.

Through the window, Gina could see huge floral sprays defining the boundaries of the impromptu outdoor chapel. Against the emerald lawn, the white-draped chairs were filling up rapidly.

The erect figure of Megan Maitland marched to a seat in the front row. Escorting her was a broad-shouldered man almost too powerful for his tuxedo. Mason.

From the third story, Gina could see his thick hair stirring rebelliously in the summer breeze. *He ought to be riding a horse,* she thought. But wait a minute. What was he doing, already moving toward the altar?

"Oh, my gosh." She glanced at her wrist, but she'd removed her watch earlier. "What time is it?"

"A quarter to five," Kate said.

"A quarter to…? Where did the time go?"

"We'd better join Ford." Her friend fiddled with her bouquet. "Ready?"

It was too late to talk to Mason privately. Too late to avoid a huge, messy, horrible scene that would repay Megan Maitland's generosity with embarrassment, and hurt Mrs. Parker, and leave Gina unable to face her co-workers.

For everyone's sake, she had to go through with this ceremony, and take the consequences.

"Ready," she said.

THE HOT, HUMID JULY DAY had mellowed by this late afternoon hour. Gina could have sworn she detected a cooling breeze as she slipped out a side door with Ford and Katie.

It was a perfect day for a wedding. Someone else's wedding, not hers.

She was marrying a stranger for all the wrong reasons. And one very right one. Or rather, two very right ones.

As they waited behind a rose trellis, Gina drew herself up to her full height of five feet three inches. The bodice of the heirloom gown fitted snugly, and the hemline teased her ankles.

"The veil!" Katie reached over and snapped it down, obscuring Gina's vision. "There—you look like the perfect bride!"

"We're going to miss you at Maitland," Ford added. "Did anyone mention that?"

"I can't remember," Gina admitted.

The recorded music playing over loudspeakers switched to a stately procession, and the minister gestured toward Katie. "Here I go. Good luck!" she said.

"Honestly, I promise not to trip going down the aisle," Ford replied, misunderstanding her meaning. "And if I do, I won't pull her down with me."

"See that you don't." The nurse strode clear of the trellis and approached the center aisle.

From here, Gina couldn't see Mason. In fact, she couldn't see much of anything, just the blurred face of the pediatric surgeon beside her.

"Is it too late to change my mind?" she blurted.

"The patient is anesthetized and the first cut's been made," he replied as if they were discussing one of his surgeries. "I'd say, yes, it's too late to back out."

"I wish *I* were anesthetized." She gulped.

The music of "Here Comes the Bride" filled the afternoon air. The guests turned in their seats, craning their necks, waiting for her. Gina imagined that the whole world was waiting.

Her whole world, anyway.

"Left foot, right foot," Ford remarked in a conversational tone as they started forward. "Remember to breathe, okay? I'm a little rusty on my CPR."

Gina concentrated on maintaining a decorous pace. It was harder than she'd expected not to gallop ahead and get this over with.

A sigh went up when people spotted her. She knew it was because of Mrs. Parker's splendid dress, and was pleased to see her landlady beaming and dabbing her eyes.

The aisle stretched ahead, lined with familiar faces. Gina hadn't expected so many of her co-workers to come to see her wed.

I belong with them. What on earth am I going to do on a ranch?

In the front row sat Margaret and Stuart. Her new sister-in-law wore a stern expression, while her husband nodded distractedly. Could it be that he approved of the wedding, after all, or was he trying not to fall asleep?

Then she saw Mason, standing at the altar. The restrained elegance of his tuxedo made her even more aware than usual of the muscular contours of his body and the untamed rawness of his jet-black hair, tan skin and prominent cheekbones.

His dark eyes feasted on Gina as if he truly were in love with her. Dreamily, she moved forward, scarcely noticing the discreet photographer capturing each step.

There was a confused moment as Ford tried to remove his arm and got his cuff link tangled on a bit of lace dangling from Gina's bouquet. Sympathetic chuckles ran through the watchers, followed by a smattering of applause when he finally freed his wrist.

"Who gives this woman in marriage?" asked the minister.

Ford cleared his throat. "I do." He gazed around, uncertain where to go next, until Katie jabbed her forefinger in the direction of the front row. Abby Maitland, who was sitting beside her mother, caught Ford by the sleeve and pulled him into an empty chair.

With a trace of shyness, Mason took Gina's hand. She caught a whiff of aftershave lotion that smelled like newly polished leather.

"When I first met Gina Kennedy some fifteen years ago, she was barely a teenager," the minister began. "It's a pleasure to see her grown into such a mature young woman, making a valuable contribution to society and moving into a new and very special role as wife and mother..."

She didn't hear the rest of what he said. She was lost in Mason's warm, reassuring gaze.

Maybe this was real. At least, for a little while, she could let herself fantasize that it was.

The groom sensed his bride's inexperience, in spite of

her twenty-nine years. That she'd never been with a man, and that tonight would be very precious to her.

As soon as courtesy allowed, he would take her away from their friends and family to a romantic hideaway. There, just for one night, they could be alone with no intrusions.

He knew he had promised to keep the marriage platonic, but he could no longer abide by that condition. Instinctively, he knew that she loved him and wanted to be his wife in every way.

The moment he got her to himself, he would frame her face with his work-roughened hands and claim her mouth with long-suppressed desire. Easing the gown from her body, he would stroke her breasts until they grew heavy with longing...

"Do you, Gina Marie Kennedy, take this man, Mason Blackstone, to be your lawful wedded husband, to love and to cherish, in sickness and in health, until death do you part?"

With a start, she came back to reality. A flush heated her cheeks, making her grateful for the veil. "I do."

"Do you, Mason Harper Blackstone, take this woman..."

She hadn't known his middle name was Harper. What other important facts didn't she know about him?

Gina swallowed hard. She wanted so much for her fantasy to come true.

"I do." Mason turned to the squarely built man beside him, who must be his cousin, Ed Whitlaw, and collected the ring. Mason had explained earlier that it was his parents' wedding ring. Neither his brother nor his sister had chosen to use it because of the old-fashioned setting.

Gina loved the square cut of the diamond and the simplicity of the design. It suited her wedding dress and it suited her.

The ring slipped on easily. It was a trifle loose, nothing that couldn't be fixed with a little ingenuity. Maybe she would have it resized, if their wedding night turned out to be all that she hoped.

"You may kiss the bride."

The crowd sucked in its breath. The effect was so noticeable that a few people chuckled.

Mason fumbled with Gina's veil.

He lifted it until Gina could see him clearly. Then his lips grazed hers, the kiss ending much too quickly.

"I now declare you husband and wife," said the minister. "Ladies and gentlemen, may I introduce to you Mr. and Mrs. Mason Blackstone."

Cheers and applause washed over them. Everyone was smiling, Gina saw as they faced their guests.

Suddenly unsteady on her feet, she clung to Mason's arm, and barely made it down the aisle with his help. Gina had reached the end of her self-possession. She could no more figure out what to do next than she could perform a strip-tease in her wedding gown.

As they reached the end of the aisle, thank heaven Elly Maitland scurried around to join them. "Receiving line!" she informed them both.

"Gina? Are you off in a daze?" Mason said.

"I must be," she admitted. "If I say something stupid, could you pretend I'm drunk?"

"Don't worry," he said. "It's your husband's job to protect you."

She felt better already.

Chapter Six

Although he'd spent the past two months at Maitland Maternity, Mason had never realized how many people worked there. Dozens of people filed through the receiving line, offering congratulations, while their names sifted into and out of his brain without leaving a trace.

Give him a herd of spring-born calves any day. He could easily recollect which one had had difficulty being born, which one possessed a mean temper and which one tended to stray.

Then there were his own relatives. Margaret and Stuart wore sour expressions, as if they'd sucked lemons during the ceremony. "Quite some wedding," Margaret said. It was difficult to tell whether she meant the remark as a compliment.

"Beautiful house and grounds," added her husband, more diplomatically. "It was gracious of Megan Maitland to offer her hospitality."

"She values Gina's work," Mason explained. "And, of course, everybody at the clinic is very fond of her, as you can see." He slipped an arm around his wife's waist.

At least Gina didn't pull away. In fact, she moved a tiny bit closer. He could feel his skin coming alive where she pressed against his tuxedo.

After the Waldmans departed, Gina murmured to him, "Was your sister ever the sweet, cuddly type?" They had a momentary break while the best man's family held up the line to exclaim over what a great job he'd done.

"No. I think she was born a grown-up," Mason said. "Of course, by the time I was five or six and old enough to remember anything, she was already a teenager."

As he leaned close to speak to Gina, he caught the fragrance of her skin. His masculine response was immediate and intense.

He wished their friends and colleagues would go away and leave them alone. But Ed's wife, Linda Alvarez Whitlaw, had finished complimenting her husband and was moving toward them.

She had the bronze skin that comes from life on a ranch, along with sharp, chocolate eyes and dark hair shot with silver. Throwing her arms around Mason, she said, "We needed some joy, after all we've been through these past two months. I'm so pleased for you both."

It was hard not to be able to tell her the truth. But if anyone found out the marriage was a sham, word might reach Margaret. "I'm glad you're here, Linda," Mason murmured.

She turned to Gina. "You're a brave woman to take a chance on this buffalo."

"Hey!" Mason protested. "How dare you insult the groom?"

"It's better than calling you an ox," she teased.

Linda introduced her fourteen-year-old son, Kevin, and her seventeen-year-old daughter, Jennifer, a budding horse trainer. "I was hoping she'd choose to be an artist, like me," she said, "but she's good at what she does."

"Linda's a potter," Mason explained. "She sells her work through Margaret's gallery."

"Really?" A tiny pucker formed between Gina's eyes. "I didn't realize your sister represented people from the ranch."

"Marge sells Bonita's weavings, too," Linda said. "The gallery gives most of its thirty percent commission to charity, you know. But we're holding up the line! We'll chat later."

"What's wrong?" Mason asked Gina when the Whitlaws had moved on.

"I can't help wondering if…I mean, it would be natural for them to feel loyal to your sister," she said.

"It would be even more natural for them to feel loyal to me." He dismissed the matter without a second thought. Margaret might have a long-standing business arrangement with his cousin's wife and the housekeeper, but his sister was no longer part of the close-knit ranch community.

Next in line, Gina's landlady showered her with hugs and good wishes. "You look ravishing in the dress! I'm so pleased!"

"We'll send you photographs," Gina answered. "The Maitlands have promised to have the dress cleaned and returned right away."

"No hurry!"

Behind Mrs. Parker came Maddie and Sam Winston, the couple whose twins had been born at the same time as Lily and Daisy. From their mellow expressions, Mason gathered that whatever differences they'd experienced had been resolved.

The Winstons were, as it turned out, the last people in line. Mason suggested they head for the food table, and Gina glanced around for somewhere to put her bouquet.

Spotting Katie less than a dozen feet away, she tossed it to her. "Good catch!"

"How could I miss?" called her friend.

"I couldn't take a chance on anyone else landing it, could I?"

"Thanks!" The maid of honor waved the bouquet happily.

They'd barely taken two steps toward the food table, however, when Gina said, "Oh, look! The twins are here!"

Across the lawn, the day nurse was pushing a double perambulator. She stopped repeatedly to let guests exclaim over the tiny creatures.

"I asked her to bring them down," Margaret said, appearing beside them. "I know people would want to see them."

"It was kind of you, but they really shouldn't be out in a crowd."

"Don't be stuffy," Marge sniffed as the stroller neared them. "Babies are resilient."

"Their immune systems aren't mature yet," Gina replied. "They could easily catch an illness, and what would scarcely faze an adult could be very serious for a preemie."

His sister drew herself up as if to argue, and Mason was weighing how best to intervene when the nurse reached them. "I didn't let anyone get close," she assured them, as if reading Gina's concern. "And the fresh air should do them good."

"You see?" Margaret stroked the cheek of one little girl. They wore matching pink gowns that Mason hadn't seen before, perhaps a gift from the Maitlands. "There's no sense in overprotecting children. It makes them fearful!"

No one could accuse Marge's kids of being fearful, he conceded silently. Blair, a twenty-year-old university student, was as bossy and as civic-minded as her mother. Gray, at eighteen an incoming college freshman, rarely went anywhere except in a crowd of noisy, athletic friends. The youngest, sixteen-year-old Sandra, got elected queen of everything at her high school, according to her mother's gossipy Christmas letters.

"I guess a brief outing won't hurt them." Gina lifted a baby to her shoulder.

"In your wedding dress?" Marge said. "What if she makes a mess?"

"It has to be cleaned anyway," the bride replied.

"There's a practical attitude," said Stuart. Catching a frown from his wife, he added, "But surely you'll want to have babies of your own, Gina. You and Mason may find the twins a burden."

Gina's jaw dropped. "Lily and Daisy could never be a burden," she said when she found her voice again.

"Not for us, either." Picking up the other baby, Margaret held her in the crook of one arm, keeping the tiny face turned away from her expensive, tangerine-colored suit. "Isn't she darling? I certainly miss having little ones around."

"You'd like more children of your own?" Gina asked.

"I'm too old to have more. I'm forty-two, and you know how the risks increase with age," Marge said. "But I've got a lot more love to give, and you have to admit the educational opportunities are better in Dallas than in Horseshoe Bend."

"With all the educational computer programs and the excellent books that are available, I'm sure we can make up the difference," Mason said.

"Computers and books are no substitute for a stimulating environment," his sister pressed. "What kind of high school clubs do they have? It's too bad Lily can't speak for herself.''

''That's Daisy,'' Gina said.

''I'm sure I could tell them apart if I'd spent as much time with them as you have!''

With an effort, Mason refrained from pointing out that his sister could have spent a lot more time with the twins if she'd chosen to. That fact must be obvious to everyone except Marge herself.

THE WALDMANS DIDN'T really want these children, that much was evident to Gina. Perhaps Margaret felt she owed it to her youngest brother to raise his daughters, or maybe she was locked into a lifelong game of one-upmanship with Mason.

Regardless of the woman's motive, the results could be disastrous. Gina volunteered at a youth center, and some of the most troubled youngsters came from homes in which the parents had raised them from a sense of duty rather than love.

Her arms tightened around Lily. She was doing the right thing by these babies. She would stay with Mason for however long it took to secure their future.

Maybe, after tonight, we won't need to worry about this temporary marriage business. Maybe we'll be a real husband and wife.

She stood beside Mason, letting the conversation flow around her. In the background, a country rock band began to play. The aroma of hot food drifted on the summer breeze as the caterer, who had no doubt turned her schedule upside down for the benefit of the Maitlands, set out chafing dishes for a light supper.

The appetite building inside Gina had nothing to do with dinner. Her whole body prickled with longings she'd denied for too many years, and with readiness for an experience she couldn't quite imagine.

Since adolescence, she'd held herself rigidly in check. She hadn't wanted to be one of those girls who remained a virgin in name only. She'd considered anything more than a kiss and a little light fondling to be unfairly teasing the boy and taking too great a risk of breaching her own resolve.

Not that any man had affected her the way Mason did. Just the sight of his hands, the traces of scars on the backs and the callused skin on the palms, made her want to be handled by him. To be introduced into a world she would risk only with him as her guide.

Her concentration shattered as a group of young women descended on them. "How could you just *hand* that bouquet to Katie?" teased Beth Maitland. "I mean, how many chances do the rest of us get to be the next to marry?"

"Bridal bouquets are practically an endangered species around here!" agreed Lana Lord, who owned the Oh, Baby! boutique. Her brother, Michael, was head of security at the clinic.

Katie hugged the bouquet. "I'm not giving it up! Although I might be tempted to sell it for a simply outrageous fee. But...not really!"

"Once it's been caught, the magic's gone, anyway," returned Beth. "We can't buy our good luck."

"It's still a very pretty bunch of flowers," Lana noted, taking a sniff.

To Gina's relief, Margaret relinquished Daisy, and she and Stuart headed for the food line. Gina was less thrilled when Mason, after returning Lily to the stroller, made a slight bow toward the ladies and accompanied his nieces and their nurse back toward the house.

It felt lonely, standing here without him. How odd, she thought, since she was surrounded by friends.

"He's such a devoted father!" said Elly Maitland, who, being more or less married to her work, had refrained from commenting on the bouquet. "Now that the girls are no longer our patients, I can admit that I do hope you two get custody."

"So do I," Gina said. *But not too quickly.*

IF HE WEREN'T CAREFUL, he would frighten her off, Mason warned himself as he helped the nurse angle the stroller into the mansion's elevator. That was why he'd left Gina so abruptly.

He itched to touch her. Indeed, he had touched her, numerous times—at the waist and on the arm.

For any other bridegroom, bestowing that sort of caress would be the most natural thing in the world. He'd made a vow to Gina, however, that this marriage was only for the sake of the girls.

If he hadn't seen so clearly yesterday, in her eyes and voice and manner, that she'd decided to refuse him, he might have hoped there was a possibility for more. But he was resolved not to lie to himself, or to take advantage of her.

Gina had set aside her own wishes to rescue the girls from his sister. Now Mason had to rise above his own wishes, too.

It wasn't going to be easy. The pressure inside him had started building the moment he saw her in that exquisite white gown.

Despite the demure veil, he'd noted the swell of her breasts beneath the silky fabric. When Gina reached his side, he'd detected something new about her, not quite a fragrance, more of a womanly note that touched him at an elemental level.

He ached in every cell to explore her at a leisurely pace that would drive them both mad. And then to take her, praying that his instinctive masculine drive wouldn't prove too rough.

She was everything unattainable, delicate and perfect. She was his wife. And he had promised not to take her to bed.

In another minute, he would burst. With a growl deep in his throat, Mason strode into the nearest bathroom and splashed cold water on his face.

He didn't know what explanation he would give for his drenched state. He just knew that, unless he cooled off, he might do something that would drive Gina away forever.

A man had to master his impulses. If he couldn't, he became a slave to his weaknesses.

WHEN MASON DIDN'T RETURN, Gina wandered over to the buffet. By now, the guests had been served, so she didn't have to wait in line. It was a good thing, since she discovered she was starving.

The Maitlands hadn't troubled with the usual catering foods like chicken wings and stuffed mushrooms. They'd splurged on poached salmon, portobello mushrooms and fresh asparagus.

She had to force herself not to overstuff. She didn't want to feel lethargic later tonight.

Where had Mason gone? His tall frame should have been obvious even in a crowd, but she didn't see him.

Maybe he'd decided to tuck the girls into their cribs. He didn't need to stay with them, though. Surely the Maitlands had arranged for a nurse for one more night.

Doubt nagged at her. Mason had plainly stated that he wanted to marry her only because of his nieces. Even though his behavior toward her had been affectionate these past few days, that might be his natural manner around female friends.

She didn't know him very well, Gina realized. She didn't know what time he arose in the morning, or what he ate for breakfast, or what his home looked like.

His cousin's wife, Linda, might be able to fill in a few blanks. Looking for her, Gina surveyed the people dotting the lawn.

As dusk faded, diffuse lights had come on. The shadowy effect was disorienting, and it took her a moment to spot Linda standing with a small group of people.

She and her husband were conversing with Margaret and Stuart. Although Marge towered over the other woman, she stood with her head cocked, listening intently to whatever Linda was saying.

Were they discussing business? Or the babies?

A shiver ran through Gina. Despite Mason's deep trust in his ranch family, she wasn't so certain who would be their allies. Certainly she couldn't go asking questions that would reveal that she and her bridegroom were practically strangers.

With relief, she caught sight of Mason coming out of the house. His hair looked a bit damp around the edges and freshly combed.

Halfway to her, he stopped to shake hands with R.J. Maitland, the president of Maitland Maternity. The nephew of Megan's late husband, he and his sister had been adopted by their aunt and uncle after their own father abandoned them.

During a lull in the general buzz, Gina saw Mason run a hand through his wet hair and heard him explain ruefully, "I was in the wrong place at the wrong time. When a baby wants to spit up, well, there's no stopping her."

She went to join them. "Are the girls all right? They're not sick, are they?"

"Perfectly fine." Mason's arms twitched in her direction, and a tingling ran down her spine as she prepared to feel his hand at her back. Instead, however, he withdrew it as if he'd changed his mind. "I just had to clean up a bit."

"Projectile vomiting could be a sign of something serious!" she persisted.

"It wasn't that bad," he said. "More a matter of Daisy's aim improving." He and R.J. laughed, and a moment later, she joined in.

Megan Maitland swung by. "Ready to cut the cake?" she asked. "We can break out the champagne anytime."

"Oh, yes!" Gina spoke more quickly than she'd intended. "Not that I'm in a hurry for people to leave or anything."

Their hostess couldn't suppress a grin. "Of course you're not, my dear. That's the husband's usual state at this point, I believe."

Mason ducked his head. Gina wished she could read his thoughts. Usually, she could assess people's mental states intuitively, but today her emotions were getting in the way.

The cake, having been ordered late, was a modest, two-tier white creation decorated with pink and blue ribbons of icing and topped by figures of a bride and groom. Several additional sheet cakes promised more than enough dessert for everyone.

The guests clustered around as Gina and Mason cut the first slice. She wasn't sure how they should handle the tradition of feeding each other a bite, which had always seemed clumsy to her.

Mason, apparently, didn't know that tradition, and was waiting with a puzzled air to see what came next. His cousin Ed raised his glass of champagne to make a toast.

"May the joy of this occasion mark a new beginning in our family and in our lives," said the stocky man.

There were exclamations of agreement all around, and the clink of glasses. Everyone must be mindful of how much the Blackstone family had lost. Gina only hoped she wasn't going to disappoint them too badly when her marriage turned out to be short-lived.

The caterer moved in to finish cutting the cake. Mason downed his slice quickly. "Aren't you hungry?" he asked, noticing that she'd taken only one bite.

"It's a bit sweet for my taste," Gina admitted.

His dark eyes met hers. They were standing very close. If he kissed her now, she thought, no one would criticize them. More likely, people would applaud.

But he didn't. "We need to change clothes," he said.

"I've got my suitcase upstairs."

"Great," Mason said. "I'll carry it down when you're ready."

"See you in a few minutes." She paused, in case he had anything to add, then went upstairs.

Katie apparently hadn't noticed her quiet departure, so Gina undressed by herself. Kicking off her pumps and unpinning the cloche hat were minor details. She wasn't so sure how she would manage the gown.

The simplicity of the design proved a boon. She was able to reach back, grasp the zipper and pull it down without catching any lace.

She felt every quiver of the silken bodice as it slipped away from her shoulders and fell clear of her breasts, leaving only her wispy bra and slip. She wished Mason were here. Her bridegroom should be the one undressing her.

As Gina stepped out of the dress and draped it on a hanger, cool air raised tiny bumps on her arms. How warm his hands would feel, smoothing her arms and shoulders.

To be married and loved had always been her dream. To be touched and held by a man who adored her. To discover the secrets that lovers knew.

She had waited such a long time. Tonight should be the night, and Mason had been born to be her husband.

From outside, she heard the strains of country music and the buzz of voices. Alone in the room, Gina hugged herself. She felt a little frightened about what was going to happen, and excited, too.

Across the guest bed lay her going-away outfit. She'd chosen a summery blue dress, knee-length, with broad straps that crossed on her back and chest, leaving arms and shoulders bare. If it weren't for the elegance of the fabric, it might have passed as a simple sundress.

A soft white cardigan, embroidered with seed pearls and white ribbons, lay beside it, in case she got cold. But she was counting on Mason to keep her warm.

After slipping into her clothes, Gina donned a pair of medium-heeled white sandals. She'd already transferred her purse contents into a woven blue-and-white bag.

She was brushing her hair when a knock at the door startled her. In her haste to answer it, she half stumbled on the carpet, and her hand slid over the doorknob twice before she wrenched it open.

Mason filled the door frame, his lean body at home in a dark blue shirt tucked into tan jeans. His lips formed an admiring whistle as he assessed her.

"Is this—appropriate?" she asked breathlessly.

"You look like a dream." He fingered her hair. "I can't believe you're mine. I mean that you, well, agreed to go through with this."

As boldly as she dared, she shifted toward him. Surely he must notice how her breasts tightened beneath the clinging fabric, and that her lips were parted, waiting for his kiss.

His eyes deepened, drawing her closer. He angled his hips toward hers, and she could feel the heat radiating from him.

Suddenly he drew his hand away from her hair and took a firm stance, like a boxer preparing for a bout. "We'd better get started." He nodded toward the interior of the room. "I'll collect your bag, if you're ready."

The signals were unmistakable. For whatever reason, he'd decided to keep his distance.

Struggling to hide her disappointment, Gina stood aside. "Thanks. Where—where are we going tonight, anyway?"

He hoisted the oversize suitcase as if it held only feathers. "To the ranch."

"Now?" Then he didn't intend for them to spend any time alone.

"It's only a two-hour drive," he said. "Don't worry, I asked Bonita to fix the guest room for you. I explained that you'll need a place to sleep when the twins are fussy, so we don't keep waking each other. You should be perfectly comfortable."

"But—I mean, aren't we—"

"The girls can ride with us." He swung the suitcase into the hall. "Ed and Linda promised to bring the wedding gifts in their van. I'm sorry you'll be getting your first glimpse of the Blackstone Bar after dark, but we'll make up for that soon enough."

Without a backward glance, he headed for the elevator.

Chapter Seven

If he had stayed one moment longer, Mason knew, they wouldn't have left that room for hours. Maybe not until tomorrow morning.

He'd never seen Gina look so sensual. How could a woman convey earthly passion and angelic innocence at the same time? She'd aroused him almost past bearing.

Her hair had been spun silk in his hands. His mind had traced the natural progression from a kiss on the lips, down her bare throat to the point where the flesh began to swell into alluring mounds.

How easy it would be to lower those straps and bare her breasts. His tongue flicked over his lips as he imagined the taste of them, the shape, the texture. Her moans would be soft and ladylike at first, but then…

Damn, he was making himself hard. How was a fellow supposed to get into a small elevator with a large suitcase and an even larger—well, appendage?

Mason felt as if he'd left parts of himself scattered around the Maitland mansion. He'd have to go back upstairs and fetch the Stetson he'd left in the groom's changing room. And what about the palpable longing that was no doubt still thickening the air around Gina?

He hadn't even fetched his bride downstairs with him,

he realized as the cramped elevator carried him below. What kind of a groom was that careless?

One who was trying his best to keep his end of the bargain, he reminded himself.

THE WHITE SWEATER FAILED to purge the chill that settled over Gina. Restlessly, she paced around the bedroom, picking up fallen garments and making sure she'd taken everything she would need at the ranch.

Regret knifed through her. Had she made a complete fool of herself? She'd been so certain that Mason was responding to her, that he wanted her as much as she wanted him.

Maybe, at some level, he did. Men were different from women, she'd observed as she comforted friends through broken romances. Men separated their sexuality from emotional bonds, or at least a lot of them did.

She ought to be grateful Mason wasn't the type to take advantage of the situation. His sheer masculinity must make it difficult for him not to satisfy himself, when she'd shown so plainly that she was willing.

She'd practically thrown herself at him. Gina's cheeks burned at the thought.

There was no reason to reproach Mason. He'd behaved exactly as a man ought to under the circumstances.

Gina sat on the edge of the bed and took several deep breaths. It would be easier, she conceded, if she could be angry with him, if he'd done something wrong. But he hadn't.

He was observing their agreement, to the letter. From now on, she would do the same.

It made no difference that she was in love with him.

SHE AWOKE WITH A START when the pickup truck turned off the highway and rumbled across a cattle guard. Beyond the windshield, the night was swathed in brilliant spangles.

"Where are we?" she asked groggily.

"Welcome to the Blackstone Bar." In the darkness, a small gleam reflected from Mason's teeth as he spoke. "You must be exhausted. You slept most of the way."

"How are the twins?" Turning in her seat, Gina inspected the two car seats behind her. Between the girls, green lights showed reassuringly on the monitors.

"They've been sleeping, too. No alarms, thank goodness," Mason said.

"Babies love car rides." So Gina had heard, anyway. "Some parents take them out for a spin to calm them when they're colicky."

Straightening, she stared at the private road, which meandered between spiny mesquite trees. The pungent aroma of cattle reached her, along with the dusty scent of range plants. The moonlit sprawl of the landscape was as alien to her as the high-rises of Tokyo had been when she'd visited there as a child.

To her right, she made out several large fenced enclosures. "What are those for?"

"Those are the horse and cattle corrals." Mason pointed to some structures that loomed blackly beyond them. "That's the equipment shop over there, along with the garage for farm vehicles. Closer to the big house, you'll find the horse and cattle barns."

Through the trees to their left, Gina glimpsed more structures. "Is that your property, too?"

"Yes. That's the village I told you about," he said. "There are four houses. Three of them are occupied by Ed's family, Bonita and her mother, and Bart Manners and his son."

The fourth, she assumed, had belonged to Rance and Amy. Judging by the way Mason fell silent, he was thinking about them, too. "What does Bart do?" she asked, partly to distract him and partly from curiosity.

"Whatever's needed," Mason answered. "Same as the rest of us." Here in his native habitat, he looked more at home than in Austin. His Stetson rode a bit farther back on his head, and he sat more loosely, with one arm resting on the window's edge.

They passed the corrals. Gina made out a couple of barns, as he'd said, and, beyond them, a long low structure set on a rise. "What's that?"

"The big house, where we live," he said. "My office is in a separate building in front, where I can keep an eye on things. Not that I spend much time there. I'm mostly outdoors."

Gina had had some vague notion, gleaned from cowboy movies, that a ranch consisted of a house and a barn, period. This place was more like a business complex. "You don't really ride around lassoing steers all day do you?"

A low chuckle rumbled from his chest as they swung into the driveway that ran in front of the house. With the aid of a couple of exterior lights, she could see that the stone-and-wood structure consisted of a modest original house with a couple of additions cobbled on to the far side.

"Right now, we're in one of our busiest seasons," Mason told her as he braked at the foot of the sloping lawn. "We've got haying underway, we're about to start branding the calves and there's always fences to mend and equipment to fix. I've missed nearly two months' work. I've got a lot of catching up to do."

That, she gathered, was Mason's way of warning her

not to expect to see much of him. Gina took a deep breath and unsnapped her seat belt.

She'd come here to take care of the twins, hadn't she? And that's what she intended to do.

MASON COULD FEEL his muscles tightening as he described the work cut out for him. Although he'd come home nearly every night, he'd been able to accomplish little beyond handling paperwork and making a few key decisions.

Furthermore, with Rance gone, they were short a ranch hand. His brother hadn't just been a major help in the day-to-day operation, he'd been in charge of their selective program of breeding and training horses.

It would have to be shut down. Mason had neither the time nor the aptitude to take it over. Besides, so far they'd barely broken even on it.

But it wasn't only the work ahead that made his muscles bunch like a spring wound too tightly. While Gina slept in the truck, Mason had drunk in her warm female presence. In spite of his resolve to keep his distance, his gaze had wandered to the peachy softness of her cheek, and the rise and fall of her chest.

How was a man supposed to hold himself in check for months with a woman like this living in the same house? Normally, the hard physical labor of the ranch burned off much of Mason's unresolved yearnings. He wasn't sure it would be enough this time.

Opening the passenger door of the truck, he reached up to help her. In that slim dress and those sandals, Gina would most likely twist an ankle if she tried to jump down unaided.

She hesitated briefly, then placed her hands on his shoulders. "I guess I do need a little help, don't I?"

"You're on a ranch now," he said. "I hope you brought some jeans."

"One or two pairs." She slid down gingerly. The brush of her body against his was a fire that flashed away so fast it left only the memory of heat.

If she'd brought only a few pairs of jeans, what else was in that huge suitcase? Mason hoped Gina didn't intend to walk around in figure-hugging clothes like she was wearing now. If she did, he was in for some painful moments in the saddle.

THE HOUSEKEEPER HAD LEFT a vase of roses on a low table near the front door, along with a note that said, "Welcome home, Mr. and Mrs. Mason Blackstone!"

"How thoughtful." Holding back her hair, Gina leaned down to smell the rich, old-fashioned scent.

The ceramic vase commanded her attention. A striking Native American motif was worked in black against a terra cotta background. "Did Linda make this?"

"That's her work, all right."

"It's stunning. And it was kind of your housekeeper to leave these flowers."

"I'm sure Bonita would have stayed up to greet us, except that her mother's in frail health." Mason set Daisy's car seat on the stone floor of the entryway. "I'll be right back with Lily."

"Which way is the nursery?" Gina asked, but he was already gone, down the walkway into the starry darkness.

Only a safety light illuminated the entryway. Beyond it spread a low-ceilinged living room, casually decorated in Southwestern colors.

The wooden floor was partially covered by a large rug that resembled an Indian blanket, a motif echoed in a weaving that hung on the back wall. Linda had said Bonita was a weaver, Gina recalled. If this was her work, it was very skillfully made.

At the back, the living room opened into a den. Although from outside it was obvious the house had been built in stages, the interior had been remodeled so that the spaces flowed naturally into each other. The twins would no doubt enjoy tearing through these rooms, scattering toys around, when they got older.

Gina's chest squeezed. Until now, she hadn't pictured the girls growing up, had only thought about those years in the abstract. But this would be their home. She could see them here, laughing and thriving, long after she was gone.

Why was she worrying about that now? she scolded herself. She'd just arrived. She didn't even know which way the bedrooms lay.

A scuffling on the porch marked Mason's return. When Gina opened the door, she saw that he had Lily's car seat on one hip, the monitor under his arm and a box with the girls' supplies in the other hand.

"I'd have started getting settled, but I wasn't sure where to go," she said.

In the quiet house, she could hear his deep breathing as he slid the box to the floor. "There's no need to apologize. You're not the hired help, Gina."

"I guess I'm not sure what I am," she said.

He gave her a rueful smile. "Boy, I wish I knew," he admitted. "There's no term in the English language for a temporary wife, is there?"

She checked the monitors, making sure the lights were green. "You're not going to tell anyone? Not even Ed?"

"Too risky," he said. "Besides, I don't want to put him in the position of having to keep secrets. Gina, I can't tell you how much I appreciate what you're doing."

She didn't want to be thanked. What she wanted was something she couldn't have. "You can show your appreciation by leading the way to the nursery."

"Yes, ma'am." He scooped up an armload of stuff and led her into a hallway to their left.

A few minutes later, both girls and their supplies were ensconced in a cheery white-yellow-and-tan room bordered with teddy bear wallpaper. Two white cribs sported checkered yellow-and-white quilts that matched the curtains, as well as the pads on a pair of rocking chairs.

"Is this what you've been doing in the evening?" she asked. "It's delightful."

"Most of the credit belongs to Bonita and Linda. Bonita's mother, Nan, made the quilts." He unstrapped Daisy from her seat and lifted the tiny girl to his shoulder. "Time for a feeding, wouldn't you say?"

"Way past time," Gina agreed. For the first week, the girls would need to be fed every three to four hours. "We want some great weight gains when we take them to see Dr. Rogers next Friday."

"Next Friday?" Balancing his niece, he fumbled with the box. "Where's the formula? Oh, shoot, I should have fixed a bottle before I picked her up."

"No problem." Gina began preparing two bottles as she talked. "I thought you knew about the one-week checkup. It's because they're so small."

"I don't mind," Mason said. "Frankly, I like having the doc make sure they're doing well. It gives us extra ammunition against Margaret, if we need it."

The two adults settled into the rocking chairs. This whole room, Gina reflected, had been designed to accommodate not only the children but also their caretakers.

Maybe Linda and Bonita weren't as likely to take Mar-

garet's side as she had feared. Why go to so much trouble
if they expected the twins to be whisked away to Dallas?

As for Mason, he'd spent a few uncomfortable minutes
lodging his large frame into the rocking chair. Now that
he and Daisy were getting into a rhythm, though, he re-
laxed with her in the crook of his arm and made low,
friendly noises as he rocked.

The sight of the big man absorbed in the tiny baby
entranced Gina. His tenderness was all the more endearing
for the contrast to his rugged appearance.

One of his ankles, stretched across the carpet, brushed
her bare leg. The contact made Gina acutely conscious
that, in her concern over Lily, she hadn't paid attention
to how she was sitting. The strappy blue dress bared not
only her lower legs, but half of her slender thighs, as well,
and she'd kicked off the sandals to reveal bare feet.

Mason didn't appear to notice. He was angling the bottle to make sure Daisy didn't swallow an air bubble.

He had to be aware of her, Gina thought. They'd never
been alone this way before. No one else was in the house,
except the babies.

How on earth were they going to keep their distance?

SHE CHANGED EVERYTHING. The air currents, the colors,
the silences, even the memories. She replaced them with
a vitality that made Mason tinglingly aware he was alive.

Even though his groin tightened until it ached, he felt
grateful. One of the reasons he'd spent so much time at
the hospital was that it hurt beyond bearing to stay at the
ranch without his brother.

Although Rance and Amy had lived in their own home
for the past two years, the boys had grown up in this
house. The nursery used to be Rance's room. The Stable,

Mason had called it, because of the posters and the bulletin board crammed with photographs of horses.

His brother had thought nothing of dragging a saddle or a bit of tack that needed repairs into the room, to work on when he took a break from his studies. Dad hadn't cared how roughly the boys lived.

After Rance's marriage, Amy and Linda had insisted on redecorating the big house. No woman would marry Mason if he lived in a barn, they'd clucked. Bonita had enthusiastically seconded their decision.

Well, a woman had married him. An incredibly beautiful woman with slim legs and smooth bare feet. It would have been unthinkable to bring her into the nest of run-down furniture and peeling wallpaper that had been Mason and Rance's bachelor pad.

His ankle pressed against her calf. Even through his sock, he could tell how soft her skin was. He hoped she didn't notice his surreptitious glances at her legs. They were spectacular. And inviting.

But Gina wasn't the kind of woman who indulged in passion for its own sake. She needed care and sensitivity, and a man who could stop whenever she asked him to.

Mason knew he couldn't hold himself in check past a certain point. He didn't lose control often, but when he did, it was like a dam bursting. Once he lowered this woman to a bed and felt her hot willingness around him, he would be like a wild bull. He might even hurt her.

If they were going to stay together, there would be time to work things out. To adjust to each other. To ease her into lovemaking. But not tonight. Not the way he was straining at the bit.

He would do anything to avoid hurting Gina. No matter what it cost him.

GINA SLEPT UNTIL nearly nine the next morning. Not wanting to risk late-night encounters with Mason, she'd insisted on handling the feedings herself, and had spent half the night up with the girls.

The guest room proved comfortable, and she'd fallen asleep instantly each time she lay down on the quilt-covered double bed. Although she regretted being alone on her wedding night, she found it reassuring to know that Mason was just a room away.

She was glad she'd come here. Glad for this chance to spend time with Mason. Glad that she could pretend, for a little while, that everything she wanted actually did belong to her.

Gina yawned and stretched. Snapshots of yesterday's events floated through her mind. Mrs. Parker's beautiful gown. Katie's longing glances in the direction of Ford Carrington. Megan Maitland's encouraging smile. Mason, bringing the twins into the ranch house in the dark.

Reluctantly, she forced herself to get out of bed. The girls should have been fed half an hour ago. She must have forgotten to reset her alarm clock after the earlier feeding.

No, it *was* set, except that the alarm button hadn't been activated. Or had been turned off, she discovered when she read the note beside it.

"Dear Gina. This one's on me. Mason."

Bold black handwriting slashed across a sheet of buff stationery. He had come in here last night. It gave her a disconcertingly shivery sensation, to think of him watching her sleep.

Determined not to dwell on the thought, she went to the closet to figure out what to wear. Jeans, her very first day? Something practical, of course, with the babies to care for, but Gina preferred to dress nicely.

She decided on a pink-and-white blouse and a pair of crisp pink shorts. With a ribbon to tie back her hair, she'd be prepared to handle both the July heat and her nursery duties.

Gathering bathroom supplies, Gina went to shower and change. Then she'd be ready to face her new world.

Chapter Eight

After she checked on the girls and found then sleeping, it occurred to Gina that she didn't know where the kitchen was. On the far side of the house, she guessed, and set off with the sense of venturing to another continent.

In the living room, she glanced outside. The large picture window was shaded by partially open blinds that gave her a striped view of Mason's kingdom.

In the yard, chickens pecked for food, guarded by a flop-eared, splay-footed hound so droopy that Gina doubted it could rouse itself if a fox came to call. A ginger cat, ignoring the birds and the dog, pounced on a whirling leaf near the small building that must be Mason's office.

Past the office lay two barns. One, she recalled, was for horses, the other for cattle. Beyond them sprawled three corrals of varying sizes, the farthest one edged by tight, high-sided corridors that she guessed were cattle chutes.

Outside the complex, the ranch spread out like a scene from a movie. On green rangeland, cows grazed beside their gawky calves. Trees grew in clumps, and a meandering row of them marked the course of a stream. Here and there an oil well pumped steadily, its modern intrusion ignored by the cattle.

Her gaze returned to the office building. Mason stood

in front of it, talking to two men Gina didn't recognize. One was in his late forties, with deeply creased, tanned skin. The other, a smooth-skinned twentyish fellow with the same lanky build, listened attentively.

These must be Bart Manners and his son, Paul. The pair dressed alike, in baseball caps, jeans, boots and red bandannas. The only difference was in their yoked shirts. Bart's was blue. His son's was tan.

Their slim builds contrasted with Mason's broad shoulders and powerful legs. He stood half a head taller than them, too, not to mention the height added by the crown of his Stetson. His jeans and blue-and-white shirt molded to his frame with a blatantly sexual air.

Gina hugged herself. She had to stop gazing at him this way. She needed to give others the impression that she was a happy, satisfied wife.

Taking a deep breath, she walked on through the house, her sandals clicking against the wooden floor. On the other side of the living room, a short corridor led to the open, modern kitchen.

With its butcher-block counters, tile floors and gleaming steel appliances, it blended a rustic charm with up-to-date conveniences. The scents of coffee and bacon whetted her appetite.

At a round wooden table in the center sat two women drinking coffee. One was Linda's daughter, Jennifer, her dark hair tucked beneath a scarf and her large-boned figure garbed in faded jeans and a polo shirt.

The other woman had gray-streaked brown hair pulled into a bun. She wore a flowered shirtwaist dress, belted at the waist.

They both greeted Gina with welcoming smiles, although she read a certain reserve in the older woman's eyes. "You must be Bonita. I'm Gina." She crossed to the floor to shake hands.

Bonita rose to greet her. "Welcome to the Blackstone Bar Ranch. Care for coffee and scrambled eggs? There's some bacon left, too."

"Coffee sounds great. All I eat for breakfast is toast. Whole wheat, if you've got it." She took a seat beside Jennifer. "What time did your family get back?"

"They didn't," she said. "Paul brought me home last night so we could see to the horses. Now that Rance is gone, the breeding and training project is up to us."

Gina wondered if the young man and Jennifer were an item. So many new people and connections to absorb!

"We were talking about a barbecue," Bonita said as she returned with a mug of coffee, a loaf of dark home-made bread, margarine and jam. "I hope you don't mind. Linda and I thought it would be nice to have a reception for you here. We all want to celebrate someone finally slapping a saddle on Mason, so we called a few people yesterday and invited them."

Gina chuckled at the image of Mason wearing a saddle. "I'd hardly say I had to thrust a bit into his mouth."

"That man was tougher to break than any horse I've ever seen!" Jennifer chortled. "And believe me, I've seen plenty."

"Jennifer's an expert horse trainer," Bonita explained. "Rance's been teaching her since she was twelve."

"I'm hoping you can persuade Mason to give Paul and me a fair chance with the horses." Jennifer stopped at a glance from the housekeeper. "Well, we can talk about that after you get to know us better."

"About the barbecue," Bonita continued. "It'll be next Saturday, out back on the patio. You don't need to worry about a thing. We'll barbecue steaks and hamburgers, and everybody'll bring a covered dish. Linda's our one-woman decorating committee.''

"It's a wonderful idea.'' Gina would have preferred to attract as little attention as possible, in light of the fact that she wasn't going to stay. But, of course, no one must suspect that. "Will there be a lot of people?''

"Just twenty or so,'' Bonita said. "With us still being in mourning, so to speak, we didn't want to make it too festive.''

Gina finished a bite of toast. "This bread's amazing. Did you bake it?''

"My grandmother's recipe.'' Bonita beamed. "Whole wheat, too. By the way, at the barbecue…'' She hesitated, and exchanged glances with Jennifer.

"What is it?'' Gina asked.

"Well, we, uh, had to invite the town veterinarian, Cliff Lee,'' Jennifer said. "He's one of the people we see a lot of.''

"Is that a problem?'' She wondered if the man tended to get drunk and make scenes.

"Cliff's terrific,'' Bonita said. "We just didn't realize that his sister was visiting.''

"Francine,'' Jennifer added.

"Francine Lee,'' said Bonita.

There was a pause. "An old friend of Mason's,'' Bonita said at last.

"It happened a few years ago,'' the teenager added. "For a while, people figured they'd get married, but it didn't work out.''

Gina wondered what had happened between those two. Did Mason still have feelings for the woman? Was that why he didn't want a real marriage now?

She refused to let herself sink into jealousy. Mason was

too ethical to have married her, even for the girls' sake, if he loved Francine Lee.

Bonita's and Jennifer's reactions didn't mean that Francine still meant anything to him, just that Mason meant a lot to them. Around here, everything he did loomed large. He dominated the landscape of the ranch the way he dominated her own thoughts, Gina mused.

"It should be interesting to meet her," she said. "I'll look forward to it."

The conversation moved on to other topics. A few minutes later, Jennifer carried her mug to the sink. "You'll have to excuse me. I've got work to do," she said. "I'll see you both later."

"It was good to see you again." As Gina finished her breakfast, she realized she didn't know what to do for the rest of the day in what spare time she might have. "I'd appreciate your telling me about the routine around here," she told the housekeeper.

"Sure. What would you like to know?" asked Bonita, who was sorting through a box of recipes.

Gina hardly knew where to start. "For one thing, does everyone eat their meals together?"

"We each cook at our own houses," Bonita said, "although people like to drop by here for coffee. I usually have a few baked goods around, too."

"Does Mason eat his meals here alone? I mean, did he used to?"

"He packs a lunch, most days," the housekeeper said. "The man's gone a lot. I hope you're prepared for that."

"Surely the ranch isn't that big, that he can't come home for meals!" Gina didn't know why she objected. It wasn't as if Mason were really her husband. Besides, most men were off at work all day.

"It's nearly eight thousand acres," Bonita said. "In an

SUV you could get home easily enough, I guess, but there's places even a four-wheel-drive can't reach. Plus motors can panic the cattle. People still rely on horses a lot.''

"Then why is Jennifer worried about Mason selling them off?" Gina rose to bus her dishes.

"I'll answer your question if you sit back down!" The housekeeper stood up.

"Beg pardon?" She paused, plate in hand.

"The kitchen is my domain." Bonita let out an exasperated breath. "I didn't mean to say that. Leastways, not so boldly. Please excuse me."

"Of course," Gina said. "Are you worried that I'm going to take over in here? Because you needn't be."

"Lots of women, when they get married, they want their kitchen to themselves," the housekeeper said.

"Not me." Gina laughed. "I'm used to living in a boardinghouse. And with the girls to take care of, I'll have my hands full. I only know how to cook a few things, anyway."

"That's a relief." Bonita smiled. "Now I meant it. Sit back down and I'll explain."

"About the horses?" she said, obeying.

"Right. You see, Mason wouldn't sell the five regular riding horses." The housekeeper busied herself clearing the table. "Jennifer's talking about the six animals that Rance acquired for breeding."

"Are they different from the others?"

"They're more spirited, if you ask me," the housekeeper said. "I guess he picked each one for its specific traits. Rance would go to livestock auctions and visit horse farms. Sometimes he'd get a top-quality horse cheap because no one could ride it. In no time, he'd have it trained. I guess he meant to make the Blackstone Bar a big name in the horse world, one of these years.''

"Even if he got some good buys, it must be an expensive program," Gina mused.

"It is," Bonita agreed. "Most years it barely breaks even, and some years it loses money. Plus, the program has memories of Rance written all over it, and that's got to hurt."

"Seeing Jennifer continue the horse operation must be like having salt rubbed in an open wound," Gina commented.

The older woman loaded the dishwasher. "You're a smart gal. I can see why Mason likes you."

"Thanks." She dared at last to broach the subject that had been troubling her. "Bonita, I know Margaret sells your work and Linda's. It must be hard for you, with her and Mason taking opposite sides. About the babies, I mean."

"Hard?" Wiping her hands on her apron, she closed the dishwasher. "Not hard at all. I can't figure out what that woman wants with two newborn babies. She's never been the stay-at-home type to begin with. Besides, Rance and Amy would have wanted their daughters to grow up here on the ranch. Believe me, nobody wants those young'uns here more than I do!"

Reassured, Gina was happy to accompany Bonita on a tour of the house. She grew increasingly impressed by the emphasis on self-reliance.

The utility room featured a large freezer stuffed with food, as was a second refrigerator in the garage. The pantry held a dazzling array of preserves from spring and the previous summer.

The chickens she'd seen earlier provided a steady supply of eggs and the occasional chicken dinner, Bonita explained. The splay-footed hound, Tippy Toes, had a deceptively lazy air that masked a good watchdog. He knew better than to bark at familiar people, though, which was why he hadn't sounded the alarm when they'd arrived last night.

Behind the house, Bonita pointed out two large water tanks, one for human residents, and one for the animals, which could be uncovered to double as a swimming pool. There was a shallow manmade pond, a rose garden up the hill, a satellite dish and a windmill, one of several Gina had seen on the ranch.

Closer to the house lay a vegetable garden and an underground tornado shelter. "Do you get many tornadoes?" Gina stayed close to the open back door so she could hear if a baby's monitor sounded. The beeping was loud enough to be heard even at this distance.

"Every few years," Bonita said. "We've had twisters knock over trees, and once we lost a couple of heifers. Those are young females that haven't had a calf yet."

She didn't seem worried, so Gina decided not to belabor the subject. "The rose garden—is that where you picked the flowers for the bouquet by the door? It's lovely."

"Bart picked them and I made the arrangement," she said. "Mason's father, George, put in the rose garden for his wife. Rance and Amy were married up there two years ago."

"It sounds like a special place," she said.

"When Mason called to say he was marrying you, he asked me to make sure there are always fresh flowers in the house for you," she said. "But he hasn't gone up there himself since Rance died."

"That was very thoughtful of him. Thank you for telling me about it,'' she said. ''And for showing me around.''

''Now I have a favor to ask of you,'' Bonita said.

''Of course! What is it?''

''I'm dying to get my hands on those babies.'' The woman's eyes lit up with anticipation. ''May I help you with them?''

''Of course,'' Gina said. ''They're about ready for a feeding.''

FROM HIS OFFICE, Mason saw Gina observing him through the living room window. Later, he noticed Bonita showing her the chickens in the front yard.

Did his wife have any idea how enticing she looked, her legs bare beneath the form-fitting shorts, her breasts shaping the demure blouse? The air vibrated with her. His body vibrated with her.

He made a point of staying away from the house. A man could endure only so much temptation, especially a man as hard-driving as Mason.

In any case, he had more work than he could handle, complying with government regulations, ordering supplies, balancing the books. As soon as Ed returned from Austin, they needed to assess the horse operation and figure out the best way to cut it back. Mason wanted advice on whether to seek a single buyer or sell off the breeding horses individually.

Breeding and training the animals had meant a great deal to Rance. Now that he was gone, there was no reason to continue.

An image of his brother's face shone in Mason's mind. Rance, five years his junior, had been Latin-lover handsome, with melting eyes and a musical way of moving.

He could have had women lined up around the corral, but he'd never wanted anyone except Amy.

Mason knew exactly how that felt. He could scarcely remember Francine anymore, except for his chagrin that he'd lost his temper in front of her. Since he'd met Gina, he couldn't imagine ever wanting anyone else.

His hands tightened, hovering over the keyboard of his computer. He couldn't keep her. He'd known that ever since he saw how she avoided his gaze at the hospital nursery when he'd come for her response to his proposal.

She hadn't even wanted to spend a few months here with him. For his daughters' sake, he'd avoided giving her the chance to refuse him, and her sympathetic heart had come to his rescue. Now he had an obligation not to take advantage of her, even if proximity and her inexperience made her vulnerable.

In the past, Mason had sometimes lost control of his impulses. He couldn't and wouldn't allow himself to do so with Gina.

It was a relief when he glimpsed Ed's motor home rolling along the ranch's main road. His right-hand man was back. For the next few weeks, Mason was grimly determined not to allow himself a moment to brood.

IT TOOK BONITA a couple of tries to get the angle of the bottle so Lily didn't take in any air. ''I've changed a few diapers in my day, but I never did much feeding,'' the housekeeper admitted.

''Mason said you raised your nephew.'' Holding Daisy tummy-down on her lap, Gina rubbed the infant's back.

''He was already nine years old when he came to live with me.'' The woman's lined face softened at the memory. ''Sweet kid. He's in the Air Force now, stationed in Germany.''

"Did something happen to his parents?" She hoped she wasn't prying.

Bonita shrugged. "My sister's been divorced three or four times. She sure can pick losers. I wish I could have helped some of the other kids, too, but Bennie's the only one that was willing to move out here to the ranch. My sister, well, I can't really blame her. She's got a soft heart. A soft head, too, sometimes."

Gina wondered how people would talk about her after she and Mason got a divorce. The prospect gave her an uneasy twinge.

She'd grown up determined not to fail at marriage. Maybe that was naive.

Still, she'd made a point of avoiding men who were overly controlling, the kind who might turn abusive. She'd figured she would know the right man when she met him, and that no matter what went wrong, they would work things out.

Unfortunately, she'd met the right man, but he didn't love her. He liked her, and perhaps he desired her. That wasn't enough. So in a few months, she would find out what it was like to be a divorcée, after all.

In the living room, the front door opened. "We're back!" Linda's announcement was followed by the thud of boxes hitting the wooden floor. "We brought the wedding presents!"

When Gina arrived, she was astonished by the pile of beautifully wrapped packages. She'd been in such a daze at the wedding, she'd hardly noticed them.

"You certainly have a lot of friends," Bonita said.

"Oh, my goodness." Gina sank onto a couch. She couldn't accept them, not when she and Mason weren't going to stay married. She couldn't return them, either, nor could she leave them wrapped without arousing curiosity.

"Worried about the thank-you notes?" Linda handed her several boxes of notecards and books of stamps. "Megan Maitland sent these along. She thought there might not be a post office handy."

"That woman is a saint." Gina felt like the lowest rat in the world for exploiting such generosity. But then, she supposed the Maitland Maternity founder would sympathize with her goal of helping Mason keep his nieces.

Bonita removed a notebook from her apron pocket. "I'll write down the names and addresses as you open the gifts."

"It's like that wedding shower I had, remember?" Linda said as she handed the nearest box to Gina.

"Margaret gave you pots of chemicals for your glazes," the housekeeper recalled. "Everyone else thought it was strange."

"I loved it. And my sister sent that ridiculous frou-frou lingerie from El Paso!" Linda said. "Ed nearly choked when he saw it."

"On or off?" Bonita asked.

"Ask me no questions, I'll tell you no lies!"

Chuckling, Gina began opening the gifts. It amazed her that so many people had gone to so much trouble.

There were kitchen appliances, most of which she wouldn't need, although Bonita exclaimed joyfully over a popcorn popper and a food processor that chipped ice and kneaded bread. Next came piles of fluffy towels, sheets, cookbooks, baby clothes, children's books, and, from Katie, a battery-operated swing to soothe a fussy baby.

A compact refrigerator for storing formula in the nursery would certainly prove useful. So would a bottle warmer. Mentally, Gina sorted them into items that could be stored and later returned, and those that should be used.

By late afternoon, everything had been cleared away and the thank-you notes written. The girls ate well and had gained more than an ounce since their release from the hospital, she found when she weighed them on a baby scale.

Bonita began to fix dinner. She would take two portions home for herself and Nana, she explained as she fried a chicken. In the evening, she enjoyed working on her weaving.

"Is your mother okay, alone there all day?" Gina asked.

"I phoned her twice, and I dropped by with lunch," the housekeeper said. "Sometimes I bring her to the big house with me. Would you mind?"

"Of course not! I'd love to meet her." An insight came to Gina. "You probably bring her every day, don't you? You left her at home on my account."

"I wasn't sure how you'd feel, being the new mistress of the house," the woman admitted.

"I expect to see your mother here every day from now on!"

To Gina's astonishment, the housekeeper gave her a hug. Thank goodness she'd discovered Bonita's concern.

Gina reflected that she'd been so absorbed in her own concerns that she hadn't given much thought to how others must feel about this marriage. Apparently Mrs. Mason Blackstone loomed almost as large as her husband in the lives of the ranch family.

After the housekeeper left for the day, Gina waited until nearly six-thirty, hoping Mason would join her. There was no sign of him, though. Through the front window, she saw no lights in his office, so figured he must be out on the range.

She fed the girls again, reheated her dinner in the microwave and ate it in front of the TV set. Thanks to the satellite dish, she could keep up with the news of the entire planet.

Except for the one thing she most wanted to know. CNN couldn't tell her what Mason had found to keep him busy so late.

Chapter Nine

Mason ached all over as he stumped uphill toward the house. His empty stomach didn't help his frame of mind, either.

Taking a long-overdue ride around the ranch, he'd found one of the pastures overgrazed. He, Ed, Bart and Paul had spent the rest of the day moving one of the herds to another section.

The men had kept up with fence repairs while he was gone, but there were calves to inoculate and brand, and the equipment was eternally in need of maintenance or repair.

To his surprise, Ed hadn't been keen on the idea of selling off the horses. He'd asked Mason to give Jennifer and Paul a chance to show what they could do.

The man was letting fatherly affection sway his judgment. Mason intended to put out the word through some of Rance's contacts that he was looking for a buyer.

Earlier today, he'd seen Ed's daughter working a bay mare Rance had bought shortly before his death. The animal must have been mistreated once, because she'd thrown the girl and kicked at her viciously before Jennifer rolled to safety.

It was one thing for a nearly thirty-year-old man who

co-owned the property to put his neck on the line. A seventeen-year-old girl was another matter. The animal might be beautiful, but Mason didn't want anyone on the ranch to run that kind of risk.

Darkness had descended while he was stabling his horse. His lighted watch face indicated it was past eight o'clock.

He wasn't sure he could stay awake long enough to shower and eat dinner. There was, mercifully, no question of any close encounters with Gina.

A SHARP BEEPING WOKE HER. Befuddled, Gina glanced at the clock. It was 2:17 a.m. Time for another feeding already?

The noise came again, and she sat bolt upright. It wasn't the alarm clock, it was a baby monitor.

She jumped to her feet. Without bothering to pull a robe over her nightgown, she yanked open her door and ran across the hall.

As she entered the nursery, the beeping stopped and the red light on Daisy's monitor switched to a steady green glow. It appeared the problem had corrected itself. Clicking on the lamp, Gina checked the baby's skin color and was relieved to find it a healthy pink.

Heavy footsteps announced Mason's approach a second before he burst into the room. Bare-chested, he towered like a hero from Mount Olympus. "What happened?"

"Daisy's alarm went off." She double-checked the wire connections to make sure nothing was crossed. "She's fine."

"How can she be fine?" He ran his fingers through sleep-mussed black hair. "Something must be wrong. Otherwise it wouldn't have sounded."

"The alarm goes off if she takes too long between

breaths or if her heartbeat speeds or slows," Gina reminded him as she picked up the baby. "The doctor decides how cautious to be. Dr. Rogers set the parameters very conservatively because he knew we'd need time to wake up and get in here, not like at the clinic, where someone's always on duty."

Her husband began pacing. "So she might just have taken a long breath?"

"That's right. I'm going to clear her nose, to make sure she doesn't have any congestion." She found a suction bulb in the changing table and went to work. "I'll check her temperature, too, and make a note to tell Dr. Rogers about this on Friday."

"We'll take turns sitting up with her all night." He walked over to examine Lily. "Maybe there's nothing wrong, but maybe there is."

From experience, Gina knew that babies' alarms sounded frequently, and usually meant nothing. Yet this time, with a child she loved, she shared his concern.

"We don't need to sit up, but I'll bring my quilt in and sleep here," she said. "That way I'll hear the alarm sooner. You should rest."

She'd been in the living room, reading, when he returned home about eight o'clock. Stiff and exhausted, he'd exchanged no more than half a dozen words with her before taking his leave.

Now Mason stood, legs apart, studying Daisy in her arms. And, Gina suspected, studying her as well.

She was acutely aware that she'd rushed in wearing only her nightgown. The thin fabric must show her outline clearly against the lamplight.

As for Mason's nude torso, its contours were tantalizingly highlighted by strips of tanned skin where the sun had burned between his shirt collar and his bandanna.

Lower down, his waist narrowed to lean hips, partly covered by low-slung pajama pants.

With a jolt, she discovered she was staring at a bulge lower down. A reaction to her, and a very marked one.

A longing for him seared through her. She had never felt anything quite so intense before.

There were only the two of them, alone in the house except for the babies. And they were married. Even if it couldn't last, she ached for him to initiate her into the wonderful, fearful secrets that she'd denied herself for so long.

She would never want any man but Mason. She didn't care where it led or how badly she got hurt. She wanted to be his wife in every sense of the word.

Was she crazy? She'd practically thrown herself at him in Austin, and he'd pulled back. He would surely lose respect for her if she behaved that way again.

Reluctantly Gina averted her gaze. And ordered herself, from now on, to sleep in her bathrobe.

UNTIL THE LAST FEW MONTHS, Mason wouldn't have worried over the monitor once he could see that the baby was breathing normally. Rance's and Amy's deaths, however, had sensitized him to the fragility of life, and he couldn't return to bed until he made certain Daisy was truly problem free.

At least, that was his initial reason for lingering in the nursery. The silhouette of Gina's slender body and firm breasts beneath her gown, and the vulnerability in her eyes, held him longer than he'd expected. Held him a captive of his own longings, and hers.

He read the signs of desire in her quickened breathing and the hardening of her nipples. And in the hunger with which she stared at his body.

Why shouldn't the two of them simply slake their thirst? It would be so natural to carry this woman to his bed.

To brush back Gina's pale hair and gaze into her sweet face. To take his woman, his wife, simply and directly.

Then she looked away. It was an agonizingly familiar gesture. Just as she'd declined his proposal—or made it clear she intended to—she was now signaling her withdrawal from temptation.

Mason itched to ask her what was wrong. He wasn't sure, though, that he wanted to hear the answer.

Was it simply a matter of two people coming from incompatible backgrounds? Or did she sense the danger in him? She might be afraid without knowing why. And she might be right.

"I'll see you in the morning, then," he said gruffly, and tore himself from the room.

THE NEXT DAY WAS SUNDAY. The occupants of the Blackstone Bar Ranch drove in a caravan to the Church of the Grove, a nondenominational house of worship located outside town on a curve of Black Horse Creek, the watercourse from which Horseshoe Bend derived its name.

About a hundred people showed up for the service. On her way up the walkway toward the church entrance, Gina shook hands and exchanged greetings with so many people she couldn't remember their names.

Her pink linen suit and drape-collared white blouse appeared to meet with everyone's admiration. And she didn't have to answer many personal questions, because folks mostly wanted to talk about the babies in their double stroller.

Mason stood beside her, making introductions and

greeting friends. No one else seemed to notice that he stood far enough away so the two of them didn't touch.

Gina became aware of him suddenly straightening, and wondered why. Approaching them, she saw a couple who resembled each other enough to be brother and sister. The man, slight, with unruly blond hair, had an open, friendly expression. The woman was petite and perky, with short, honey-colored curls.

In a blur, Gina heard Mason pronounce their names: Cliff and Francine Lee. The town veterinarian and his sister, who was visiting from Houston.

"I'm pleased to meet you." Francine's gray eyes assessed Gina. "I just heard the other day that Mason got married. What a...pleasant surprise."

The tightness around her lips told Gina otherwise. Had the woman come to Horseshoe Bend in hopes of reconciling with Mason? But it had been a few years since they parted, she recalled.

"I was pleased to hear you'll both be attending the barbecue next Saturday," Mason said. "We'll look forward to seeing you."

The pair nodded and moved on. It was time to take seats and get settled for the service.

Mason paid the Lees no further attention. Still, Gina wished she knew why the couple had broken up. On Francine's side, she suspected that old affections hadn't died.

Halfway through the service, the girls started fussing. Linda waved Mason back into his pew and accompanied Gina to the cry room.

Neither Bonita nor Jennifer had had much to say about Francine. Gina hoped Linda might have more information.

It didn't take long to work the conversation around to the Lees. As the two women rocked their charges, with the Reverend James Farkas's sermon buzzing incomprehensibly over a faulty intercom system, Gina admitted to Linda that she was curious about Francine.

"This morning, I got the impression she was disappointed to learn that Mason is married," she said. "Do you suppose she's still—what's that old-fashioned term?—carrying a torch for him?"

"If she is, she has only herself to blame." Linda brushed a kiss across Lily's forehead. "Mason was quite taken with her. Then one evening, while she was visiting, he blew up and pounded the heck out of a ranch hand. Gus deserved it, by the way, but it upset Francine."

Gina shivered at the image of Mason flying into a rage. The sight must have been terrifying. "Why would he do such a thing? He didn't hurt the man seriously, did he?"

"For years, Gus had been presuming on his old friendship with Mason's father. Slacking off. Making careless mistakes. He had a mean streak, too, although he rarely showed it," Linda said. "That night, he got drunk and rode one of Rance's favorite horses half to death."

"I hate to see a helpless animal abused," Gina murmured. "But that's hardly an excuse for violence. What exactly did Mason do?"

"He gave Gus a black eye and a split lip, according to Rance," Linda said. "And fired him."

"Francine broke up with him because of that?" In a way, Gina sympathized with the woman. "She must have been shocked."

"She said she couldn't bear the way he lost control." Linda's rocking intensified. "She was afraid he might do it again, toward her. But Mason would never hurt a woman, or a man who couldn't fight back. Gus was a big guy."

Still, Gina gave Francine the benefit of the doubt. "She

might have thought he blows up a lot. Had they been dating long?''

''Only a few weeks,'' Linda said. ''It was very intense. After they met, he drove into town almost every day.''

''That sounds like us.'' She and Mason had been thrown together for two months under unusual circumstances, Gina reflected. How well did they really know each other?

''Courtships don't always need to last a long time,'' Linda said.

''Sometimes they can last too long.'' Gina was thinking of Katie and Ford. That wasn't exactly a courtship, though. ''How long did you date your husband?''

''Not long. I met Ed at a rodeo.'' The other woman's expression softened at the memory. ''I went to cheer on my boyfriend, who fancied himself a tough guy. Ed was with some friends, watching. His eyes met mine, he quirked an eyebrow and I fell in love.''

''Just like that?''

''I let him pursue me for a few months,'' she said. ''But I could tell right away that he had a sense of humor, which is important. And he possessed a certain maturity. Plus a cute rear end. Don't you think?''

Gina laughed. ''I never noticed.''

''Mason's isn't bad, either.''

''*That* I noticed.''

This time they both laughed.

Gina wasn't sure why, but she no longer felt so apprehensive about Francine Lee. True, Mason hadn't been the one to end the relationship, and it appeared Francine might be interested in renewing it if he were available. Yet, in the long run, the woman was too easily intimidated to stand up to, and stand beside, a man like him.

And I'm not?

She wasn't sure. She did know that seeing Mason lose his temper at a man who deserved it wouldn't be nearly enough to drive her away.

Linda slipped out a minute later to join the church choir, which was giving an informal performance at the end of the service. It surprised Gina that such a small congregation could muster eight women and five men for a choir, and she was even more impressed when she heard their singing.

Not only Linda, but Ed, Jennifer and fourteen-year-old Kevin also participated. Ed's baritone voice lent strong support to the group.

She had seen a notice on the bulletin board outside about a trip to another town in two weeks for a joint choir performance. Apparently these folks took their singing seriously.

After church, Mason drove her and the twins through the town of Horseshoe Bend so she could see what kinds of services and merchandise were available. "You're welcome to take one of the vehicles into town whenever you need to shop," he said.

"Thanks." Although Gina didn't suppose she'd be here long enough to make many expeditions, she was impressed by the well-kept appearance of the shops.

The bookstore's display window featured child care, Western themes and bestsellers. Signs at the supermarket advertised specials on summer melons, grapes, kiwi fruit and tomatoes. One boutique specialized in Indian jewelry and handicrafts, belts, embroidered vests and custom-made boots.

"I've been meaning to ask you," Mason said as they headed home. "Did Daisy have any more problems last night?"

"No more alarms, and you can see she squawked just as loud as Lily at church."

"How do you feel after sleeping on the floor?" he asked.

"I'm a bit stiff, but not bad." Gina had slept better than she'd expected last night, rolled up in a quilt. She'd found it reassuring to be so close to the girls, after the monitor alert.

"Take a nap this afternoon if you need it. I'm afraid I've got to work. We're missing a couple of cows and calves and I think they're hiding out near the creek," Mason said. "Bart and I found a tear in the fence, so we'll fix that, then look for our renegades."

Gina had been hoping to cook dinner for him, since Bonita had Sundays off. There were a few dishes she'd mastered, including spaghetti with artichoke sauce. "Another late night?"

"Yes. Bart and I might even sleep in a trailer we keep in one of the hollows, in case we get stuck out there after dark." Mason sped along the two-lane highway. "No sense in risking a horse's neck, or our own."

"Of course not." Gina tried not to dwell on the possibility that she might be alone with the babies in the big house. There were plenty of people to call if she needed them.

But the only one she wanted was Mason.

Still, she felt an unexpected glimmer of pride at the prospect of demonstrating her self-sufficiency. Like it or not, she was becoming a ranch wife.

SUNDAYS, Gina soon found, weren't much different from any other day once people returned from church. No one on the Blackstone Bar wasted time sunbathing or watching television.

After Mason and Bart headed out, Linda showed Gina around the ranch village. The houses were comfortable structures with two and three bedrooms. The one that had been Rance and Amy's stood empty, everything but the furniture removed, she saw through the curtainless windows.

"I doubt Mason will hire anyone to move in here soon, although he could use the help," Linda said. "He hasn't even looked inside this house since the accident. He asked Ed to clear it out and give away anything the rest of us didn't need."

"I hope he does hire someone. He works so hard," Gina said.

"It's good for him to keep busy, though. It stops him from brooding."

"Everyone needs to mourn." Gina had learned that lesson after her parents' death, when she tried to persuade herself that they were in a better place and she should be happy for them. Not until she allowed herself a few good long cries beside their graves did she emerge from a tense, anxious state of mind she later identified as depression.

"I guess Mason has to find his own way to grieve for Rance and Amy," the other woman conceded. "He's not the type to discuss his emotions with others. Want to see where I work?"

"I'd love to."

Linda led the way to her covered patio. A potter's wheel had been set up in a sheltered corner, near an electric kiln. Pots, teapots and plates, some wet and some nearly dry, sat on a series of card tables. They were awaiting bisque firing and glazing, she explained.

"These are beautiful." Gina was afraid to touch any of the smooth shapes. "But doesn't the weather pose a problem out here?"

"Yes. When it gets bad, I have to carry things inside. We're thinking of enclosing the patio," Linda said. "Would you mind if I go to work? I'm having a one-woman show at Margaret's gallery next month...."

"Of course! Go right ahead." Gina indicated the twins, awake in their stroller. "I need to get these guys fed again."

On her walk to the big house, she could hear a thud-thud from Bonita's house that must be the loom at work. If she stayed here long enough, Gina thought, she might start knitting and crocheting again. Her mother had taught her how to make sweaters long ago, but she hadn't had anyone to make one for.

This winter, Mason might enjoy a soft wool sweater in turquoise and tan and mauve. It would give him something to remember her by, she thought, and she resolved to pick up the yarn the next time she went into town.

Austin seemed very far away. She had only been gone a few days, yet she had to think for a moment to pry up the image of herself on a Sunday afternoon, reading the newspaper at a café where she might run into friends.

A shrill whinny caught her attention. Gina stopped and gazed into the nearest corral.

Jennifer stood in the center, holding the end of a long rope. At its other end, a beautiful golden mare had planted her hooves in the ground and was refusing to run in circles.

Paul sat on the fence, watching. Positioning the stroller in the shade of the barn, Gina went to stand beside him. "What's going on?"

"They're making friends." Now that he pointed it out, Gina could see that the girl was talking softly, and the horse appeared to be listening. "She'll make a terrific riding animal one of these days."

When the horse nickered again and jerked her head, Gina said, "What's she so nervous about?"

"She's not nervous, she's high-spirited," Paul said. "Her name's Darter, because she's so quick."

"What breed is she?"

"Quarter horse," he said. "The best kind for ranch work."

At last Jennifer moved back to the center of the corral. At her verbal command, the horse began to lope in circles. When her pace settled to a steady canter, Jennifer called to Gina, "Do you ride?"

"Not since I was a kid," she called back. "I took lessons when I was thirteen." Her involvement in choir and candy-striping had taken all her spare time after that. Impulsively she added, "I'd like to learn, though. It could be useful around here."

"Essential, sometimes." In Austin, Jennifer had looked young and a bit gawky. Here in her element, however, she became confident and thoroughly adult. "I'd be happy to teach you. You did bring jeans, didn't you?"

It was time to break them out, Gina could see. "Sure. Would tomorrow be all right?"

"I could spare some time around ten," Jennifer said.

"Great! Thanks." Gina, revitalized, headed home with the babies.

THE WEEK WENT BY with surprising speed. Mason spent most of his time on the range, and although Gina missed him tremendously, she was glad he wasn't around to witness her clumsiness at riding.

The first day, she fell off a placid old mare that was hardly moving. The only injuries were black-and-blue marks on her rear end and a distinct blow to her pride.

She kept at the lessons, though. Jennifer was a patient

teacher, and it buoyed Gina to gain a sense of the balance and rhythm of riding. She wasn't sure why it seemed so important to learn, except that she wanted to absorb as much of the ranch experience as possible.

Bonita and Nana loved playing with the babies, which enabled Gina to take some time off. She taught them both infant cardiopulmonary resuscitation, using a doll from the nursery in place of the anatomically correct model she would have demonstrated with at the hospital.

She hoped the technique would never have to be used. But it was a valuable precaution.

On Wednesday, Gina drove into town and found yarn and a pattern for a man's sweater. Between caring for the children, riding and knitting there didn't seem to be a spare moment after that.

The best part was seeing the way the little girls gained weight and motor coordination. Thanks to the stimulation and attention they enjoyed on the ranch, they were making up for any lags caused by their lengthy hospitalization.

Mason continued to work long days, often into the evening. He always took time to visit his nieces, though, early in the morning and during their nighttime feedings.

He would sit beside Gina, holding Daisy or Lily and plying a bottle expertly. He would talk about the cattle or the ranch business or the girls in a friendly, companionable tone.

He never touched Gina, except by accident. He never discussed his brother's death, or his sister's custody battle, or how long he expected Gina to stay at the Blackstone Bar.

He didn't do anything to make her fall more deeply in love with him. But she did, anyway.

Chapter Ten

"This baby is doing splendidly." Dr. Rogers beamed as he finished examining Lily. "She's thriving, I'm delighted to say."

"Wouldn't you expect as much, with Gina taking care of her?" Mason asked, moving to dress the little girl in her cheerful yellow gown. He was pleased at the doctor's comment, but not certain it would mean anything to a judge if his sister pursued a custody battle.

When he removed Lily from the table, Gina laid Daisy in her place. The two of them coordinated their movements with a smoothness that came from taking care of the girls together night after night.

"I wouldn't take it for granted, even with expert supervision," the pediatrician said in answer to Mason's question. "Some babies, especially preemies, fail to thrive for reasons we don't entirely understand. They need appropriate care, of course, but it's no substitute for love. That's what children need most. And adults, too."

He seemed to be referring to Gina. Mason had to admit she looked happier than when she'd worked here at the clinic. Had the sunshine touched her pale hair with bright golden strands, or was he imagining it? Certainly her smile was broader and came more quickly than before.

Dr. Rogers was mistaken in his assumption that Gina owed her blossoming to marital bliss, though. It was the other way around. Her warmth had brought a new sunniness to the Blackstone Bar.

Everyone went out of the way to drop by the big house for a chat. Linda, Jennifer, even Paul and Ed felt comfortable visiting the girls and talking to the new Mrs. Blackstone. Nana and Bonita positively doted on her.

Although Gina had settled in better than expected, Mason had been apprehensive about today's visit to Austin. Amid her friends and her familiar surroundings, she might become impatient to return, he feared. So far, though, she'd stayed focused on the twins.

All week, Mason had struggled to stay as far from Gina as possible, so she wouldn't be in a hurry to leave. It might have worked, but the lack of time together had only made him miss her more. Not only that, but he'd driven his men so hard that Ed had declared he, Bart and Paul were taking this morning off while Simon Legree was away from the plantation.

Dr. Rogers examined Daisy next. "This surgical wound is almost healed," he said. "She'll have a scar, but that should fade. By the time she's a teenager and wants to wear a bikini, it may not even show."

His comment jarred Mason out of his reverie. "A bikini? On my daughter?"

"Not anytime soon," Gina said with a laugh.

"These girls aren't going to wear anything like that!" Mason declared.

"Even if all their friends are doing it?" she teased. "What if they beg and plead? 'Oh, Daddy, how can you be so mean?'"

"And no strapless dresses at the prom, either!" His

daughters were not going to show up half-naked in public. "Or skirts cut up to you-know-where."

"Just try to keep them from getting tattooed on their you-know-wheres," the pediatrician said. "Tattoo inks can interfere with some of our medical scanning equipment."

"Tattoos?" Mason hadn't even contemplated this potential threat. He could feel himself working up a head of steam, when he realized he was amusing the others. "Okay, so I'm overdoing it. But I don't intend to let my daughters run wild."

He wished Ed would show the same caution with Jennifer. Mason had seen her riding that mare again, and while the horse had behaved itself this time, he was glad he had a potential buyer coming to look at the operation tomorrow morning.

"I'm giving these girls a clean bill of health," the doctor said. "Let's see them back in two weeks, though, just to make sure everything's on track."

Mason let out a slow breath. He'd been worried that the doctor might find something wrong. Something unexpected, as Daisy's hernia had been.

But they were doing wonderfully. And the well-being of the twins was what mattered most.

Now he yearned to whisk them and Gina back home immediately. He had to force himself to remember his manners.

"Is there anything else you want to do while we're in Austin?" he asked as they left.

"I need to see Mrs. Parker, my landlady," she said. "When I called to make sure the wedding gown had been returned, she said she'd packed some of my mother's china figurines for us to take."

"You're bringing them to the ranch?" Quickly, Mason

added, "You're welcome to, of course. I just didn't think…"

"I can't see any way around it. If I leave my things here, people may start wondering why." Gina moved ahead of him, pushing the baby stroller down the corridor.

"Of course."

They were nearing the lobby when girlish squeals stopped Gina in her tracks. A moment later, two nurses were hugging her and peppering her with questions. He recognized one as her maid of honor, Katie Toper. The other woman was someone he didn't know.

The two had just left when Dr. Carrington stopped to look at the babies. Then it was Megan Maitland's turn, and Elly waylaid them in the lobby.

Gina greeted everyone affectionately. As closely as Mason observed her, though, he didn't see any sign that she wanted to stay.

He knew he ought to leave well enough alone. In the truck, however, he asked, "Do you wish you were back here?"

Gina stared at the clinic's impressive front, where slightly over a week ago she had declared her intention to marry Mason. "Not exactly."

"Not exactly?" He started the engine. "What does that mean?"

"I've worked here for so long, I thought today would feel like coming home," she admitted. "But everyone's caught up in their routines, and I'm not part of it. I was…almost an outsider."

Gruffly, he said, "Do you feel like you belong at the ranch, then?"

"I don't know where I belong," she admitted.

With me. He was on the point of saying the words, when caution stopped him.

He didn't want to frighten her by acting too possessive. It was best not to give her any reason to withdraw from him or the Blackstone Bar.

FROM THE LIVING ROOM, Gina could hear Linda, Bonita and Nana chattering in the kitchen. Cooking smells filled the house as they prepared potato salad and brownies for tonight's barbecue.

Earlier this morning, Mason had found a china hutch in the basement, one that had belonged to his mother. He'd wiped it off and positioned it in the living room for Gina.

Finding herself all elbows and thumbs in comparison to the other women, she'd abandoned her attempts to prepare food. First she'd attacked the cupboard with glass cleaner and wood oil, then she'd set to work unpacking.

Freshly cleaned and polished, the dark wood and the glass windows sparkled. The hutch didn't match the casual decor, Gina had to admit, yet it looked at home, as if the room had been awaiting its return for years.

Mrs. Parker had wrapped each figurine in blank newsprint. The little people emerged dust free, their clothing alive with color and their familiar faces stirring fond memories.

Here was Cinderella in a tattered dress, and the fairy godmother waving a wand. The prince had dark hair and eyes, like Mason, although it was slighter of build. Next came a charmingly gowned Cinderella, about to step into a pumpkin-shaped carriage.

Gina had watched every movie and TV version of *Cinderella* that came out. She always identified with the women, but none of the princes ever equaled her fantasies.

Maybe the problem was that no one told the story properly.

The prince wore cowboy boots, tight-fitting jeans and a Stetson. As he leaned against the door frame of the dance hall, he displayed the muscles of a man who spends the day riding the range, replacing fence posts and lassoing errant calves.

As for Cinderella, she felt a trifle self-conscious in her ruffled gingham dress as she approached along the town's dusty Main Street. Or maybe she was smoothing down a fringed denim skirt and vest. Or—well, how would a fairy godmother dress a cowgirl princess, anyway?

Stumped, Gina abandoned her daydreams and positioned four tiny mice-figurines in livery next to the coach. She flinched as footsteps clomped through the front door, and looked up to see Jennifer and Paul.

"I can't believe it! That arrogant..." Jennifer stopped in midsentence. "I mean, he doesn't have to treat us like children!"

"He does own the place," her boyfriend said, more mildly.

"I know, but..." The girl took in the china hutch. "Oh, how cute! Is that yours?"

"The figurines belonged to my mother," Gina said. "The cabinet was in storage here."

Linda's daughter came to kneel next to her. "May I unwrap some for you?"

"Sure."

"I'm going to get some coffee," Paul said, and disappeared into the kitchen.

"What's this?" From the paper Jennifer had opened, a very different sort of princess emerged, one with a ruff around her neck. "Oh, it's Snow White!"

"Mom started collecting fairy-tale figures when we lived overseas," Gina explained, retrieving one of the dwarfs. "They're small enough that we could ship them when we moved."

"I've never seen anything so delicate." Jennifer lifted out a scowling china witch.

"You don't think they look out of place here?"

The girl glanced at her in disbelief. "Heck, no. My mother and Amy decided on the contemporary look because they figured it wouldn't get ruined as fast if Mason put his boots all over it. It's your house now! Whatever you put here, it belongs."

Gina wished it really were her house, but she couldn't say so. Besides, she wanted to know what Mason had done to make the young woman so angry a few moments ago. "If you don't mind my asking, what was that business about being treated like a child?"

As Jennifer set the witch on a shelf, her dark eyes glistened. "Mason's doing something with the horse operation. He won't say what, just that he wants to take stock of it. But he wouldn't let us stick around the corral this morning."

Gina couldn't help sympathizing with the seventeen-year-old's dedication. It was important not to take sides, though. Mason had to do what he believed was best, and Gina certainly wasn't qualified to interfere with the running of the ranch.

"Is your father with him?" she asked.

"Well, yes," the girl conceded.

"He'll present your point of view, won't he?"

"I suppose so." But she didn't seem happy to leave her fate in the hands of the men. Gina couldn't blame her.

Wailing from down the hall announced that the babies were awake. "Can I help?" Jennifer jumped up so fast she banged her thigh on the cabinet door and had to grab the hutch to keep her balance. "Ow! I really whacked myself. What a klutz."

"Let me take a look at it," Gina said. "I'm a nurse, remember?"

"Okay. Then can I feed one of the babies?"

She smiled at the girl's single-mindedness. "Of course."

As they went down the hall, Jennifer hardly seemed to notice she was limping. The girl was made of tough stuff, Gina thought, and hoped Mason didn't underestimate her.

THE POTENTIAL BUYER, a rancher from Montana who'd been attending a championship rodeo in Mesquite, proved a disappointment. He wanted to cherry pick, offering to buy only Rance's favorite stallion and a promising colt.

Had he offered for the dangerous mare, Mason would have sold her. Otherwise, however, he decided selling the six breeding horses as a unit would be more profitable, even though the rancher's offer sounded fair.

Keeping the animals together would also honor Rance's judgment in acquiring them in the first place. Mason knew his brother had had a plan, choosing each horse for particular reasons.

His brother had intended to breed outstanding animals and school them for excellence in ranch work. He hadn't been interested in racing them, although he sometimes picked a fast horse to improve his stock. He'd also hoped to build on his reputation as a trainer so more and more ranchers would pay him to train their animals.

Eventually, the operation would have paid off modestly, although nobody got rich breeding ranch horses. It would have brought considerable prestige, though, in the proud world of Western ranchers. In their pursuit of money, city folks sometimes forgot there was such a thing as taking pride in one's work for its own sake, Mason reflected.

"You can't keep my daughter in the dark forever," Ed pointed out that afternoon as the men changed the oil on a tractor in the farm vehicle garage. "She's going to blow a gasket when she finds out what you're planning." Catching Mason's dark look, he added hastily, "But she won't find out from me!"

Mason saw no reason to explain his running of the ranch to a teenage girl. Heck, it hadn't been more than a few years since Jennifer had pigtails and big gaps in her teeth. "I'm not running a girls' horseback riding club here," he said. "This is a business."

"Paul's interested, too," his foreman pointed out, wiping more spilled oil with a rag. "He's got a level head on his shoulders. We figure they'll get married one of these days. They might be needing a house of their own, too."

It was obvious which house he meant. Rance's house. Well, it couldn't stay empty forever. "We'll see." Mason bent to his work. "Meanwhile, we'd better hurry. I expect the ladies will have us setting up chairs and tables for the barbecue the minute they figure out where we're hiding."

"Is that what we're doing?" Ed asked. "Hiding?"

Mason grinned. "It's not my fault some fool put this garage so far from the house that they can't hear us. And that tractor's been whining about needing an oil change all week. Right?"

"Absolutely," said his cousin.

DESPITE HIS JOKE TO ED about hiding, Mason made a point of returning to the big house in time to set up chairs and tables for the guests. It was the least he could do, with the women so busy cooking and arranging crepe paper streamers around the patio.

In the bedroom, he changed into clean jeans, a fringed shirt and dress boots. He wore a leather belt and silver buckle he'd bought some years ago on a trip to Mexico.

From the guest bathroom, he could hear Gina humming a song he didn't recognize. It had a pleasing melody, made all the more attractive by her pretty voice.

She'd once mentioned having sung solos in a high school chorus. Mason himself couldn't hit a tune with a shotgun, but he admired those who could.

It was time to fire up the barbecue, so he didn't wait to escort his wife. Outside, Jennifer was setting a tray of cut vegetables and dip on the table.

The way she avoided meeting Mason's gaze told him the girl was still irked about being shooed away this morning. He wasn't looking forward to hearing her reaction when she learned the truth.

When the girl crossed toward the back of the house, she limped noticeably. Mason's jaw tightened. That mare must have thrown her again and kicked her. The sooner he got rid of that one, the better.

He believed Rance would have understood. In any case, Rance wasn't here, and it was painful to watch his brother's beloved project stumble along without its master.

Soon the guests began to arrive, bringing covered dishes and baby presents. The other ranchers came first. Will and Emmaline Bonney were their closest neighbors. They and two other couples had known Mason all his life, while some newer neighbors had also become good friends. Their children, faces washed and hair combed, said shy hellos and then scampered off to play.

The townsfolk came soon afterward. There was Bess Millet, the mayor of Horseshoe Bend, and her husband,

Abner, who ran the dry-goods store. Reverend Farkas brought his wife, Miranda, and their two youngsters.

The last ones to arrive were Cliff and Francine Lee. In the late-afternoon light, Francine's blond curls and white, off-the-shoulder blouse stood out.

Mason was pleased that he could observe his former girlfriend without feeling the regret that had dogged him for so long. He was sorry she hadn't found a husband yet, and wished her well.

Then he spotted Gina, maneuvering the stroller across the screened porch toward the steps. She'd done something different with her hair—parted it and woven the top into two French braids that lay demurely atop the flowing blond tresses. A touch of smoky shadow on her lids brought out the radiant blue of her eyes, while her lips, darkened to the color of wine, seemed fuller than usual.

The dress was one he'd never seen before, dark-red fabric gathered between her breasts, short cap sleeves and a knee-skimming hemline. The scooped neck and sensual fabric, and the way it clung to her bosom, stirred hungry male impulses.

Others, he realized, were also staring. And, no doubt, wondering why he didn't rush to her side.

Proudly, Mason stepped forward to claim his wife.

Chapter Eleven

From the porch, Gina could see bowls and platters crowding the buffet table. The scent of barbecuing steak filled the air.

She nearly lost her appetite, though, when she noticed the way everyone was regarding her. Was that curiosity, or disapproval? Maybe she shouldn't have chosen this dress for a barbecue.

She was grateful when Mason ascended the steps to join her. His powerful presence made everyone else fade to obscurity.

When he flashed her the edge of a smile, prickles ran through her. Together, they lowered the stroller to the yard.

Yesterday, in Austin, he'd asked if she thought she belonged at the ranch. She hoped there was a hidden meaning to the question, that he was beginning to enjoy having her in his home.

Several guests headed their way, people she didn't recall meeting at church last Sunday. Introductions were made, and Gina tried to keep straight who lived on which of the nearby ranches. They all seemed friendly, so she supposed her earlier apprehension had been misplaced.

The babies, of course, were the center of conversation.

Half the guests said they resembled their mother to a tee. The other half thought they looked exactly like their father. It was clear that everyone had fond memories of Rance and Amy.

Across the patio, Francine Lee stood with her brother, gesturing animatedly as she chatted with Bart. Although her gaze kept straying to Mason, he gave no sign of returning her interest. Gina began to relax on that score.

"Who wants steak?" called Ed, who was manning the barbecue. "We've got rare and medium. And there's hamburgers for the kids."

People began lining up with paper plates. Gina left the stroller by a table and accompanied Mason to the buffet.

Linda slipped into place beside them. "I didn't want to interrupt you while you were welcoming your guests, but there's something I think you should know."

Her tone of voice drew their full attention. "What is it?" Mason asked.

"Margaret called awhile ago to discuss my ceramics show," the dark-haired woman said. "Just before she hung up, she mentioned that she and Stuart are driving down next Saturday for a visit."

"This is the first I've heard of it." Irritation colored Mason's voice.

"That's what I figured," Linda said.

The Waldman couple hadn't informed him before they came to hospital, either, Gina recalled. "Why don't they have the courtesy to tell you their plans?"

"Marge figures she's got as much right to come here as anyone, even though she sold Rance and me her share of the ranch years ago." He shrugged. "I figure she likes to call the shots, and so does Stuart."

"In other words, it's a power struggle," Linda said.

A power struggle that extended to the babies, Gina

thought with concern. Did Margaret still intend to fight for custody, despite their marriage?

A court battle would mean Gina and Mason could stay married longer. But it would take its toll on him, and she didn't even want to contemplate the possibility that the Waldmans might win.

Mason remained quiet while they served themselves from the buffet. Judging by his distracted manner, his thoughts were a million miles away.

After dinner, Bonita offered to keep an eye on the babies so Gina could enjoy the party. She thanked the housekeeper and went to move the desserts to the front of the buffet table.

"I'll stack some of these empty bowls to make more space," offered a voice beside her. Although Jennifer had been standing there a moment ago, Gina saw that she'd been replaced by the petite Francine.

The woman was a froth of blond curl and white ruffles. Above a denim skirt, the off-the-shoulder neckline bared the curving tops of her breasts. It was easy to see how a man could find her attractive.

"Thanks," Gina said. "It's kind of you to help."

"Everyone pitches in around here," the smaller woman said.

"But you're from out of town. I didn't expect you to join in the work," Gina explained.

"Mason seems to prefer women from out of town," Francine said with a touch of irony.

Was the woman trying to needle her, or merely making conversation? Gina decided there was no point in skirting the issue. "I understand the two of you used to be involved."

Francine sliced a cake into neat, thin wedges. "Three

years ago. It took me a ridiculously long time to come to terms with what happened.''

Several guests glanced toward them with interest, but no one approached. ''I heard he lost his temper,'' Gina ventured.

''He's got a nasty one.'' The woman finished slicing the cake and began rearranging some cookies that didn't need rearranging. ''Not that I'm criticizing your husband. You see, it took me a long time to realize what it was that upset me so much.''

She seemed to want to talk, and Gina was intrigued to hear the whole story. ''Oh?''

''When I was younger, I was married briefly,'' the woman said. ''The man I'd believed was a doting husband lost his job and started drinking. Then he began hitting me. I stood for it longer than I should have.''

''Mason's hot temper reminded you of your ex-husband?'' Gina spotted his brawny figure some distance away, amid a group of other ranchers. ''He didn't hurt you, did he?''

''Mason? No, but when I saw him punch that man...'' She caught her breath. ''It terrified me. I also remembered hearing that Mason's father used to get drunk occasionally. I decided to have nothing further to do with him.''

''And you regret it?'' Gina asked.

A startled expression greeted her remark. ''Is it that obvious?''

''I noticed the way you look at him,'' she said.

Even in the fading light, it was clear that Francine was blushing. ''When I planned this trip to Horseshoe Bend, I didn't know he was getting married.''

''We...made our plans rather suddenly,'' Gina said.

''I hope I'm not intruding. My brother invited me to

come with him tonight and I—well, I guess I was curious to know more about you.''

''I was curious, too.'' Gina felt only sympathy for what the woman had experienced. ''Thanks for confiding in me. And you're more than welcome as our guest.''

''Thanks.'' Francine smiled. ''Maybe it was for the best that we broke up. Anyone can see that he's crazy in love with you. He never looked at me quite that way.''

Gina debated how to respond. To deny that her husband loved her would be to reveal too much. Yet obviously Francine had misunderstood something in Mason's expression.

''I've been lucky,'' she said at last. ''I hope you find the right man for you, too.''

Bart and Paul were making a beeline for the desserts. Gina moved out of their way, and, with a friendly farewell, Francine went to find her brother.

As the sky darkened, outdoor lights switched on. Bonita stopped beside Gina. ''Do you think the girls should be fed and put to bed? I'll be happy to do it.''

''I don't want you to miss the party,'' Gina told her, although she wasn't eager to tear herself away.

''Actually, my mother is rather tired,'' the housekeeper said. ''I want her to lie down on a couch, and I can keep her company while I take care of the twins. I'd enjoy it.''

''You're great with them. Thanks!''

After helping lift the stroller onto the porch, Gina heard the strum of a guitar and turned to see who was making music.

It was Ed, who sat on a folding chair, tuning his instrument. The party chatter hushed and people gathered around.

''It's kind of a Blackstone Bar tradition to have Ed sing at parties,'' Linda explained when she joined Gina. ''My husband earned his way through community college as a folksinger.''

"He was wonderful in the choir," Gina said. "I look forward to hearing him solo tonight."

"Oh, we'll all join in," said her new friend. "You should, too. I'm sure you'll know some of the songs."

Gina would have liked to sit with Mason, but the other ranchers had drawn him off to one side, and it looked like they were talking business. She hoped they weren't offering to buy the horses. It would break Jennifer's heart.

Ed's strong but untrained baritone proved perfectly suited to "My Darling Clementine" and "The Streets of Laredo." Soon everyone was singing along to "The Yellow Rose of Texas."

Gina didn't mean to show off, but she instinctively provided a high harmony line. Ed caught her eye and, after the song ended, said, "We'd love to recruit you for our choir."

"More singing!" someone cried, and the cheer was taken up by many others.

"Something cheerful," Linda instructed her husband.

Soon Gina was leading the guests through "She'll Be Comin' Round the Mountain." Then, happy to return the musical focus to Ed, she slipped through the crowd to her husband.

His arm went around her waist, and he pressed his cheek against her hair. "Beautiful," he said.

Ripples of anticipation ran across her skin. She wanted him to kiss her. She wanted him to do much more than that.

They stood at the back of the group, near the vegetable garden. To one side lay the pond, and in the faint light she could see ducks floating along its banks, settling down for the night.

A faint rustling sound was the only warning before cold drops of water danced across Gina's shoulders. "What the—?"

"Who forgot to turn off the garden sprinklers before the party?" Mason grumbled, then added ruefully, "I guess I'm the culprit."

Fortunately, the jungle of sunflowers, trellised tomatoes and other edibles lay far enough from the lawn that the spray didn't reach most of the guests. "No harm done," Gina said as she scooted out of reach of the water.

A few other people shifted away, too. Most were out of range and too absorbed in singing "Blue Bayou" to notice the mild disruption.

"I'll shut the water off." Shaking his head at his omission, Mason strode onto a gravel path that led behind the garden.

Gina spent a split second contemplating the possible damage to her shoes, and decided she wanted to stay near him anyway. By hurrying along the gravel path, she caught up in time to see Mason duck into a toolshed.

The sprinklers didn't stop. Softly, she called, "What's wrong?"

His voice echoed from inside. "The light's burned out and I can't find the blasted sprinkler switch."

She heard him fumbling, but when she peered in, she saw only pitch black. "Can I help?"

A thin beam broke the darkness. "I found a flashlight. Good, there's the switch." Outside, the rustle of water cut off. At the same time, she heard a muttered curse.

"What's the matter?" Gina called.

Mason appeared in the doorway, the heel of his hand pressed to his mouth. "Cut myself."

"Let me see."

"It's nothing."

Gently, Gina lifted the flashlight from his other hand and trained it on the injury. "A cut is never something to disregard, especially in an old shed like this. When did you have your last tetanus shot?"

"Two years ago. Maybe three." That put him well within the ten-year limit.

"Let me look, anyway. It may need a bandage."

Reluctantly, he allowed her to take his hand. Beneath the pale flashlight beam, Gina saw a thin upwelling of blood. "It doesn't look very deep."

From his pocket, Mason handed her a large handkerchief. "Just tie it up and I'll put a bandage strip on it later."

"It needs to be washed."

"There's a faucet inside. You can rinse it."

Returning the flashlight to him, she followed his directions as he illuminated the way. The shed had a deep metal sink and a faucet that issued ice-cold water. "We really should go in the house and get an antiseptic."

"If I ran for cover every time I scraped myself, I'd never get a blamed thing accomplished," he said.

"Okay, tough guy. Hold still."

She concentrated on winding the handkerchief into place and tying it securely. It was tricky, working by flashlight without a proper bandage.

Gradually, she became aware that Mason was breathing shallowly. His heartbeat reverberated abnormally loud in the small space.

The darkness intensified the heat of their bodies. The air around them ripened as he switched off the beam and set the flashlight aside.

Instinctively, Gina raised her mouth to receive Mason's. There was nothing halfway about his approach, she discovered, when one arm caught her and a hard, questing mouth probed hers.

He enveloped her, big and hot, one hand cupping her buttocks as he tipped her chin toward him. She grasped his shoulders, barely able to keep her balance as she lost herself in the kiss. Gina had never experienced so many colors at once, the scalding red of his touch, the white ferocity of her desire, the brilliant gold that flared across her skin.

She ought to draw away. She ought to hold herself in reserve. But every instinct drew her tight against him as his mouth teased hers.

Her curves received the imprint of his hard chest, of his lean hips, of his unabashedly masculine readiness. Years of vague longings and romantic daydreams hadn't prepared Gina for this sheer, overriding physical need.

Every cell and membrane called out for satisfaction, and the only man who could give it to her was Mason. She understood now why women yielded to temptation, even against their own best interests.

Yet what was *her* interest? She wasn't only a physical being, but an emotional and spiritual one as well. She didn't dare go any further while she was so unsure in her own mind.

With a sound halfway between a groan and a sob, Gina twisted free. "We...we have guests...." It was hard to speak. And the loss of his embrace chilled her.

At the threshold, she stopped. She couldn't see Mason's expression in the dark, but she could hear his ragged breathing.

"You're my wife," he said. "Some things are natural between a man and a woman, Gina."

"Natural, but not necessarily right," she said. "We have to control ourselves."

"I'm tired of controlling myself!" Mason moved forward so quickly she barely had time to scoot out the door.

Maybe he was right, she thought as she stood indecisively in the moonlight. Maybe she shouldn't be so eager to preserve her virginity when she wanted him so much. As for her heart, what need would she have of that once this man no longer claimed her?

From the direction of the yard, she could hear people laughing as they struggled to coordinate rounds of "Row, Row, Row Your Boat." There was another noise, coming this way: footsteps marching on the gravel path.

Gina wavered between being grateful and feeling annoyed. In the end, it didn't matter. Whoever was heading their way had a purposeful stride and was not about to be dissuaded.

"Damn!" Mason muttered as he emerged from the shed. "Company. What timing."

A ray of moonlight caught Jennifer's young, taut face as she came around the corner of the garden. "Mason!" Her voice was tight with anger. "I want to talk to you!"

"Right here," he said.

The girl limped closer. Spotting Gina, she hesitated. "I didn't realize you were here, too. Dad mentioned Mason came this way. I don't mean to make trouble at a party, but I just found out..."

"This isn't an appropriate time to talk business." Mason's knife-edge tone made it clear he knew exactly why his young cousin had come.

"Then you should have told me earlier instead of letting me find out from gossip!" Jennifer planted herself on the walkway, addressing Mason from a distance that would have been suitable for a duel. "Emmaline Bonney says she heard you had a horse buyer come by this morning."

"That's right." Mason spoke stiffly. "We didn't make a deal, so it doesn't concern you."

"Those horses are my whole life!" the girl flared. "I've never wanted to do anything but work with them! And Rance wanted me to do it!"

"Don't tell me what my brother wanted!" Mason's dark shape loomed. "I'll run my ranch any way I see fit, Jennifer. Frankly, selling the operation is in your best interest, even if you're too young to see it."

"I'm nearly eighteen."

"You're a baby, and you're acting like one," he snapped. "If you had any perspective, you'd be making plans for college."

"Yeah, sure, you're doing this for my own good! Well, I know better. It's the money, isn't it?" Tears sparkled on her cheeks. "You're selling out Rance's dream. He wouldn't have stood for it, and you know it!" She turned and stumbled away.

Gina held her breath, wondering if Mason would explode. He stood, fists clenched, staring into the night. His chest rose and fell in short bursts that revealed his fury louder than any words could have.

As the silence lengthened, she wondered if there was room for compromise. "Is the horse operation losing a lot of money?" she asked.

"It isn't a matter of expenses." His voice came out in a low, feral snarl. "It's a question of judgment. And when it comes to the ranch, mine is the only one that counts."

Every instinct warned Gina to back off. Yet the horses, after all, had been close to his brother's heart. Although seeing Jennifer work with them every day must be painful, that wasn't a good enough reason to destroy the girl's dreams.

"Maybe you shouldn't be in such a hurry," she said.

"When we lose someone we love, it's best not to make major decisions right away. And you can see how deeply Jennifer's affected."

"I've known her since the day she was born," he growled. "You've known her, what, a week? It's easy to sympathize with her, Gina, but you're not going to be around to take the consequences, are you?"

You're not going to be around. No, she wouldn't, since it appeared he had no intention of asking her to stay. She'd started to care about his family and his ranch, and he was throwing it in her face.

"I'm sorry." She tried to steady the quaver in her tone. "From now on, I'll mind my own business."

She walked off, crunching across the gravel with as much dignity as she could muster. She had to swallow hard several times before she could face the guests.

MASON CURSED HIMSELF in the darkness. He'd let his temper get the better of him, and he'd upset Gina.

If only Jennifer hadn't confronted him at the very moment when the two of them were finally getting close. His body throbbed at the memory of his wife's nipples taut against his chest and her heat igniting a blaze inside him.

He'd forgotten all that, though, when the girl arrived and he saw the way she was limping. Like most young people, Jennifer had no sense of her own vulnerability. It probably never occurred to her that a kick in the head could end her life when it had scarcely begun.

Maybe he should go explain his concerns to Gina. But as Mason's mood leveled, common sense warned him not to expect too much.

His wife had ended their embrace even before they were interrupted. She'd said that lovemaking might be natural, but that didn't make it right.

She'd been reminding him of their agreement. She'd come to the Blackstone Bar for the sake of the babies, not to become his soul mate and life partner.

He wanted her so badly he could scarcely hold himself in check. It hurt like fire to know she didn't feel the same way.

Yet he needed her now more than ever. Under other circumstances, Margaret's decision to visit might not mean she still intended to seek custody. The fact that she'd told Linda instead of informing Mason directly, however, convinced him that his sister was still playing power games.

Without Gina, the twins would get shuffled off like pawns to a couple who hadn't bothered to pay them a single visit in the first two months of their lives. How loving could they be?

If he had to sacrifice his pride or his heart to save his nieces, Mason was prepared to do it.

Chapter Twelve

When she finished weighing Daisy, Gina made a note on her pad and put an exclamation point after it. Like her sister, the baby had shown a healthy gain in the six days since the party.

Gina only wished there'd been a comparable improvement in her relationship with Mason. Instead, it seemed to have gone backward.

He hadn't touched her since last Saturday, and he no longer gazed at her with that melting expression she sometimes used to catch on his face. They'd reached a tentative, unspoken pact in which they fussed over the girls, speculated about Margaret and Stuart's plans and treated each other with the pleasant, distant air of acquaintances.

Even though she saw Mason several times a day, she missed him keenly. It was as if a wall had gone up between them, and Gina didn't know how to break it down.

Her arms tightened around Daisy as the little girl snuggled into her lap. "I don't know what I'd do without you." Gina's throat caught. "You're so sweet, you know that?"

Peering directly into her eyes, Daisy quirked a corner of her mouth. Her first smile!

Gina's spirits soared. "Next thing we know, you'll be running in marathons and writing poetry," she said, and made another notation on the paper where she was recording the girls' development. "Obviously, you're showing early signs of genius."

"Are you talking to yourself?" From the hallway, Bonita sauntered in. "Living on a ranch can do that to people."

"I was talking to Daisy," she informed the housekeeper. "She smiled. Honestly!"

"Did she crack any jokes? Now, that would be impressive." Bonita shifted her armful of sheets to get a better grip.

"I thought you changed the linens on Wednesdays." Gina lifted the little girl into the stroller.

"Margaret and Stuart are arriving tonight, remember?" she said. "I'm fixing the guest room for them, and their younger daughter is coming, too. She can sleep in the den."

"Fine," Gina said automatically. But her thoughts were flying in an entirely different direction.

It hadn't occurred to her that since there were only three bedrooms in the house, Margaret and Stuart would take the room that Gina herself usually occupied. That meant she'd be sharing quarters with Mason for two nights.

The two of them would be alone in one bed. It was a situation they'd studiously avoided in the two weeks since their marriage, and now it was being forced upon them.

"You can hear the monitors from the master bedroom, can't you?" the housekeeper asked.

"Of course." There hadn't been any alarms since the first one, anyway.

"If you wake Mason every time you get up and down

at night, he might be grumpy with his sister," Bonita said, chattering on. "Which is exactly what she deserves."

"I suppose so."

"Worried?" the housekeeper asked. "I don't see how a judge could take their side, I really don't."

"How well do you know Margaret?" Gina asked, tucking Lily into the stroller beside her sister. "Did you work here when she was at home?"

The housekeeper hugged her load of sheets. "I came twenty-two years ago, when Mason's mother was dying of cancer, to take care of her and the boys. Margaret was already married."

"What was their mother like?" Gina asked. "I picture her as a true Texan, at home in the saddle and a crack shot with a rifle." *Everything I couldn't dream of becoming.*

"Not even remotely." Bonita walked to a shelf and straightened a couple of dolls that had tipped over. "She was English."

"English?"

"From Bath. Isn't that a strange thing to call a city? Her name was Lainie, which I guess is a nickname for Elaine," she said. "When she was about twenty, she got a notion to tour the American West all by herself. She was in San Antonio when she asked George Blackstone to take her picture at the Alamo."

"What was he doing there?" Gina asked curiously.

"Attending a livestock show, I think," Bonita said. "Lainie said she was fascinated to meet someone of Indian descent, and they started talking. I guess one thing led to another."

"How old was she when she died?"

"In her early forties," Bonita said. "Not very old. She saw her daughter married, but her sons were still young."

"So you helped raise them," Gina said.

"Not Mason. At twelve, he was already practically a grown-up." Bonita's expression warmed. "But Rance, he was seven. I sure miss that sweet boy. And I love his little girls. I hope you don't mind my saying it, but I feel as if they're my granddaughters."

"Why would I mind?" she asked. "Mason and I have both lost our parents, so you're the only grandmother Lily and Daisy have."

"And you're the perfect mother," Bonita replied. "They're lucky little girls. You're wonderful with them. I'll do anything I can—short of breaking the law, of course—to keep them out of Margaret's hands."

"I wish I understood why she wants them so badly," Gina said.

"People don't always know what's good for them," Bonita agreed. "Well, you let me know if there's anything I can do."

"Thanks." Gina gave her a smile. "I will."

"I'll put your things in the master bedroom for you," the housekeeper added. "If that's all right."

"I'd appreciate it." She remembered the sweater she was making as a surprise for Mason. Doggedly, she'd continued working on it this week, even though she doubted she'd be around next winter to see him wear it. "Would you mind hiding my knitting?"

"I'll put it by the washing machine," the other woman said. "A man would never look there."

They both chuckled. When Gina glanced down at the twins, she saw to her astonishment that they were smiling, as if sharing the mirth.

"A matched set!" she said. "Look at that."

"They have happy natures," Bonita observed. "They must get it from their mother's side. It certainly isn't a

Blackstone trait!'' She clucked to herself as she went out with the linens.

Gina pushed the baby carriage through the house and eased it down the front walkway. The air was steamier than usual, thanks to an electrical storm that had struck in the early morning hours. The thunder had awakened her, but she'd been so exhausted by middle-of-the-night feedings that she'd fallen immediately back to sleep.

Today, she decided to circle the corrals and take a look at the barns. Each day she varied her walks, although, with the stroller, she was limited to paved areas and well-worn footpaths.

Gina liked the slower pace of the country, the intimate interaction with the weather and the myriad of sounds and scents. It was as if, after being wrapped in a cocoon all her life, she was feeling a breeze on her skin for the first time.

On her way past Mason's office, she glanced at the window. There was no sign of activity inside, but then, he usually confined his bookkeeping to the evening hours when he couldn't do other work.

By the chicken coop, which was attached to the cattle barn, Tippy Toes the hound raised his head to stare at her. He'd barked at Gina once or twice when she first arrived, but now accepted her as a fixture.

The ginger cat, named Owl because of her huge eyes and preference for nighttime activities, woke from a nap and surveyed her surroundings. A chicken wandered by, blithely ignoring her. Through the window, Gina had seen Owl stalking wild birds, but the cat knew enough to leave the chickens alone.

''You can learn a lot, living on a ranch,'' she told the girls. ''Such as that different creatures can learn to get along with each other.''

She pushed the stroller around the cattle barn. From inside came the lowing of a few cows that had been confined due to injuries. Their earthy, comforting smell wafted through the open doors.

Farther on, by the farm vehicle garage, Ed was revving up a tractor. When the noise abated, he called from his high seat, "Got to plant some hay. Might as well take advantage of the soil being wet."

"Where's Mason?" Not that she expected to see him before dinner, but Gina always liked to know where he was. And rarely did.

"He and Bart went out to the north pasture to check on a lightning strike." The foreman patted a walkie-talkie in his shirt pocket. "They just called to say there's no fire. That's a relief."

"A fire on the ranch?" The idea scared her. "I can't imagine anything worse."

"Twisters aren't any picnic, either," he said. "Frankly, that thunderstorm last night had me a little worried, but we got lucky."

Even though the sun was warming her shoulders, Gina shivered. "I guess so."

Ed leaned down from his seat. "Could I talk to you for a minute? About something personal?"

"Sure." She stood back and gave him room to swing down.

He landed nearby. After wiping his forehead with his bandanna, he said, "It's Jennifer. I have a request, sort of. Girls that age, they listen to their friends more than they listen to their parents."

"I'll do anything I can to help." She was flattered that he considered her a friend of his daughter's.

Certainly they'd gotten to know each other well in the past two weeks, thanks to daily riding lessons. They'd

gone out on the range nearly every day, Gina's placid old
horse trailing the lively Darter.

She'd asked Jennifer to take her around the ranch, and
was finally beginning to recognize the natural landmarks
as well as the manmade ones. It was a big spread, and
she had to concentrate hard, but Gina was pleased that
she could sometimes pick out a route by herself.

"We'd prefer that she choose college rather than stay
here, but some people aren't the academic type, so we
don't push," he said. "Anyway, she's so tied up in those
horses, well, we're trying to prepare her for the possibility
of losing them. Linda and I, we're afraid she'd be devastated."

"What could I do?" Gina asked.

"Just…help her see that there's a larger world, that's
all," Ed said. "Talk about Austin, and what life is like
in the city. About college. So that, if the worst happens,
maybe she won't feel lost."

"I'll do my best," Gina promised. In fact, she'd already talked quite a bit about her previous life. Jennifer
was curious about everything, but it was obvious that she
had a special connection to the animals she trained.

Mason hadn't said any more about selling them. On the
other hand, he might be merely biding his time until another buyer came along.

Ed climbed to his seat and set off on the tractor, and
Gina resumed her walk. For all its isolation, or perhaps
because of it, the ranch was a close-knit community. She
had become involved in these people's lives even without
intending to.

Her thoughts strayed to Mason's mother and her fateful
encounter, more than forty years ago, with George Blackstone. How exotic the ranch must have looked to Lainie

when she first arrived! Had she loved it from the first moment, or had it grown on her gradually?

It had certainly grown on Gina. And so had its owner.

She'd known the risks when she said yes to a short-term marriage. But she hadn't anticipated the depth of her own feelings.

Next week she would celebrate her thirtieth birthday. For so long, she'd feared that she would never find the right man to marry. Now she'd found him, yet she was as lonely as ever.

If only Mason were really hers. If only tonight, when they shared a room, he would make her his wife in every sense of the word.

She would be sitting at the dressing table, brushing her hair, when their eyes met in the mirror. She would feel his lips graze her neck, and his hands would gently seize her shoulders. Caressing her. Turning her toward him.

Before she could guess what he had in mind, he would lift her in his arms and carry her to the bed. Their bed. The one they would sleep in, together, for the rest of their lives.

Gina tore herself from the fantasy. She was only setting herself up for disappointment, the way she'd done on her wedding night. Yet she couldn't help hoping.

A few minutes later, she rounded a row of cattle chutes and caught sight of the main ranch road. A late-model sedan, its shiny paint marred by mud splatters near the wheel base, was jouncing past the village toward the big house.

In the passenger seat sat Margaret, recognizable by her tall figure, straight shoulders and dark hair. That was Stuart driving, and, in the back seat, the teenage girl with short, sandy hair must be their daughter.

Gina glimpsed something else, too. A pair of infant seats, strapped into the back next to the girl.

Margaret and Stuart had come prepared to take the twins home with them.

THE LIGHTNING HAD shattered a tree stump and, judging by the charring, started a small fire. Mercifully, the rain had put it out.

Calling to reassure Ed, Mason had to shout to make himself heard over the static on his walkie-talkie. One of these days, he'd like to replace these old devices with cellular phones. Rance had insisted the cost was prohibitive, but these aging relics of their father's era were barely serviceable.

After making sure no sparks remained around the stump, Mason rode on alone to check other areas for signs of damage. Along Black Horse Creek, he found a mudslide that had turned a steep stretch of bank into a slippery plunge. An animal coming to drink here could get injured or, at the very least, trapped down by the water.

The area needed to be fenced off. Mason made a mental note to take care of it as soon as possible.

He didn't dare spend too long on the range this weekend, though. If he knew his sister, she'd keep a record of how much time he spent away from the girls, and use it against him in court.

He rode home early, arriving at the big house about four o'clock. The sight of the Lincoln out front, and the two infant seats in the back, told him all he needed to know.

Wanting to appear at his best in front of his relatives, he'd left clean clothes, soap and a towel in a shower stall located in the garage. Freshly washed, he made his way through the utility room and past the kitchen, where Bonita and Nana were preparing dinner.

It struck him, as he stepped into the living room, how much the place had changed during the past two weeks. The china cabinet, with its lovingly placed figurines, warmed the impersonal space. A riotous arrangement of flowers exploded from a vase on the coffee table, and the air hinted of roses and baby powder.

"Mason!" Gina rose to greet him. In a pink linen suit, with berets clipping back her blond hair, she had a tailored crispness that even his sister couldn't fault.

Not that his wife's sophistication, or anything else, was likely to help their cause. Once Margaret set her mind to something, she hung on like a bulldog.

At the moment, his sister was holding Daisy rather awkwardly on her lap, while sixteen-year-old Sandra cradled Lily. Although he'd seen the Waldmans' younger daughter at Rance's funeral, Mason had been too distracted to notice how she'd sprouted from an awkward girl into a self-possessed teenager.

Her layered haircut, printed blouse and skirt, and painted toenails peeping from stylish sandals shouted "city girl!" Despite the differences in age and coloring, the tilt of her chin and the assurance in her expression reminded him of Margaret.

Stuart stood up to shake hands, his grip firm and dry. As always, the man had an air of detached amusement, as though he were an observer in his own life.

"They're so cute!" Sandra cried, bouncing Lily on her lap. "Uncle Mason, I can't wait to dress the twins in little gowns! Mom and I are going to take them shopping at Neiman-Marcus."

"Of course, they have darling outfits from Austin already," her mother added with a rare attempt at tact, which she spoiled by adding, "But now that you're living out here and they're growing so fast, they'll need new clothes you can't possibly find in Horseshoe Bend."

Mason felt himself bristling. If Gina had had to put up with more than a few minutes of this condescension, she deserved a medal for self-control.

His annoyance displayed itself as irony. "I'm glad you're getting acquainted with your nieces at last," he said, "since you didn't manage to visit them during their two months at the hospital."

Marge pressed her lips together. The battle was on and she knew it.

"I had no doubt they were receiving excellent care at Maitland Maternity," she said at last. "What infants need in their early days, any skilled person can provide. It's their later years that I'm concerned about. They'll need a decent education, and an exposure to culture and the social graces."

His internal pressure rose yet another notch. While Mason valued an education as much as anyone, he wasn't impressed by his sister's idea of social graces. Snobbery, that's what she meant.

"But the girls are still infants," Gina pointed out. "For the next couple of years, they'll need constant supervision and a lot of patience. If you're mainly interested in their education, why are you in such a hurry to take them to Dallas?"

"Because they're so darling!" Sandra burbled. "I can't wait to take them for a walk and let my friends see my cute little...what are they to me, anyway, Mom? Cousins? Nieces?"

"First cousins," Marge said. "Jennifer, Linda's daughter, is your second—no, third—cousin. You know, that scruffy-looking girl we saw riding horseback a few minutes ago.''

''I've met Cousin Jennifer before,'' her daughter said. ''We went swimming once when I was twelve. She's nice, but hasn't she put on a little weight around the hips?''

''It's the riding,'' said Marge, who had been afraid of even the most docile mare since she fell off one as a child. ''It's not a proper form of exercise. She needs to join a gym.''

Mason's sympathy for Jennifer took a huge leap. He'd forgotten how catty some females could be about women who didn't conform to their ideas.

''I've been learning to ride, myself,'' Gina interjected smoothly. ''Jennifer's a wonderful teacher. I think it's healthy for girls to grow up on a ranch where they can learn to be self-sufficient. You know, it's fine to study nature in a classroom, but experiencing it firsthand is even better.''

''Then why not raise them in a rain forest? Or go live in Antarctica?'' Margaret snipped.

This was too much even for her daughter. ''But Mom, you grew up on the Blackstone Bar. It didn't hurt you.''

''That's because I left as soon as I could!''

''Let's be frank here,'' Stuart said to Mason. ''There's a lot to be said for your lifestyle, but when it comes to the girls, you can't compare the rough-and-tumble of the ranch with what Dallas has to offer.''

''Aren't you forgetting something?'' Mason demanded. ''It's called love. It's what makes people drive four hours a day round-trip to be with someone in the hospital. The girls need parents who love them a lot more than they need trips to Neiman-Marcus.''

''Of course we love them.'' Margaret gave him a smug smile, as if she'd already won. ''That's a given.'' She didn't notice that Daisy had slid to an awkward angle on her lap and was squirming in discomfort.

"Exactly when have you spent enough time with them to know whether you love them or not?" He was about to continue his tirade when, from the corner of his eye, he caught Gina's slight frown. He interpreted it as meaning "simmer down."

She must have a plan. At considerable cost to his blood pressure, Mason yielded.

"Stuart, Margaret," Gina said, "I think you should know that, as a medical professional, I have some concerns about the babies' care." To illustrate, she crossed the room and shifted Daisy so that her head was supported against Margaret's arm. "Her neck muscles haven't matured yet. It's very important to pay close attention to the babies when you're holding them."

The smugness vanished from his sister's face. This was one arena in which neither she nor her husband could claim superiority.

It didn't take her long to rally, though. "Having raised three children, I think I know something about infant care," Margaret said. "Plus, we know a first-rate pediatrician in Dallas. Certainly you can't find anyone like that in Horseshoe Bend."

"We take them to a doctor in Austin." After making sure Daisy was secure, Gina returned to the couch. "Now, before we come to any agreement, or decide to fight it out in court, I'd like for the two of you to take charge of the girls for a couple of nights."

"What fun!" Sandra squeezed Lily a bit tightly, but the baby didn't seem to mind.

"You mean, here at the ranch?" Stuart asked.

Gina nodded. "I'll have to train you both in infant CPR. And I'll teach you to use the apnea monitors. You realize the girls have to be fed every three to four hours, even if you have to wake them in the middle of the night to do it.''

Margaret waved her hand airily. ''We can always hire a baby nurse.''

''You can't always find someone reliable right when you need her, and nannies have been known to quit without notice.'' Gina's professional manner brooked no quibbling. ''It's imperative that the twins' parents be able to care for them.''

''Well, naturally,'' his sister said.

Stuart cleared his throat, a sign of discomfort. He obviously hadn't intended to take a hands-on role in this parenting business. Mason wondered if his brother-in-law had ever changed a diaper in his life. ''You should realize that, regardless of what happens here, we intend to file for custody as soon as we return home,'' the lawyer stated.

''We just wanted to give you the chance to avoid a court battle,'' Margaret added. ''It would be so much more pleasant if you would yield to the inevitable.''

''And we want to make certain you're capable of dealing with these babies,'' Gina continued. ''You should understand that they must at all times be in the care of an adult over the age of eighteen, who's trained in CPR.''

''Only for a few weeks, isn't that right?'' Stuart said.

''For as long as the doctor believes they need the apnea monitor,'' Gina corrected. ''That could be months.''

''We'll work it out, won't we, Mom and Dad?'' Sandra begged. ''But does that mean I can't take them for a walk by myself?''

''It does,'' Gina said.

''Blair could come with me! My sister's twenty,'' the girl explained.

"That's enough, Sandra." Stuart met Gina's gaze straight on. "My wife and I have decided we're the best people to raise Rance's children. We'll be happy to learn CPR, and we can curtail our social activities for a few months if that's necessary."

Mason had known they wouldn't fold easily. Still, he hoped Gina's remarks would at least make the Waldmans think more clearly about what they were doing.

"I can train you in CPR after dinner," Gina said.

"That would be fine." Margaret stood up. "Now we'd like to unpack."

"Of course."

"Can I help feed the babies?" Sandra asked.

"Sure. Come with me." Expertly, Gina transferred the pair into their stroller.

The house, Mason discovered as he made his way toward his room to shave before dinner, had suddenly become far more crowded than he would have expected with only three visitors. He had to wait for Gina and Sandra to angle the carriage into the nursery, and then stand while Stuart lugged two huge suitcases into the guest chamber.

With a sense of relief, Mason finally entered the master bedroom and closed the door behind him. Verbal fencing games exhausted him more than a day's work on the range. He needed a break....

His gaze flicked over the room as it dawned on him that this was no longer his solitary refuge. Atop the handmade quilt lay a soft nightgown that he'd seen Gina wear once in the nursery.

Through the partly open door to the closet, he glimpsed a cluster of pastel colors. Her clothes. Of course, with his sister and brother-in-law in the guest room, she had to sleep here.

For two nights, he was going to lie beside her in bed. How would he keep his distance now?

Mason could feel his body hardening in response to her faint perfume. His palms itched to smooth out the silky fabric of the nightgown.

Tonight was going to be a tough one. But he could handle it. He would have to.

Chapter Thirteen

Gina saw the tension in Mason during dinner but, mercifully, he avoided an outright quarrel. Although it was clearer to her than ever that the Waldmans had no real emotional bond to the girls, she shared his misgivings about how matters might fare in court, given Stuart's ability to twist matters to support his position.

The one bright spot in the ordeal was Sandra. Her good nature and cheerful adoration of the girls were a pleasant change from her parents' self-absorption.

Gina trusted her enough to let her watch Lily and Daisy while she herself taught the parents CPR in the living room. Bonita, sensing a storm brewing, had wisely left immediately after finishing the dinner dishes.

Stuart handled the practice doll as if it oozed slime, and endured the training session with a mocking smile on his face. Margaret tried harder, and mastered the procedure as well as most inexperienced parents Gina had seen.

There was a key difference, though. Neither Margaret nor her husband showed any concern when Lily started crying in the next room. There were none of the anxious glances or general agitation that a real mother and father might display.

When the baby quieted, no doubt soothed by Sandra,

Stuart's only response was "Thank goodness. That screaming gets on my nerves."

"We have a large house," Margaret added quickly. "His home office is at the opposite end from the nursery."

Mason never complained about the girls' crying, but Gina saw no point in mentioning it. She'd given up on persuading the Waldmans with logic. Her hope was that experience would provide them with a more rational perspective.

After completing the CPR training, she took them into the nursery and reviewed the procedure for responding to the apnea monitor. Attaching the Velcro belts was one area that Stuart seemed eager to tackle.

"You've got these on a little loose," he told Gina. "Let me show you." He pulled Daisy's belt tighter. "Let's check the other one. See, you've got that one loose, too."

The girls were squirming but not in any real distress. If she intended to let the Waldmans get a taste of what it was like to be in charge of the babies, Gina decided, she should avoid interfering unless absolutely necessary, so she left the belts alone.

"You've set your alarm clock for the 1:00 a.m. feeding?" she asked.

Stuart tapped his watch. "It keeps perfect time. Doesn't vary by more than a second each year."

"I doubt the girls will notice if we're five minutes late," Margaret said dryly.

"By tomorrow night, you'll feel like old pros," Gina assured them. "If there's an emergency, of course, you should call me."

"We won't need to." Stuart's blandly confident smile was becoming more irksome by the minute. "We've got it wired."

"Good night then," she said, and ducked down the hall.

Earlier, Mason had gone out to make a last-minute check on an ailing calf. As she retreated, Gina wondered when he would return. And in what frame of mind.

Maybe it was for the best if they didn't make love. After all, he'd made it clear last Saturday that, for him, sex meant nothing more than doing what came naturally. To her, making love meant making an emotional commitment.

Inside the master bedroom, Gina collected her nightgown. Then she stood motionless, transfixed by the masculine essence that infused this private space and filled her with a sense of Mason's nearness.

She wanted so much to lie beside him and feel his strength dominating her. She wanted him to awaken her in ways she might never again experience.

She was ready to take the risk. Or at least she thought she was.

THE INJURED CALF, which had run into a barbed-wire fence during the recent storm, was recovering nicely and didn't really need special attention. Mason stayed in the barn longer then necessary anyway.

He needed to let his temper simmer down. Margaret and Stuart had a knack for rubbing his nerves raw. In the past, their air of superiority had been only a mild irritant, but now something he valued more than life itself was at stake.

Daisy and Lily. Rance's daughters were the heirs to his parents' and grandparents' legacy, to all the love and dreams and heartbreak that had gone into building the Blackstone Bar Ranch.

Even if the girls someday chose to move elsewhere,

they ought to carry inside them the values and the ideals of their forebears. In spirit, they should always belong to the ranch.

Without Gina, he knew he would have lost the battle already. He only hoped that her tactic of putting Margaret and Stuart's sleep on the line would pay off.

By the time he left the barn, twilight had deepened to starlit darkness. Although it was the beginning of August, night came earlier than it had around the summer solstice in June. Out in the country, a man noticed even the smallest signs of the changing seasons.

When he entered the house, Mason took off his boots and left them near the front door. Aided by the glow of safety lights, he moved quietly across the living room and past the den where his sixteen-year-old niece slept.

At the nursery, he glanced inside. The monitors showed a reassuring green light. Much as he would have enjoyed visiting with the babies, he was reluctant to risk provoking Margaret to accuse him of interfering while she was in charge.

At the master bedroom, he turned the doorknob and eased inside. Moonlight showed Gina's blond hair spread across her pillow, gleaming like spun gold.

Mason caught his breath. She was a figure straight out of his dreams, with skin as clear as porcelain and dusky lashes trembling against the sweet curve of her cheek.

With difficulty, he drew away and went into the bathroom to put on a pair of pajamas. It was a brand-new set that Bonita had given him last Christmas. No doubt she'd be happy to see from the laundry that he'd finally worn something to bed besides his old pj bottoms.

A few minutes later, he crawled beneath the covers and lay stiffly, hardly daring to breathe. Despite the few inches that separated them, Gina's warmth played across his skin, and the rise and fall of her breathing lured his body rhythms into a subtle dance.

He ached to put his arms around her, from behind. He wanted to hold her in what his parents would have called spoon-style, two people nestled together.

A fiery urge in his midsection warned that it wouldn't stop there. Not by a long shot.

Grimly, Mason scooted closer to the edge of the bed.

THE PIERCING BEEP of the apnea monitor pulled Gina up from the well of sleep. She awoke in a disoriented blur. The dimensions of the room, the whisper of breathing beside her, none of it was familiar.

In the hall, a door creaked open. A muffled voice called, "Get up, Stuart! For Pete's sake!"

As the monitor continued beeping, Gina's throat clamped. She had to check on the girls.

Balling her fists, she forced herself to remain in place. She shouldn't get up unless the monitor kept going a lot longer, or she heard Margaret scream....

Light footsteps crossed the hall, followed a moment later by heavier ones. That must be Stuart, finally awake.

The beeping stopped. Did that mean the baby was all right, or that the monitor had been switched off? Which child had set off the alarm?

When Margaret spoke, her voice was shrill with worry. "She's breathing okay. See? Her color's nice and pink. That's what Gina said to look for."

"What about the other one?" Stuart asked gruffly. "Maybe we should wake her up, too."

"It's time to feed them, anyway."

"Not for another half hour."

"So? What's the point of going to sleep for half an hour?"

As the squabbling ended, Gina hoped the pair would remember to check for wet diapers. The little girls' delicate skin could easily develop a rash.

Beside her, Mason sat up. "What's going on?"

"One of the monitors went off. I think everything's fine," she said.

He shifted position. The mattress echoed with his movement, tipping Gina slightly downhill. As she tried to catch her balance, her leg grazed his.

"Sorry," she said.

He chuckled. "That's hardly worth apologizing for."

"I guess not," she said ruefully. "After what we did last Saturday…"

She stopped, realizing as the memory of their close encounter flared through her that she shouldn't have mentioned it. Apparently her comment had a similar impact on Mason, because, in the act of turning over, he halted in profile. Fierce tension bunched his muscles, as if he were a half-tamed animal about to pounce.

"I'm sorry," she said. "I shouldn't have said that."

He didn't answer. Just dropped flat onto his front and lay there, forehead pressed to the pillow.

IN ONE SWIFT ACTION, he could be on top of her, his mouth probing hers, his hands and hips caressing her. She was aroused; he'd come to know her well enough that her facade of control no longer fooled him.

It would be sheer heaven to take her. And she would enjoy it, too. There was so much longing pent up inside this woman that she would match his passion point for point with her own.

But she'd said it herself, a week ago. Just because something was natural didn't make it right.

Even without turning his head, he had a clear image of

Gina's trusting blue eyes and silken fragility. At this moment, he might be the man she wanted, but he wasn't the one she needed. He could never be careful enough, gentle enough to avoid hurting her.

Mason knew his own violent nature and the explosions that propelled him beyond control. He would never forgive himself if he hurt Gina.

Worse, he might get her pregnant. At the moment, he had no means to prevent it. What if he trapped her here, on a ranch where she hadn't wanted to live, with a man she hadn't intended to marry?

She would make the best of it. She might even lay the fault on herself. But the unhappiness might destroy her.

His father had blamed himself for his mother's early death, despite the fact that cancer could strike as well in an English city as on an American ranch. Years later, on a night when he'd drunk too much, George had confided to Mason that the adjustment to ranch life had been hard on his wife.

"Depression weakens a person," he'd said. "Weakens the immune system. She was everything to me, but sometimes I wish we'd never met. For her sake."

Mason would never take such a chance with Gina's life. She hadn't intended to marry him, even temporarily. She'd done it for the girls' sakes.

And tonight he would control himself, for her sake.

AT 3:07 A.M., a monitor went off again. This time, as Margaret and Stuart slogged across the hall, Gina had an easier time holding herself still. She'd gained a little more confidence that they could manage.

"It's the other baby," she heard Stuart grumble as the beeping stopped. "She's fine. Why can't they make this equipment work right?"

"Maybe you didn't attach the belts properly," his wife said.

"Of course I did! These doctors don't know what they're doing. Stupid piece of equipment."

"Maybe we should feed them," Marge said.

"It's too early. And don't tell me there's no point going back to bed for an hour!" He was clearly working himself up to a rage.

"Did you change Lily's diaper last time?"

His tone switched from anger to bewilderment. "Lily? I thought I was feeding Daisy."

"Did you change *anybody's* diaper?"

"No, and if it's waited this long, it can wait a little while longer!"

After a few more words, the two of them retreated across the hall. Ordering herself not to intervene, Gina fell asleep, and scarcely heard the Waldmans get up an hour later for the next feeding.

SHE AWOKE ON SATURDAY morning with sensual longings tickling the back of her mind. In her dreams, she'd been making love with Mason. He'd been right on the verge of…of…

The dream evaporated like fog in sunshine. Beside Gina, Mason's pillow carried a dent and the covers were partly thrown back. Those were the only signs that he'd even slept there.

Ranch work started early. Still, a void gaped inside her where Mason should be. Where the *knowledge* of Mason should be, the sense of completeness that making love might have provided.

Restlessly, Gina collected her clothes and went to shower. This determination to make love with him, despite his reticence, was unlike her. Usually she held back from confronting anyone, preferring tact and persuasion.

But she wanted Mason more than she'd ever wanted anyone or anything. As the hot water hit her skin, she imagined him standing with his chest pressed against her.

His hands would reach around and cup her breasts. Those callused hands that could be incredibly gentle with the babies would be that way with her, too.

A shudder ran through Gina. Tonight, she had no intention of lying there hoping that Mason would act. She intended to make sure nature took its course.

In the meantime, she must deal with the Waldmans. Gina dried off, brushed her hair to one side and fixed it with a silk flower clip. Then she put on a lavender sundress. By the time she emerged and went to the nursery, there was no outward sign of her turmoil.

The Waldmans had left out a half-empty can of formula that should have been stored in the minirefrigerator, she discovered, and the lid was ajar on the diaper pail. Otherwise the nursery looked pretty much as usual.

The girls were awake, Lily playing with her fingers, Daisy staring wide-eyed at a Winnie-the-Pooh mobile. "Where's your aunt and uncle?" she asked as she cleaned up and began preparing fresh bottles. It was nearly eight o'clock, time for the next feeding.

Of course, she could guess where Margaret and Stuart were. Sleeping off their restless night.

Gina didn't have the heart to go knock on their door. For one thing, she didn't want them to suspect her of intentionally making things as difficult as possible. And she hadn't. It was Stuart's own fault that he'd pulled the belts tight enough to set off the alarms more easily than usual.

Half an hour later, Gina was eating breakfast when a

drawn-looking Margaret stumbled into the kitchen in her bathrobe. "Coffee," she gasped.

"Sit down and I'll bring it over," said Bonita, who'd been bursting with curiosity this morning. She scarcely managed to conceal her merriment as she added, "Didn't you sleep well?"

"Who could sleep?" It would take a liberal application of makeup to hide the dark circles beneath Margaret's eyes. "Those babies certainly don't!"

"You'll get used to it," Gina advised. "The trick is to take naps during the day so you'll be ready for tonight."

"Tonight?" Mason's sister stared at her blearily.

"You were planning to take care of them again tonight, weren't you?" On the verge of pointing out that every night was going to be like this if they won custody of the girls, Gina halted. Rubbing it in would only get Margaret's back up.

Stuart joined them a few minutes later. Unlike his wife, he'd showered and changed. The night's toll didn't show as clearly on his face, but his voice had a ragged edge. "Doesn't anybody around here have a Saturday paper?"

"All we get is a weekly, and it comes out on Thursday." Bonita set a plate of pancakes on the table. "Anyone care for eggs?"

Margaret shook a finger as if someone had said a dirty word. "Who eats all that cholesterol?"

"It's the saturated fat that gets you," her husband muttered as he speared a stack of pancakes. "Nobody's proven that cholesterol in food translates into cholesterol in the bloodstream."

"Go ahead then!" flared his wife. "Eat your way to a heart attack."

"Thanks anyway, Bonita," he said wearily, yielding to his wife. "I'll pass on the eggs."

The housekeeper handed them each a mug of coffee, and set a sugar bowl and creamer on the table. Marge stared at the white liquid accusingly. "Don't you have nonfat milk?"

"You tell me how to raise nonfat dairy cows and I'll bring you some," was the tart reply.

"Gina, you're a nurse," Margaret said as she fished a packet of artificial sweetener from her robe pocket and added two droplets of cream to her coffee. "The girls should get nonfat milk as soon as they graduate from formula, shouldn't they?"

"Actually, no, they shouldn't," she said.

Both of the Waldmans fixed their attention on her. In Stuart's face, she thought she detected a gleam of hope. "Really?" he said. "That watery stuff's not all it's cracked up to be?"

"For you, yes." She'd noted him happily pouring a dollop of cream into his coffee, along with two heaping spoonfuls of sugar. "But children need fats for proper brain development. You should ask your pediatrician before putting them on a low-fat diet."

"Are those the latest findings?" Margaret asked.

"The doctors change their minds every five minutes, anyway," added her husband. "Who can believe anything they say?"

"I do, for one," Gina told him.

No one answered. They never got the chance, because right then Sandra banged through the kitchen door, followed closely by Jennifer. Both girls wore jeans, although Sandra's clingy halter top made a sharp contrast to her cousin's loose T-shirt.

"I'm starved!" Sandra announced.

"Bacon and eggs?" Bonita asked.

"You bet! All I usually get is cereal." The sandy-haired girl made a face.

"I wouldn't mind eating again, either," said Jennifer. "Thanks."

They crowded around the table. For a while, the talk was about their early morning horseback ride. Despite her mother's condescending reference the previous day to Jennifer's scruffy appearance, their daughter had obviously been itching to follow her cousin's example.

"She actually trains the horses herself!" Sandra explained to her parents. "Do you think I could stay here for a few weeks?"

Marge shook her head. "With all that's happened in the past few months, I think your uncle has his hands full."

"Well, next summer, then? Could I, Aunt Gina?"

With a twinge, Gina reflected that by next summer, she wouldn't be here, and she wouldn't be Jennifer's aunt, either. Not wanting to discourage the girl, however, she said, "That's up to your folks."

"We'll see," said Stuart.

The eggs and bacon arrived, along with a refilled platter of pancakes. After stuffing herself, Sandra said, "Let's have a picnic this afternoon! We could all ride out on horseback."

Her mother's expression tightened. "Not on your life!"

"Don't worry, we're not going riding again, Cousin Margaret," Jennifer said. "Sandra, didn't you notice the clouds? There's a storm brewing. We need to stay near the house."

Bonita peered out the window over the sink. "They're getting darker by the minute. I'd better turn on the radio in case there's a tornado alert."

"You see?" Margaret told Gina. "This isn't a safe place for children."

"A twister went right through Dallas in, what was it, '57?" Bonita replied from across the kitchen. "And one smashed a bunch of high-rise buildings in Nashville, Tennessee, just a few years ago. Don't think you're safe in the city!"

"We could have a picnic in one of the barns," Gina suggested, hoping to guide the conversation to safer ground. "It's stimulating for the babies to be near the animals, and I'll bet we can find a comfortable spot to eat in one of the haylofts."

"Not exactly my idea of hygienic," muttered Stuart.

"Compared to what, Daddy?" asked Sandra. "You've been getting awfully stuffy since you turned forty."

"That was three years ago. You never mentioned it before."

"That's because you get worse every year!"

"A picnic in the barn would be fine," said Margaret.

The rest of the morning passed quietly. Worn-out from their busy night, Margaret and Stuart took a long nap after breakfast. Jennifer and Sandra went off to work with some horses in the corral, while Gina, Bonita and Nana planned their luncheon expedition.

Although there'd been no sign of funnel clouds, Mason, Ed, Bart and Paul were on the alert. Bonita explained that she'd packed lunches and the men probably wouldn't be in until dinnertime or later. "They want to get some of the weaker animals moved to shelter before the rain hits, and make sure none of them gets stuck down by the creek in case it overflows."

By midafternoon a light rain began falling. Gina was grateful for Sandra's suggestion of a picnic. Even in the gloomy half-light, there was something comforting about the patter of rain on the barn roof and the steamy smell of horses and leather.

The friendly isolation reminded her of the times in Alaska when her family had been virtually snowbound. Neighbors would come to visit, and they'd tell stories and sing around a fire.

Gina told the others about her experiences living in Alaska, Japan and Kuwait as a young girl. Margaret, to her surprise, indulged in a fond memory of fishing with her father and falling into the creek. Even Stuart got into the spirit, although his account of winning a medical malpractice suit somehow lacked the warm flavor of the other stories.

When the twins began fussing, Gina sang one of her favorite lullabies to them. Sandra and Jennifer joined in, and soon they were singing their way through pop and show tunes, fudging the lyrics they'd forgotten and occasionally changing key without warning.

"I'd forgotten how much fun being in the country was," Margaret admitted as, beneath umbrellas, they made their way up the lawn to the big house. "My mother, well, she liked the idea of living out here, but the reality of it depressed her."

"It did?" Gina had imagined Lainie Blackstone embracing the exotic—to her—setting, and turning into an English version of Annie Oakley.

"She was a strong woman." Margaret led the way into the utility room, which had its own entrance. "Once she'd made her decision to marry Dad, and especially after they had us children, she never considered going back to England. But she would sink into dark moods sometimes. 'It's so lonely out here,' she'd say."

"Times have changed," Gina said. "Now we've got

the Internet and satellite TV and all kinds of connections.''

"You've only been here a few weeks," warned her sister-in-law. "You're practically still on your honeymoon."

I wish! "Austin's two hours away. Unlike your mother, I've got friends there. If I find myself getting too gloomy, I can always drive in for the day."

"I suppose that's true." Marge arranged their umbrellas so they dripped into a plastic bag. "But I love being in Dallas. So many things to do! Important people to meet, and cultural events to attend!"

Not if you have two babies demanding your time. She bit her tongue, though. Either Margaret would grasp the point on her own, or she'd refuse to get it at all.

They played cards that afternoon, and watched a TV newscast. Dinner was delayed until seven because of their late lunch, but even then, Mason didn't come home.

"He's probably holed up somewhere till the rain stops," Bonita said as she prepared to drive back to her house with Nana. Usually they walked, but today she'd brought her car.

"What will I do if there's a tornado warning?" Gina asked.

"The storm's starting to clear," the housekeeper said. "It doesn't seem likely now."

Gina waited up until eleven o'clock, but, although the rain had stopped, there was no sign of Mason. He might be playing it safe, sleeping out in a shelter to avoid the danger of a horseback accident in the dark.

Or he might be avoiding coming home to her.

Chapter Fourteen

The storm might have been a blessing in disguise, Mason told himself as he stabled his horse on Sunday morning, but it had been a darned ugly one.

The blessing was that it had prevented him from breaking his silent promise to leave Gina alone. The cost had been a bone-jarringly uncomfortable night spent in a lean-to when it got too dark to ride home safely, and, this morning, the sight of still more erosion near the creek.

On the way back, he'd also noted some posts tilting in the soggy soil. Although it was Sunday, he and his men needed to make sure none of the fences had broken.

Grimly, Mason recalled that today the whole Whitlaw family was scheduled to participate in a choral concert fifty miles away in the town of Groundhog Station. He could sure use Ed's help, and even Kevin's, although the boy was a bit young for heavy work, but they, Linda and Jennifer formed the backbone of the Horseshoe Bend choir. He would have to handle the work without Ed until Monday.

At least the skies had almost cleared. That was no guarantee of anything, but the latest forecast on his pocket radio called for at least a two-day break between storms.

As he approached the big house, Gina came out onto

the front porch. She made such a pretty picture in her navy skirt and red-and-white blouse, with her blond hair like a splash of sunlight, that she filled his soul with contentment. Even if he couldn't touch her, he longed to keep her nearby.

Her eyes swept across his grimy figure. "There you are! I was coming to look for you."

"You were?" Remembering his manners, he swept off his hat, which had the unfortunate effect of exposing his matted hair. "I mean, I'm sorry I didn't call in, but I figured you'd know I was all right."

"Well, I didn't know!" Her voice trembled. "And look at that mess! What did you do, wallow in mud all night?" She'd been worried, he realized with a tug of pleasure.

"Oh, honey, I'm glad to see you, too!" Before he could think, he was clomping at a near-run up the front walk, spattering it with half-dried mud from his boots.

Gina launched herself at him, heedless of his grimy condition. Slender she might be, but she grabbed him around the neck with a grip like steel.

Mason didn't care that he was messing up her beautiful clothes and rumpling her perfect hair and kissing her soft mouth too hard. She tasted like springtime and happiness, and she made his heart sing.

Reality intruded in the form of his sister. She came out the front door and said, "Hey, lovebirds! One night apart and you can hardly stand it!"

Reluctantly, he released Gina. *One night apart.* How many more of those could he take?

Then he saw that her pristine blouse and skirt were smeared with dirt, and one cheek as well. Her hair, where he'd fondled it, sprouted tangles.

"I'm sorry," he told her.

"Don't be." Blushing, she picked a clump of dried brush off her skirt. "I consider it a souvenir."

"Are you two going to church?" Marge asked. "Linda just called to ask."

"I don't think I'm up to it," Mason admitted. "Unless you're eager to?"

"Certainly not!" said his sister. "I'll suggest she go on without you."

"Tell them to enjoy the trip to Groundhog Station," Mason added. "Sorry we'll have to miss the concert."

Margaret went inside. Gina waited while he pried off his boots.

"I would have liked to hear them, although I don't want to make that long a trip," she admitted. "Jennifer says they have fun in the church van, too, singing and playing word games. But your sister and Stuart are leaving around ten, and I want to be here to see them off."

"And make sure they don't take the twins with them," he added in a low voice.

She nodded but said no more until they were alone in the master bedroom. Then, while sorting through the closet for a change of clothing, she said, "You should have heard them last night."

"What happened?" Eager as he was for a shower and breakfast, he didn't want to miss the juicy details.

"The alarms went off three times." When she grinned, the splotch of dirt on her cheek gave her the air of a mischievous ragamuffin. "Stuart really does need to quit fastening those apnea belts so tight."

"So that was the problem!" He'd wondered why the monitors had suddenly become so touchy.

"They'd agreed to take turns getting up, but he kept denying that it was his turn," she recounted. "One time I heard him shout, 'This was your idea, you know. I'll have to be in court. I can't go without sleep.' And she said, 'Get a grip, Stuart. Tomorrow's Sunday!'"

Mason chuckled. "It doesn't sound as if you got much sleep, either."

"It was worth it," she said. "They were very entertaining."

If he stood here any longer, he was going to hug her again. He headed for the bathroom.

"I learned one more thing," she said.

"What's that?"

"Sandra and I had an early breakfast together." From the closet, Gina plucked a pair of tan slacks and an off-white top embroidered with flowers. "She says one of your sister's friends just had a baby from her second marriage, and another has a new grandchild. The moment they heard about the twins, they started twittering about how cute it would be to take all their babies to the park together. As if they were playing dolls!"

"That's why she wants Daisy and Lily?"

"That's part of it, anyway," Gina said. "I also wonder if she feels a little guilty that she didn't do more for Rance when he was growing up."

"Interesting notion," said Mason, and retreated with much to think about it.

HE HADN'T STAYED AWAY last night to avoid her, Gina was certain of that. She'd seen joy illuminate his face when he'd spotted her on the porch. And the way he'd covered her mouth with kisses, well, he hadn't even tried to hold back.

Tonight their guests would be gone. They'd have all the time in the world to work things out.

After changing and fixing her hair, she went to the

guest bathroom and washed her face. Then she peeked into the nursery.

Sandra was rocking Daisy and humming a lullaby while, through the bars of her crib, Lily watched intently. Gina smiled at them and went on.

Since Bonita had the day off, she wanted to make sure their guests were finding enough to eat. She also wondered what they might be discussing. Two nights with the girls had tried their patience, but had it been enough to knock sense into their heads?

In the living room, the sound of raised voices from the kitchen halted her. "I'm sure we can find a nurse in less than a week!" Margaret was saying. "Stuart, you're making way too much of this. Once we settle into a routine—"

"Nurses are expensive, and they can quit. Do you realize we're not even taking full care of those girls now?" her husband demanded. "Gina gets up and feeds them at 8:00 a.m., and during the day there's always someone around changing them and burping them and doing whatever else they need. How long before you're biting my head off the minute I walk through the door at night?"

"Did I do that when our kids were little?" Margaret flared.

"As a matter of fact, yes!"

It wasn't right to stand here eavesdropping, so Gina walked as loudly as she could across the floor, and the conversation broke off. When she reached the kitchen, the Waldmans were sitting across the table from each other, scowling. Marge had an untouched bowl of cereal in front of her and Stuart held a piece of toast slathered with preserves.

"Good morning!" she said. "Did you talk to Linda again, Margaret? To let her know we wouldn't be going?"

"She said they'd miss us at services," she replied. "She was so excited about the concert this afternoon that I almost wish I could go. Apparently the church in Groundhog Station has grown quite a bit since I lived around here, and their choir performances attract a crowd."

"Groundhog Station." Stuart scratched his face. "I'd be embarrassed to say I was from a town with such a ridiculous name."

"Where are you from?" Gina asked.

"Oshkosh, Wisconsin," he said.

"That's not much better." His wife jabbed her spoon into her cereal.

"Well, I went to college in Boston," he replied. "Try making fun of that!"

"You two seem a little short-tempered," Gina murmured.

"And about three hours shy of a night's sleep," Stuart replied.

When Mason joined them, Gina was eager to fix something special for him, but she was a bit rusty on her cooking skills. The scrambled eggs got overdone, the bacon came out soft and the toast emerged black around the edges and soggy in the middle.

She wasn't sure how she'd managed to louse up even a regulation toaster, but her husband wolfed everything down without complaint. He even thanked her.

"You must have a lot of work to do after that storm last night," said Stuart, who had startled them all by voluntarily clearing the table and was scrubbing away at the egg pan.

Mason nodded. "Let's hope it stays clear for a few days."

His sister stretched lazily. "Well, I guess I'd better see about packing."

At the last minute, Margaret decided to collect some roses from her mother's garden, and Sandra couldn't stop cuddling the babies. Although they'd planned on making an earlier start, it was nearly noon before the Waldmans were ready to leave.

"Mom, I am definitely coming here next summer for a month!" Sandra said as she reluctantly placed Daisy back in her crib.

"They won't be so little and cute then," Margaret warned. "Toddlers get into everything."

Her husband groaned. "I'd forgotten about that."

"We'll hire a nanny." To Mason, she said, "Obviously, we're not going to try to take the twins with us today, but we'll return next weekend. In the meantime, I plan to hire some help."

"Next weekend?" Stuart said. "Wait a minute. I've got briefs to prepare."

"We'll discuss it in the car." His wife grabbed her suitcase and headed outside.

"She'll have to bring a court order if she thinks I'm going to let her walk out of here with those girls," Mason said.

"Do you have any buffered aspirin?" Stuart asked Gina. "I think a thousand little monitors are beeping in my brain."

By the time he was medicated, all the suitcases got stowed in the trunk and the big car disappeared down the driveway, black clouds were thickening overhead.

"That doesn't look good," Gina said, standing on the front porch.

Mason stared upward. "Not good at all. If this turns into a downpour so soon after the last one, there'll be hell to pay."

"What can I do to help?"

His hands cupped her shoulders and he regarded her with concern. "The best thing you can do, honey, is look after the babies and listen for a tornado alert. Call Bonita and Nana and invite them to stay with you. They'll be nervous down at the village by themselves, anyway. Ed's family is halfway to Groundhog Station by now, and I'll need Bart and Paul out on the range."

A dark stain of fear spread through her. She'd never been frightened on the ranch before, but the ominous sky and his tense words had a quelling effect.

Gina swallowed hard. She wasn't going to whimper and cling. "Don't worry about me," she said. "I'll be fine."

WITH BART AND PAUL'S HELP, Mason righted the tilting fence posts and drove them deeper, then ran some wire between tree trunks along the eroded creek bank to keep the cattle out. He was worried there might be more erosion farther along, though.

"You two take the Jeep and check the fence north of the village," he told Bart. That pasture lay beside the highway and could be reached more quickly by vehicle than by horse. "That's the other area I'm worried about. I'll follow the creek south to Saucer Rock and make sure there aren't any other problems."

"What should we do once we make sure the fence is okay?" Bart asked. The walkie-talkies had so much static that they'd become almost useless, so he might not be able to call for instructions. "Want us to ride back here in case you need help?"

Mason slanted another look at the lowering sky. Those clouds looked worse than yesterday. "Go up to the big house," he said. "Help the women if they need it."

"Will do." His ranch hand wiped his forehead on his

sleeve. In this sultry weather, everyone wore a sheen of perspiration.

"You think the church group will stay in Groundhog Station?" Paul asked worriedly. "I don't like to think of Jennifer riding in the church van if we get a twister."

"Ed's got as much sense as any man I know," Mason assured him. "If they need to take cover, he'll make certain they do." Much as he missed his foreman's assistance, he was glad the man was there to protect his family.

"We'd better get moving, I guess," Bart said.

Mason waved them on their way. He didn't see any point in fretting overmuch. Tornadoes rarely touched down, and when they did, they generally made contact with the ground for less than a mile. Besides, about a mile farther down, the heavy, semicircular outcropping known as Saucer Rock was big enough to protect him and his horse.

It was Gina who concerned him. Despite her bravado, she must be frightened. Not that he didn't trust her to use good judgment, but he could see how fragile she was, the way his mother had been.

Well, he couldn't send his men out into the approaching storm while he himself stood guard over his wife. A man worthy of respect didn't behave that way. The alternative was for them all to hole up and let the ranch go to pieces, but that went against every instinct he'd developed in thirty-four years on the Blackstone Bar.

They would all be fine. It was just another storm coming, nothing more.

BONITA AND NANA ARRIVED at the house about one o'clock. Leaving Nana in charge of the girls, the two younger women went around shuttering the windows, putting lawn furniture in the garage and bagging food and baby supplies to take into the shelter.

"Jennifer must have taken care of the horses earlier, because I didn't see any of them outside," Bonita told her. "The chickens are in the coop, too."

"What else can we do?" Gina brushed dust off the jeans she'd changed into. She didn't want to stop working, because whenever she stood still, she started to worry.

"Why don't you teach me how to knit?" Bonita asked. "That's something I always wanted to learn."

"Teach you to knit?" Gina repeated blankly.

"It'll give us something to keep our minds off the storm," the woman said.

"I'd be happy to." She could spare some blue yarn left from the color-patterned front of Mason's sweater, along with a pair of smaller needles she wasn't currently using.

With Nana and the girls, they settled into the den, near the rear exit. Bonita turned on the radio to listen for a weather alert.

The two women sat side by side on the couch. "You start by casting on the number of stitches you need," Gina said. "For practicing, let's make it twenty stitches."

She demonstrated how to start the stitches on one needle, then unraveled her work and handed needle and yarn to Bonita. "You try it."

"Show me how to twist it again. I didn't quite catch that."

"You run the yarn this way…"

Bonita had been right. Concentrating on the delicate task helped both of them keep their minds off the situation.

About two o'clock, Gina heard the clicking of light rain against the roof. Bonita went onto the covered rear porch to study the sky.

''I don't like that yellowish cast to the thunderclouds,'' she said. ''It could start funneling.''

''Should we go into the shelter?''

Nana, who was feeding Lily, glanced toward the radio. ''They haven't reported anything.''

''And maybe they won't, until it's too late. We can't count on some weatherman who's miles away,'' Bonita said. ''But once we go down there, nobody can reach us by phone, and we won't pick up radio signals too well, either. I don't relish being stuck for hours, not knowing what's going on.''

Gina felt the same way. Besides, the rain was so light, she couldn't help hoping the brunt of the storm would pass them by.

They adjourned to the kitchen for a snack and a game of dominoes. Gina couldn't remember the rules, so it was her turn to learn from Bonita.

The rain got heavier after three o'clock. ''Won't the men come in now?'' Although it was fairly dark outside, there was enough light for them to ride. She hoped Mason wasn't going to take refuge in some shed, not when her nerves were raw with anxiety.

''It depends,'' Bonita said.

''On what?''

''How far away they are. And whether they've found a really big problem that they can't afford to leave.''

With a raw sense of foreboding, Gina wished Mason would return. For the first time, she glimpsed how Lainie Blackstone must have felt.

In the city, Gina had always had the comfort of knowing that, in an emergency, she could call the police or the fire department. Certainly she hadn't had to worry that someone she loved was miles away, facing the forces of nature.

Had she misjudged her own ability to adapt to the ranch? Maybe she didn't belong here. But what she hated most, she realized, wasn't her vulnerability so much as her inability to help Mason.

The phone rang. Despite the background noise of wind and rain, its loudness made her jump.

"It might be Linda, to let us know that they've reached Groundhog Station." Bonita went to answer. "Blackstone Bar Ranch. Oh, hello, Mr. Waldman. No, he's not here but…yes, she is."

"For me?" At her nod, Gina hurried over. She hoped Stuart and Margaret hadn't had an accident on their way home. "Hello?"

Everything was all right; she could tell it the moment she heard his cheerful voice. "I have some good news."

"What's that?"

"We're not even home yet, but I had to call and let you know." A faint cracking noise confirmed that Stuart was calling from a cellular phone. "We've changed our minds about the girls."

"You have?" She scarcely dared to believe it.

"The more we talk about it, the more Margaret's decided she doesn't want to curtail her good works," he said. "She raises a lot of money for charitable causes, you know."

"I'm sure she does." *And has a lot of fun planning events and running her gallery. But there's nothing wrong with that.* A bubble of excitement rose inside Gina at the discovery that the Waldmans were backing down.

Faintly, over the phone, she heard Sandra say to her father, "Ask Aunt Gina if I can come stay with them at Christmas!"

Margaret's voice responded, "You'll spend Christmas in Dallas with the rest of us, that's what you'll do!"

"I want to thank you," Stuart said to Gina. "If you hadn't insisted we take care of the twins, we might not have realized how much work they are. Double trouble, that's for sure."

"Now just a minute!" Marge sounded much clearer, no doubt because she was speaking close to the phone. "This isn't about our not wanting to take care of the babies. It's a question of deciding how we can do the most good for the unfortunate."

"Exactly." From Stuart's relieved tone, Gina gathered that he would have agreed with almost anything his wife said, as long as it meant he didn't have to be awakened at night by beeping monitors. "The sooner we get the legalities settled, the better for everyone. I'll draw up the adoption papers first thing tomorrow morning."

"Terrific!" In a fog, Gina acknowledged his thanks for their visit, and they said goodbye. When she put down the phone, she didn't know whether to laugh or cry.

"They're giving Mason...they're giving us custody," she said.

Nana beamed, and Bonita let out a whoop. "I wish we had some champagne so we could drink a toast!"

"I'll feel better when we get the adoption papers," Gina admitted. "People who change their minds once can always change them again."

But she didn't think that would happen. Without Stuart's support, Margaret wasn't likely to resume the battle.

They tried to play another round of dominoes, but Gina could no longer concentrate. Bonita attributed her distraction to the good news, which was partly true, but not in the way the housekeeper believed.

Gina couldn't avoid the implications. This news meant that her reason for coming to the ranch was about to end.

Once the papers were signed and approved by a judge, Mason wouldn't need her anymore.

She didn't doubt that he desired her physically. She'd even begun to hope that he was falling in love with her. If only they had a few more months, he might realize that they belonged together.

Now her only hope was to bring him to his senses in a hurry. She wished he would come home, that this storm would end and give them a chance to hold each other all night.

A shrill noise from the radio made her hand knock against the domino tiles. A bunch of them clattered to the floor, but she scarcely heard them over the thundering of her heart.

"That's the alert!" Bonita cried, and jumped to her feet. "Let's get the girls into the shelter before the tornado hits!"

Chapter Fifteen

"I'll call the men on the walkie-talkie," Nana said. "At least I'm good for something."

"You're good for lots of things," corrected her daughter. "We'll be right back."

Gina and Bonita threw on hooded yellow rain slickers and, together, pulled open the door of the underground tornado shelter. Even though they stood beneath an overhang, light rain slanted at their ankles and feet. Gina was glad she'd put on half boots and tucked her jeans inside them.

They descended a ladder into the concrete rooms. The air smelled musty, despite the ventilation system, but the battery-operated lamps showed her that the place was clean. Checking the corners and under the furniture, they made sure no snakes had taken refuge here.

Then, using baby slings that had been gifts from neighbors, the two women carried Lily and Daisy down into the shelter. Once the girls were settled in a portable playpen, Bonita assisted her mother in descending and Gina brought their supplies.

At last they were all safe. That knowledge failed, however, to dispel the restlessness thrumming through Gina. She needed to take action.

"Did you raise anyone on the walkie-talkies?" she asked.

Nana shook her head. "Those darn things aren't worth a hoot."

"Rance was too penny-wise about getting cell phones." Bonita sighed. "I hope the men have the sense to take cover."

The rain had slackened to a thick mist. Peering out of the shelter, Gina scanned the horizon. There was no sign of a funnel cloud.

"They might try to ride back while the downpour's let up," she said. "Someone needs to tell them to hurry directly to the shelter. I'm going to see if anyone's at the barn."

"You're worried about Mason, aren't you?" Bonita said.

Gina nodded slowly, then wondered why she felt so reluctant to let others know that she loved her husband. *Because I'm not supposed to love him. Because it wasn't part of our bargain.*

"He'd want you to stay here," the housekeeper warned.

She was probably right. Gina didn't care. "If you need to close the door, go ahead," she said, climbing out. "Don't worry about me."

Clutching her umbrella, she strode around the garage and past Mason's office, hoping in vain to see a light burning there. A glance toward the cattle barn to her left showed it, too, closed up.

If the men came back, the first thing they'd do would be stable their horses. Bending into the wind, she turned right along the driveway and headed for the horse barn.

Down the pavement, headlights swung toward her. Gina moved to the shoulder and waved.

The four-wheel-drive vehicle, barely visible through the misty air, headed toward her at a steady pace. Abruptly, it bucked. Amid the crunch of metal, it halted, and the engine died.

Gina hurried toward it. On closer inspection, she could see that the front of the Jeep had dropped into a deep pothole in the driveway.

There was only one man inside, too slim to be Mason or Bart, and he lay motionless across the steering wheel. "Paul?"

Gina opened his door and checked to make sure he was breathing. She didn't dare move him, in case he'd suffered a spinal injury from being thrown forward abruptly. Besides, although slender, the young man weighed more than she did.

To her relief, his eyelids fluttered and he lifted his head. "What happened?"

"You had an accident," she said. "Can you see all right? Are things blurry?" He could easily have suffered a concussion.

"No, but my head hurts like fire." With a groan, he straightened. She saw that his nose was bleeding, and bruises were forming along one cheekbone. "I'm supposed to be helping people, not causing problems."

"It wasn't your fault. The pavement gave way." Now that she could see he wasn't seriously injured, she dared to ask, "Where's Mason? Is he all right?"

"I don't know," Paul said. "Dad and I were in the north pasture. There's a big break in the fence and cattle all over the main road. Mason's checking the creek down by Saucer Rock. We couldn't reach him on the walkie-talkies."

His speech sounded clear, although his sentences tumbled out in a somewhat disjointed fashion. "Can you stand up?'' Gina asked. ''There's a tornado warning. You need to get into the shelter.''

''I've got to call the church at Groundhog Station,'' he said. ''To tell them not to let the van leave. If it comes down that road in the dark and they hit a steer, they could all be killed.''

''With luck, they'll hear the tornado warning and stay put,'' she said. ''But it can't hurt to call.''

With a little help, he climbed out of the vehicle. As she steadied him, Gina assessed the situation.

Bart had been left alone, on foot. In the opposite direction, Mason was following the winding course of the creek.

With the four-wheel-drive damaged, he could only be reached by horseback. She and Jennifer had picnicked one day at Saucer Rock, and had returned home via a shortcut. As best she could recall, it had taken them about half an hour to make the journey on horses.

Paul couldn't go in his injured condition. That left her to make the trip.

It was crazy even to contemplate going after Mason. She didn't ride terribly well, she'd barely begun to know her way around the ranch and there was a tornado warning in effect.

Nevertheless, he would surely want to know about the cattle on the road. Even if the van stayed in Groundhog Station, some other vehicle might come along. And in the worst case, Ed, Linda, Jennifer, Kevin and others would be at risk.

Mason would never put his own safety above that of others, and neither should Gina, she told herself. She was his partner, or at least she hoped to be. If she were to be a rancher's wife, she couldn't cower in safety at a time like this.

"I'm going after Mason," she said. "Can you help me saddle a horse?"

"I'll go myself." Paul took a step forward, stumbled and had to grab the vehicle for support.

"Maybe I should stay and take care of you," she conceded.

"I'm not hurt that bad." Using his sleeve, he wiped some blood from his nose. The flow appeared to be slowing. "Geez, I don't know what to do."

"While you help me saddle a horse, I'll observe you to make sure you're okay on your own," she said. "Then you make the call and go to the shelter." To stave off further argument, she added, "Bonita and Nana need you."

"I shouldn't let you…"

"You wouldn't try to stop Jennifer, would you?" Gina had seen how strong-minded the young woman was. "Well, I'm no wimp, either. Come on."

In the barn, she took one look at the placid mare she usually rode and knew it wouldn't be fast enough or smart enough. Jennifer had explained that horses, like people, varied in their intelligence level.

Gina needed the best. So she went to Darter's stall.

"You can't take that one," Paul said.

"Jennifer wouldn't mind."

"It's not that—"

"And she's very responsive." The instinct to reach Mason was hardening into a compulsion. Gina itched to get going. "Jennifer swears she'd trust this animal in a pinch, so why shouldn't I?"

"You're tougher than I thought," the young man admitted. "Man, I hope Mason doesn't kill me for this."

"Your speech is getting clearer, which is a good sign,"

she said. "Help me saddle Darter, and I'll give you a medical release to go call Groundhog Station."

Reminded of his mission, he hurried to the tack room. Even with his help, though, it took far too many minutes to get the mare ready.

After watching Paul negotiate the uphill slope to the house, Gina mounted outside the barn. Although the rain remained little more than spray, the wind was picking up.

I can do this. At least it means I'm going to see Mason soon.

AS HE'D FEARED, another section of creek bank had given way from two days of heavy rain. Three cows and their calves were stranded at the bottom, and the water had risen a few inches in the last hour.

Mason debated whether to try herding the cows up the muddy, unstable slope. The downpour had let up, and the area wasn't known for flash flooding. They might be safer staying down there than risking a bad fall.

On his pocket radio, he'd heard a tornado warning, and hoped that by now Bart and Paul had joined the women at the big house. With luck, they were all safe and warm, while he stood out here with water dripping from his hat and his leather jacket turning his body heat to steam. His jeans were half-soaked, and his boots and chaps splattered with mud. He'd be willing to step fully clothed into a shower just to clean off.

Although it went against the grain to leave a task unfinished, Mason was debating returning home himself when he felt the winds pick up, from the northeast. That meant more storm clouds blowing in this direction.

His black gelding, Quickstep, nickered uneasily. Mason made another of his periodic scans of the sky. What he saw changed his mind about heading for the house.

High up and some miles off, a dark cloud appeared to be boiling. A small cone-shaped section distended below it, disappearing and reappearing several times before vanishing.

It was a twister, all right. He'd heard that some ninety percent of the vortex never descended below the clouds. If he were lucky, the thing wouldn't touch down, or it might skirt the ranch.

On the other hand, he knew better than to count on luck. It was time to get Quickstep and head for Saucer Rock.

ONCE IN THE SADDLE, Gina had no trouble setting Darter on the right path. The horse responded instantly to any change in her position or touch of the knees. There was scarcely even a need to tug the reins.

Still, the late afternoon was ominously dark. Beneath the slicker hood, Gina could feel the wind intensifying against her nose and cheeks. Perhaps it was the mud or the fact that she rode an unfamiliar horse, but Darter's sudden movements nearly dislodged her a couple of times. If she weren't careful, she would fall.

She wasn't sure why she felt so compelled to go after Mason. Maybe to prove something to him about her ability to handle herself on a ranch. Or maybe because she couldn't stand to spend one more night without him.

Until a few weeks ago, Gina had worked in a meticulously clean nursery, her clothing starched and spotless. She'd had the assistance of the latest medical technology, with top-notch doctors and nurses on hand.

Now she was alone in a primitive environment. It was just her and a horse against the elements. She must have taken leave of her senses. She'd lost all judgment when she fell in love with that virile, hard-to-pin-down rancher.

She yearned desperately to hold him. The need had become deeper than hunger and more powerful than fear.

Later, Gina wasn't sure how she found her way along the trail as the rain thickened. She could barely see a dozen feet ahead through the cloudburst, and water dripping from her hood further obscured the view. Most frightening of all was the shriek of the wind and the crack of tree branches as they sheared off.

It was Darter who maintained a steady course. The horse seemed almost to share her sense of urgency.

The goal was no longer simply to reach Mason. As the minutes ticked by and the winds rose, it was to reach Saucer Rock, which, now that they'd traveled so far from the house, was Gina's main hope of safety.

Although weathered, the ancient formation had withstood the elements for millions of years. There was a fragility to its appearance, like a mushroom growing from the face of a low cliff, but surely it could hold against one more blast.

Gina didn't dare look at the sky. If she saw a funnel cloud, it might panic her.

She could see now that she'd been an idiot to make this trip. Mason couldn't do anything about the broken fence or the cattle on the road, not in this weather. If she wanted to help someone, she should have taken his pickup and gone along the pavement to collect Bart.

Well, if she ever heard the reassuring rumble of Mason's voice again, he could scold her as much as he liked. She wouldn't mind a bit.

Wrapped in her thoughts, she hardly noticed the rock in the distance until the trail ended and Darter hesitated, awaiting instructions. Gina peered toward the creek, but swirling leaves and dust frustrated her efforts to see any sign of Mason.

The whole trip had been wasted. Choking back a sob of disappointment, she nudged the mare toward the rock.

HIS EYES MUST BE PLAYING tricks on him, Mason thought as he stared from beneath the overhang. What would a horse and rider be doing out in this weather?

Gusts of wind hit the oncoming duo, nearly knocking the mare off her slender legs. She danced backward and scrabbled for balance, somehow keeping her body straight enough so her rider could hang on.

He recognized the horse as Darter, but Jennifer had left this morning for an all-day trip. Who on earth was riding her?

The slimness of her build gave him the answer even before he saw her clearly. It was Gina. What on earth had brought her here?

She had to get under the shelter quickly. In the distance, the funnel cloud was pushing downward from the cloud, probing from side to side as if questing for prey, and turning black with sucked-in dirt.

His eyes narrowed against the blowing debris, Mason ran toward Gina. A blast of rain hit him, and the wind was so strong he seemed to be stroking through water rather than air.

When the mare saw him, it shied back, startled. Gina lost her grip and fell, not a headlong tumble but a slide down the horse's flank. He grabbed her, his hands struggling to get a grip on the slicker, and she landed hard against him.

"Come on!" He yanked her toward Saucer Rock.

"Wait!" She caught a dangling rein and tugged Darter along with them. "Okay!"

A roar surrounded them as they struggled across the remaining few feet of open ground. A mat of tumbleweed shot past, followed by a thick branch that must have weighed as much as a calf.

Mason pushed Gina beneath the outcropping and stumbled after her. The horse snorted in suspicion, but followed them without balking.

Under the shelter, the air was chill and damp. Leftover rain streamed off Gina's slicker, and when Mason removed his hat, a thin sheet of water tipped from the brim.

Even in the semidarkness, droplets glittered on Gina's eyelashes. She was crying, Mason realized as he gathered her close.

"You're safe here." He felt her shiver within the circle of his arms. "Where are the girls?"

"In the shelter…with Bonita. They're f-fine."

She clung to him as if he were the only thing anchoring her to the Earth. Lord, she must have been terrified out there. What could have spurred her to ride into that deluge?

There was no time for conversation. Instinctively, Mason drew her as far from the storm as possible, although he had to crouch. The overhang wasn't more than six feet high at the outside, and more like four feet on the inside, against the rock bluff. Still, the wind was blowing so hard that he could feel a touch of spray.

Released, Darter wandered along the curve of the shelter. Quickstep uttered a welcoming nicker from out of sight.

Gina's trembling vibrated through Mason. He lowered her to sit beside him next to the pack he'd unloaded earlier from his saddle, and pulled a blanket around them both.

Outside, beyond the ledge, debris flew by at an ever-increasing rate. A small boulder rolled past, then abruptly took flight.

They might be in the path of the vortex, Mason thought.

If it scored a direct hit on Saucer Rock, he hoped the limestone ledge would hold.

Gina nestled onto his lap, pressing her face into his shoulder. Mason was glad she wasn't watching the intensifying spiral of debris outside their refuge. He would stand watch for her.

The gray haze of faint daylight went black. He heard the mutter and shriek of an unearthly voice, the voice of the tornado. Softly, he began to pray.

Close to his ear, Gina joined in. It was an old, comforting prayer they must both have learned at their mothers' knees.

Then he could no longer hear anything except the scream of the maelstrom. The world he knew vanished, and the two of them were alone in a terrifying universe.

In the utter darkness, there was no way to measure time. Maybe time itself had been sucked away. Mason gripped Gina as the howling rose until even his toughened nerves couldn't stand it a moment longer.

At last he noticed the hard slam of rain beyond the ledge. He didn't understand why the noise filled him with relief, until he realized what it meant. He could hear something beyond the wind. "The worst of the storm has passed."

"Thank heaven." Gina blinked up at him. In her face, he saw a thankfulness that matched his own.

Mason touched his mouth to hers. Life pulsed between them. They were still here, and more alive than ever.

His tongue traced the edges of hers. A quiver of longing ran through her, or maybe through him. They were holding each other so closely he could no longer separate their responses.

She released him long enough to take off her slicker.

"It's hot." Beneath it, she wore a thin blouse and tight jeans.

"Hot," he agreed, shrugging away his jacket. "Come here."

And she came. Her lips met his, and Gina's hands raised fire along his chest as she unsnapped his shirt. Fumbling, hurrying, he undid the buttons on her blouse. It was hot. Too hot to think.

Mason knew he ought to slow down. He should be gentle, but he couldn't. If he didn't strip away the barriers between them, he would burst into flames.

He yanked open his shirt and tossed it beside the jacket. Catching Gina off balance, he laid her across the blanket, threw open her blouse and slipped off the lacy pink brassiere.

Her breasts were rounder and fuller than such a slender woman had any right to have. They filled his big, rough hands, and his mouth.

Her gasp troubled him, but she didn't push him away. He could feel the nipples tightening in his mouth. Her response was as immediate, as instinctive as his.

When her back arched, it was more than Mason could bear. Reluctantly drawing his mouth away, he lowered her jeans. They stuck on her boots, so he jerked those off, too. A pair of pink panties joined the pile of clothing on the ground.

She was naked. Splendid and soft, inviting. Her eyes had gone wide and a little glazed.

The last of Mason's self-possession vanished. He had never needed anyone so much. Never known such need existed.

He couldn't stop to remove all his clothing. He shoved it down, out of his way. Separated her slim legs, angled her hips, bent to penetrate her mouth with his tongue and, at the same time, thrust himself into her with a groan of pure happiness.

Inside her, he felt a moment's resistance, and then it was gone. Her virginity. He'd believed, suspected, it was still there. Now he'd taken it.

Did it hurt? If so, she gave no indication. She was holding his upper arms, clinging to him as she'd done during the cyclone.

He kept wanting to look at her body, to touch her all over. To cherish the blond curls that encircled their joining, to relish those perfect breasts and the slender indention of her navel.

But the storm that had threatened them now raged inside him. Releasing all qualms, he drew himself in and out of her as the grief of the past months washed away amid a flood of ecstasy.

GINA HAD NEVER KNOWN she could feel such sensations. Despite all her anticipation, she'd underestimated the man. And herself.

At first she was a little afraid. Everything happened so quickly, and Mason became so fierce and primitive that he almost frightened her.

He was a big man, and he seized control of her. She didn't know what to expect. She wanted to relish each new discovery, but he gave her no time. The aching intensity in her breasts as he sucked them, the almost shocking discovery that she was naked and entirely at his command went by much too fast.

And yet his obvious passion and her own yielding raised her excitement to a fever pitch. Even as he took her, she wanted to give more. The faster he moved inside her, the faster she wanted him to move.

There was a little twinge at first. She was glad of it, glad she was a woman now. Mason's wife.

The muscles bulged on his arms as he held himself over her. She scarcely dared looked down to where he possessed her. She didn't know where to look. She only wanted to feel him, swelling inside her.

His big masculinity moved with the raw ferocity of the storm. He had become a force of nature, demanding all the wildness inside her.

Lightning flared through her body as he rocked back and forth. He wouldn't let her stop, wouldn't let her think. There was nothing in the world but this wondrous, exploding joy.

Gina heard him cry out hoarsely. Then she lost all awareness of anything except a peak of pure white light.

MASON LAY SPENT beside his wife. He could hear Gina's breaths come in shuddering gulps.

What had he done? He'd taken this delicate, trusting woman on this hard ground, with as much subtlety as a bull.

He'd always feared that this violence inside him might someday slip its leash and hurt someone he loved. And there could be no deeper way to hurt a woman than to violate her heart and her body at the same time.

Few things truly frightened Mason. But he was afraid as, very carefully, he lifted himself to look at his wife.

She lay on her side, facing away from him. Lightning flared and, by its glare, he saw the bruises on her back, traces of dark red where he'd pressed her against the thin blanket laid over rocky ground. From their angry shade, he guessed that they would quickly turn to black and blue.

A knot of regret tightened inside Mason. At the very moment when he should have introduced Gina tenderly to the beauty of lovemaking, he'd assaulted and bruised her.

He should never have brought this woman to the Blackstone Bar. He should never have exposed her to this risk.

He tried to apologize, but the words stuck in his throat. All that came out was a cough.

"Mason." Stiffly, she sat up. He could see how much pain the movement caused her. "I—I wanted to tell you that Stuart called. He and Marge are backing down. He said he'd draw up the adoption papers tomorrow."

"Is that why you came?"

"And—there's a fence break along the road. Cattle got out. It could be dangerous…"

He didn't wait for her to finish. He knew the threat this posed to the church van or any other vehicle that came by.

Cursing his own clumsiness in the semidark, Mason found his shirt and jacket. The rest of the clothing, he discovered, was still on him, down around his ankles.

He hadn't even had the decency to take off his boots when he made love to Gina. The discovery of his own heedlessness added to his shame.

"The storm's letting up." He kept his face averted. "Let me make sure there's no more funnel clouds, and then we can go."

He left her alone to find her own clothing.

Chapter Sixteen

Gina didn't know where she'd gone wrong. It was obvious she'd made Mason angry, but what had she done?

He'd made love to her on impulse. Maybe he was angry at himself for doing something he hadn't meant to do.

Maybe he had been looking forward to ending their marriage. Now that Stuart and Margaret no longer sought custody of the girls, he might not want to complicate matters.

Tears pricked her eyes. This time, they sprang from emotions far more painful than fear.

She'd given Mason everything. And she'd loved having him inside her, loved the fierceness of the man's unleashed desires. In spite of everything, she believed they belonged together.

Her whole body felt sore. She hadn't been aware of the hardness of the ground while they were lost in passion, but now her muscles ached. Still, the ache inside, and the emptiness, were infinitely greater.

It was hard to find her garments in the dark, and her fingers fumbled with the back of the bra three times before she got it hooked. She'd never felt so clumsy before.

Gina kept her distance from Mason. She didn't want him to see her tears, and she didn't want to risk an argument. If he regretted what had been the most magnificent moment of her life, there was nothing left for them to talk about.

When she was fully covered, with the rain slicker in place, she looked around and spotted him leading both horses toward the edge of the outcropping. "What on earth possessed you to ride this mare?" he asked gruffly.

Of all the subjects he might have chosen to dispute, this was the last one she would have expected. "The mare I usually ride is too placid. I knew Darter would do a good job."

"You saddled her yourself?"

"Paul helped," she said. "He got hurt when the Jeep hit a pothole. His injuries may not be serious, but I didn't consider it safe for him to ride."

Mason drew the animals into the drizzle. "He should have stopped you."

"He tried," she said, following him. "I pulled rank. What have you got against Darter, anyway?"

"She's vicious." He stood frowning at the mare, who appeared completely docile. "I've seen her try to kick Jennifer."

"Recently?" As he held the reins, Gina swung into the saddle, and immediately winced. She was sore in more places than her back, she realized.

"A few weeks ago." He scowled at her involuntary flinch. What did the man expect? No doubt he would have preferred a cowgirl who had calluses on every key point of her anatomy, but Gina was doing her best.

"Jennifer's been working with her," she said. "She rides her every day."

He handed her the reins and swung onto his own horse. "And you think that's a good idea? I saw how she was limping at the barbecue."

"That wasn't from Darter," Gina said. "Jennifer was helping me put away figurines and she banged her leg on the china cabinet."

"I didn't know knickknacks could be so dangerous," he muttered, and clucked his horse to a fast walk.

They returned home through a landscape startlingly altered. Trees lay upended, their roots torn from the ground. Small ponds had formed where impromptu dams of branches and debris blocked rivulets of water. A fence, ripped loose, draped jauntily atop a stump.

The farther they went, the more Gina's thoughts flew ahead to the twins. Surely they hadn't been harmed in the underground shelter, but she wouldn't feel easy until she saw them for herself.

Mason rode ahead, not speaking. She tried not to read too much into his silence. No doubt he, too, was consumed with anxiety over the fate of the ranch and its occupants.

The trail straightened as it neared the barns and houses. The first thing Gina saw was the equipment shop, or, rather, what used to be the equipment shop.

Glass and wood lay strewn across the ground. The building itself had been demolished down to the foundation.

Beyond it, one end of the farm vehicle garage had been torn open, providing a cutaway view of an untouched tractor. As for the largest corral and the cattle chutes, only scraps of lumber and bits of metal remained.

Darter slowed as they topped a grassy mound. From here, Gina could see the capricious damage the tornado had wrought on the rest of the complex.

The two smaller corrals and the two barns stood with no trace of damage. To her immense relief, the big house and Mason's office were also intact, although, behind them, a windmill had been tipped on its side.

Downhill to the left, three of the four houses remained standing, although Bart's had lost a section of roof. The fourth house, the one that used to be Rance and Amy's, lay smashed as if a giant had stomped on it.

She came alongside Mason, who sat motionless, surveying his property. "Relatively speaking, I suppose we were lucky," he said tightly.

"Do you have insurance?"

"So to speak." After a moment, he clarified the enigmatic remark by adding, "There's a big deductible. We might get enough money to cover the materials, but we'll have to rebuild everything ourselves."

A couple of shouts made them both turn toward the big house. Calling their names, Ed, Linda and Kevin waved from the driveway.

Mason kneed his horse uphill. Gina followed, pleased to see that the Whitlaw family had returned safely.

Ed and his wife met them at the barn. "Our van just missed hitting a cow," Linda said. "We picked up Bart, and then we caught sight of that twister. It was huge!"

"You should have seen us all crammed into the shelter," added her husband. "Reverend Farkas and his wife, Abner and Bess Millet and the rest of the choir. We were practically sitting on each others' laps. They left just a few minutes ago."

"The babies are fine," Linda added. "Jennifer's helping Bonita feed them."

"The power went out, but I got the generator going," Ed added. "We have our work cut out for us."

"I noticed," Mason said.

Amid the excited talk, and their reunion a few minutes later with the babies, no one noticed the tension between

Mason and Gina. Maybe she'd imagined it, she told herself.

She hoped so.

MASON TOOK A LONG TIME in the bedroom getting cleaned up, remaining there long after Gina had rejoined the others in the kitchen. An hour later, when he and the other men had gone outside to repair the fence along the road, she discovered what he'd been doing.

He'd moved all her clothes back into the guest room. Her toiletries, including her toothbrush, had been transferred to the hall bathroom.

Gina sat on the guest bed, her heart pounding. The man had declared his intention to keep apart from her in a way that brooked no doubt. He hadn't even given her a chance to discuss their future.

He couldn't have rejected her more plainly if he'd stood up in front of the entire ranch family and declared that their marriage was over. She'd been trying to prepare herself for a letdown like this ever since their wedding. Even so, it came as a stunning blow.

Why didn't he want her to stay? He'd held Gina through the storm as if he cared about her. The two of them had made love, and he'd enjoyed it. Then, abruptly, he'd changed.

Did she dare to ask him why? It went against Gina's upbringing to force a confrontation. In her family, people had communicated indirectly, waiting for the right moment to give someone a hint.

That system had worked because they all subscribed to it. And because they loved each other enough to stick things out. It wouldn't work now.

She and Mason needed to talk. Surely she could find a moment to bring up the subject when Bonita wasn't around, and when her husband wasn't rushing off to his chores.

Across the hall, one of the babies began to cry. They'd been fussy ever since Gina left the shelter, Nana had told her.

She hurried across the hall. It would be hours before Mason came home for dinner, and in the meantime there was no point in brooding.

RANCE'S HOUSE WAS a total loss. Ed and Bart, standing in front of it, shook their heads in almost the same rhythm.

"I'll get started clearing that glass and stuff," Bart said at last. "Okay, Mason?"

"Sure thing." Yesterday, they'd stayed out late fixing the pasture fence and bringing in the strayed cattle. Today they needed to finish surveying the buildings and animals, remove debris and order replacement materials so they could begin rebuilding.

They had a lot of work to do, and a limited amount of time in which to do it. As soon as the fields dried out, there would be hay to mow and bale for the winter. Starting next month, they needed to plant winter wheat, supervise the fall calving, wean the spring calves and prepare cattle for the annual auction.

This ranch was Mason's life, as it had been his father's before him. And Rance's. For their sakes, he wouldn't rest until he'd restored everything to peak condition.

Rebelliously, his thoughts strayed to Gina and those precious moments in her arms. It hurt to look back and admit the harm he'd done. The knowledge that he had to stay away from her burned worse than any prairie fire.

He would do what was right. That was the only way Mason knew how to behave.

ON TUESDAY, the proofs for the wedding pictures arrived in the mail, with a note from Megan Maitland. "Aren't these lovely? I hear you're bringing the girls on Friday to see Dr. Rogers. If you'd like, drop the proofs at my office and I'll order whatever you want."

Gina wasn't sure she could bear to look at the sheets filled with color images. She'd had so many hopes and dreams on that magical day, and now they were shattering, one by one.

Both Sunday and again last night, she'd fallen asleep before Mason got home, and he'd left so early this morning that she'd missed him. According to Bonita, he packed both lunch and dinner. "That man will work himself to death," the housekeeper had said with rueful admiration.

No man was so busy he couldn't stop to say hello to his wife, Gina thought. Not unless he was avoiding her.

In the den, she put the girls on a blanket to play while she sat on the couch. Already, Lily was trying to push up on her knees to crawl. So far, her efforts usually ended with a plop onto her chest or, occasionally, forward onto her nose.

Daisy kept rolling from her tummy to her back, and sometimes over to her stomach again. Other times she would get stuck, unable to complete the turn, and wail for help.

Through the rear window, Gina had a view of the garden, where she and Bonita had reerected the wind-flattened tomato trellises. Sunlight streamed over the pond and, high on the hill, the battered but proud rose garden.

She forced herself to turn her attention to the proof sheets. As she viewed them, she remembered the chubby photographer who'd reminded her of a cheerful gnome. It made the viewing a little less difficult.

The first group of shots showed Katie in her lavender

dress, beaming as she adjusted the bride's hat. Gina smiled at the sight of her own borrowed gown, sweetly reminiscent of an earlier era. She decided she looked a bit old-fashioned herself, with her straight blond hair and tremulous expression.

That uncertainty reflected the fact that she hadn't known what to expect from marriage, or from a man. Especially a man like Mason.

If she could make the same choice again, would she? Gina knew the answer even as she framed the question. Of course. She would never give up this time with him, or with the girls.

The photographer had caught many of the clinic staff dressed in their best. At the time, Gina had been too preoccupied to notice most of her guests. She would like to have prints of these, to remember them by as they'd looked on that special day.

There was Megan Maitland in a dark-blue suit, standing between her daughters Elly and Abby. And here was Gina on Ford Carrington's arm. Goodness, what a dreamy look on her face! Anyone would have thought she was marrying for love.

Well, she had been, even if she hadn't known it yet. On the next page of proofs, Mason stood proudly beside Ed. At the time, Gina hadn't known the ranch foreman and had had to guess at his identity. She could hardly believe that had been a mere three weeks ago.

Neither man was entirely at home in a tuxedo, she mused fondly. With his height and self-possession, Mason could pull anything off, but she preferred him in jeans and cowboy boots. Or out of them.

Her body tingled with forbidden memories. Last night, she'd ached for him in a way she'd never experienced before. How had she lived so long in ignorance? And how was she going to go on living without someone she needed so badly?

Surely he felt it, too. Men couldn't be that different from women, or at least she didn't think so. It must be exhaustion that was keeping his feelings at bay. Surely the two of them could work things out.

On the floor, Daisy squalled for help. Gina glanced over to see the baby stuck on her back, waving her arms and legs angrily.

No sooner had she righted the little girl than Kevin Whitlaw ambled in, apologetically holding out a bloody hand. He'd cut it clearing some glass, and his mother had insisted he ask Gina to look at it.

"She says we're lucky to have a nurse on the ranch and we shouldn't risk infection," he said. "Do you mind?"

"Of course not." Briskly, Gina put the proofs away and went to get her first aid kit.

SHE FINISHED FILLING OUT the order form on Thursday morning. Despite the pain of knowing what lay beneath the surface of this unlikely wedding, she wanted the pictures to treasure always. Maybe she would never be able to view them without a sheen of tears, but still, they belonged in her heart.

A short time later, the mail arrived, and with it a thick packet from Stuart's law firm. Scarcely daring to breathe, Gina opened it.

There were forms for her and Mason to fill out, along with a letter. Stuart assured them that, once they'd talked it over, he and his wife had agreed without reservation that the girls would fare best with Mason and Gina.

Of course, he wrote, there would be some formalities to undergo before the adoption would become final.

Reading the letter, she hoped it meant that Mason would let her stay on the ranch for another month or so.

He'd become virtually a ghost figure since Sunday. But surely even he couldn't bury himself in work for that long.

BY THURSDAY AFTERNOON, even Mason's callused hands were blistered, and a hard knot had formed between his shoulder blades. He couldn't keep working at this pace without risking serious injury.

To add to his misery, he wasn't sleeping well. Drained by physical labor, he would drop off instantly at bedtime, only to awake about 1:00 a.m. with an agitated need for Gina.

He missed her voice, and her smile, and the welcome in her eyes. Most of all, he missed her touch. At night, he could hardly bear the knowledge that she lay only a short distance away, and yet he didn't dare go near her.

The few times he'd glimpsed her, these past few days, she'd worn a troubled expression. Little puckers formed between her eyebrows, and once he saw tears in her eyes.

Yet she hadn't run out, although surely she'd wanted to. She was keeping her commitment to the girls.

Did she go to sleep afraid that he might disturb her? That she would awaken to a repetition of Sunday night's outburst?

He wanted to reassure her, to take her hands in his and promise that, as soon as possible, he would return her to Austin. But before he talked to her, he needed time to steel himself. He wasn't ready to give her up yet.

That evening, Mason worked on repairs until it got too dark to stay outside. Then he cleaned off his boots, went into his office and filled out insurance papers.

At last he saw the light fade in Gina's bedroom. He waited awhile longer, then went into the house.

While stripping off his boots by the front door, he spotted an envelope on the side table. Gina had taken to leaving his mail there.

The envelope bore the logo of Stuart's law firm. Pulling out the sheaf of papers, Mason read the letter with mingled relief and sadness.

He had won. More fairly, Gina had won. As he'd always believed, his sister and her husband didn't really want to raise two babies, and she'd made them face the truth.

As he set the letter down, Mason's attention fell on a sheet of paper bearing a note in Gina's handwriting. It said, "Don't forget the girls' appointment with Dr. Rogers tomorrow at 10:00 a.m."

That meant they'd be driving into Austin together. After dodging her all week, he found that he was suddenly eager for the chance to talk.

Maybe they could begin again. If he promised to rein in his impatience and show her the gentleness she needed, maybe she would trust him one more time.

In his sock-clad feet, Mason walked soundlessly through the house. The nighttime quiet magnified every noise: the ticking of a clock, the distant hum of the refrigerator, the whimper of one of the girls as she dreamed.

He slipped into the nursery. The monitors showed a steady green. Lily slept on her back, her little face angelic.

Daisy had turned onto her stomach, pulling the monitor wire askew. The slightest additional movement would set off the alarm, so he carefully rolled the baby over.

It was intimidating to think of managing these children without Gina. He supposed Bonita and Nana might be willing to stay over occasionally, and perhaps he could pay Jennifer to sleep in the nursery sometimes, as well.

It would never be the same, though. He wanted his wife here. The girls needed her, and so did he.

In the hallway, Mason was reaching for his doorknob when a low noise caught his attention. A heartbeat later, he recognized it as a muffled sob.

A low series of shuddering noises followed. Gina was weeping into her pillow

His hands clenched against the urge to rush to her side. A visit from the man who had injured her was the last thing she needed.

Had she been going through this every night? He cursed himself for not having noticed.

He couldn't keep on making her suffer, no matter how urgently he wanted her to stay.

GINA AWOKE on Friday morning with her eyes stinging from the previous night's crying. She'd sat up reading, hoping to hear Mason come in, until weariness made her turn off the light.

Disappointment had rushed over her. She missed him so much. It was the fourth night since they'd made love, and not once had he spoken to her, let alone held her or given any sign of affection.

To herself, she'd made excuses, but last night she'd run out of them. Desolation had reduced her to tears.

Yet this morning she felt a sense of hope. On their trip to Austin, they would have to spend two hours together each way in the truck. She intended to ask him why he'd withdrawn from her. And to tell him how much she loved him.

It was nearly seven o'clock, and they would have to leave by eight. Gina went to get ready.

Half an hour later, she had showered and dressed. Nana

and Bonita waved to her from the nursery, where they were dressing the girls in pretty green jumpers.

In the kitchen, she paused to drink in the sight of Mason finishing his breakfast. He hadn't noticed her yet, and her gaze lingered on his muscular frame and the proud way he held himself.

He was more of a man than anyone she'd ever met before, or ever hoped to meet again. She thought about touching him, and a thrill ran through her.

Then he glanced up. The coldness of his expression doused her good spirits.

"Mason?" she said. "What's wrong?"

He dropped his napkin on the table and stood up. "As soon as you finish eating, pack your suitcase," he said. "It looks like you can stay in Austin."

She could hardly breathe. His tone was so abrupt and so final. "But—"

"I'll send your other things later." He gazed past her, as if it pained him to look at her. "We can tell people you have business affairs to straighten out."

"The adoption—"

"We'll do whatever we have to do. No one here is going to shoot their mouth off to my sister." Still without meeting her eyes, he went out.

Gina stood there in shock. She couldn't even find the words to call after him.

MASON FASTENED the two safety carriers into the pickup's rear seat. He jammed his thumb into a buckle, and had barely finished muttering an oath before he squished one finger beneath the heavy carrier and came up with an even more colorful choice of words.

It had taken all his self-control, there in the kitchen, to

do what had to be done. He'd given Gina what she needed. It was the least he owed her.

He could still hear the echo of those helpless, wracking sobs. Only later in the night had he realized why they disturbed him so deeply.

His mother had cried that way once, when he was nine or ten. His father had gone to a cattle auction, leaving her alone on the ranch for a week. She must have felt as desperately lonely and isolated as Gina did.

He refused to repeat the mistakes of the past. For the rest of his life, he would never love anyone the way he loved Gina.

But he wouldn't try to keep her here. He wouldn't let the harshness of the ranch, and the hardness within himself, suck away her life.

THE FIRST HOUR in the truck, the two of them sat side by side with the radio chattering into the silence. Stunned, Gina couldn't even think how to begin a conversation.

She'd crammed her clothes into a suitcase without paying attention to what she was doing. She'd probably left half her stuff behind, and she didn't care.

To Bonita's startled questions, she'd muttered something about seeing old friends. She couldn't figure out any other plausible excuse. What kind of business affairs would require her to stay in town over a weekend, let alone permanently?

Thank goodness Mason himself had packed the girls' diaper bag. If Gina had to handle those dear, familiar baby items, she knew she'd burst into tears.

She felt as if she were abandoning Lily and Daisy. Surely Mason could understand that, even if he didn't want her around. Yet it was his ranch, and these were his nieces. Gina couldn't fight him.

Still, she had to say something. Once they reached Austin, it would be too late.

"How are the twins going to get along?" She hoped he didn't hear the catch in her voice.

"Things are slowing down while we wait for the supplies to arrive." He kept his focus on the road. "I'll make a point of getting home by the time Bonita leaves. And I'm going to order cellular phones, so I'll always be reachable."

"Are you angry with me?" Gina asked.

"Of course not." He leaned over and turned up the volume on the radio.

"Then why—"

"We'll be fine." His tone was gruff and impersonal. "Don't worry about the girls. Or anything."

Country music thumped through the truck cab so loudly that her teeth ached. *I don't want to cry. I don't want to break down in front of him.*

"I know this is what we agreed on," she said tautly. "Still—"

"It isn't your responsibility anymore," he answered, barely audible over the amplified twanging of a guitar. "Give it a rest, Gina."

She sank back, her body rigid with self-imposed discipline. He'd left her no opening to slip through, no chance of reconciliation.

Their marriage was over.

Chapter Seventeen

Gina wasn't sure how she managed to maintain her composure during the babies' checkup. Dr. Rogers glanced at her curiously a couple of times, but he misinterpreted the source of the problem.

"You should cut the number of night feedings to one," he said. "You both look like you could use more sleep."

She nodded, and tried not to think about the fact that she wouldn't be the one feeding Lily and Daisy any longer.

The babies were progressing so well, the doctor continued, that they no longer needed monitors. "You've both done a wonderful job," he said.

"You don't think they'll have any residual problems because of their prematurity?" Mason asked.

"Not at all," the doctor said. "In fact, with such a loving environment, they should continue to do exceptionally well."

He shook hands with them and recommended that the girls be brought back in a month. After he left, a nurse came in to administer vaccinations, and then Mason made a new appointment.

Gina held each little girl longer than necessary as she changed and dressed them. "I love you," she whispered to Daisy while Mason was out of the room. She would have repeated the words to Lily, but tears rose too close to the surface.

When they were out in the corridor, Mason said briskly, "Where should I take you?"

She didn't know how to answer, until she remembered Mrs. Parker's comment about not renting her room right away. "My old boardinghouse, I guess."

They were outside before Gina recalled that she needed to drop off the proofs in Megan Maitland's office. The irony of ordering wedding pictures was almost too great, and for a moment she considered not returning the form. But she did want the photographs, in spite of everything."

"Wait here," she said. "I'll be right back."

She ducked through the lobby into Megan's office. There was no one sitting at the secretary's desk, so she left the envelope in the In basket.

In the lobby, she caught sight of Katie Toper, whose face brightened. "Gina! Happy birthday!"

"It's not till…" She'd almost forgotten the special occasion looming before her, until now. "Not until tomorrow."

"Send me a slice of birthday cake, okay?" Katie said. "I slept with your wedding cake under my pillow, which is supposed to make me dream about the man I'm going to marry. So guess who I dreamed about?"

"That's kind of a tough one," Gina teased, enjoying the banter in spite of herself.

"Yeah, the good doctor himself." Katie sighed. "So much for relying on superstitions. I'm about as likely to marry Ford as to get chosen Miss America. I wonder what happens when you sleep on birthday cake."

"You get icing in your hair." Gina was considering telling Katie that she'd be in town tomorrow, so they could celebrate in person, when her friend gave a little wave and headed off, saying that duty called.

Soon she, too, would be returning to work, Gina reflected. She'd always loved nursing, yet now she dreaded the prospect of trying to fit into her old routine. She wasn't the same person she'd been.

Outside, she was still smiling over the image of Katie literally sleeping on a piece of birthday cake. Then Mason, who had been gazing fondly down at his nieces in the baby carriage, looked up and his expression darkened.

Apparently he couldn't wait to drop her off.

HE SAW THE SMILE on her face, and how it disappeared at the sight of him. He hoped she'd be smiling a lot more now that she was home.

At the boardinghouse, her landlady looked puzzled, but accepted her return without comment. Fortunately, the room was still available. Since he doubted Gina would have any trouble getting her job back, at least she would be able to resume her old life with minimal disruption.

As he left, Mason felt more lost than he had since his mother's death when he was twelve. The grief over his brother and sister-in-law's deaths had been tempered by the need to take action: to make sure their daughters survived, to keep the ranch going. Now an abyss opened inside him.

He'd accomplished his mission, hadn't he? The girls were his, or soon would be. Even the tornado damage, while daunting, wasn't severe enough to threaten the ranch.

Even so, the world had gone gray. He had to force himself to put the truck in gear and head back to the Blackstone Bar.

Mason glanced into the back seat. Daisy was sleeping, her cheeks a healthy pink. Lily stared out the window with a solemn expression. They were fine. Motherless, but fine.

The whole way home, he was dogged by a sense of

having forgotten something. Once he patted his wallet to assure himself he hadn't left it at the doctor's office.

Of course, he knew what it was that he missed. But he couldn't go back for Gina. She was where she belonged.

At the big house, Bonita came out to help him unload the pickup. She registered Gina's absence without comment, so she must have been prepared.

"I've got work to do," he said as soon as the babies were inside. "I'll be home by five."

"If you'd been home by five all week..." She stopped herself. "Never mind."

If he'd been home more this week, she thought Gina would have stayed. It was just as well she'd jumped to that conclusion. She might as well blame him, because he was at fault for Gina's departure, only not in the way she assumed.

He changed into work boots and went outside. In the corral, Jennifer held one end of a long rope while a horse he didn't recognize circled her at a fast walk.

Mason leaned on the fence next to Ed, who was watching his daughter. "Whose horse is that?"

"Will Bonney brought him over," he said, naming the neighboring rancher. "Blaze Boy has some bad habits, but he's a fine animal. Will's paying well for the training."

"Jennifer shouldn't count on the money for a living," Mason said. "There won't be much to do here once we sell off the breeding stock."

In the corral, the girl called out, "Trot!" and snapped a whip against the ground for emphasis. Startled, the horse broke into the requested gait.

Some owners still believed in "breaking" horses by throwing a saddle on them and riding a bucking bronco until it gave in. That could destroy the animal's spirit, and it certainly didn't result in a reliable, disciplined work partner.

Jennifer was teaching this horse with patience instead of brutality. Already, Mason could see, it was responding to voice commands. "She's good," he conceded.

"She's darn good," corrected his foreman. "Listen, I want to talk to you about the horses."

The project had been Rance's dream, and it hurt Mason even to think about continuing. Still, Ed deserved a fair hearing. "Shoot."

"Paul came over last night," he said. "He and Jennifer are planning to get married when she turns eighteen in October."

"They make a nice couple." The news didn't exactly come as a surprise.

"Paul's going to ask you to let him rebuild Rance's house. He'll do the work himself if you'll provide the materials," Ed said.

"Fair enough," Mason said. "I've got no troubles with them living there."

"And I'm asking you as a personal favor not to sell the horses," Ed said. "Give the kids a couple of years to show what they can do."

Mason shook his head. "It's never going to be a big money maker, and I've got enough responsibilities."

"You wouldn't have to be responsible," his cousin said. "They will."

Lifting his hat, Mason wiped his forehead. In midafternoon, the August day was hot even here in the partial shade of the barn. "They may do the physical work, but there's more to running a ranch than that. You know that, Ed. There's feed to order, farrier and vet bills to pay, insurance, you name it."

Folding his arms, his cousin met his gaze squarely.

"I've never gone against you, Mason. But I've got a few choice words I'd like to say if you don't mind."

"Nobody's stopping you," he said, and waited while Ed collected himself.

At forty-two, the foreman was eight years Mason's senior. He, and earlier his parents, had lived here as long as Mason could remember.

The men were second cousins, and the differences in their economic stations went back to their grandfathers, who had been brothers. Mason's had saved his money and invested in the Blackstone Bar. Ed's had enjoyed the life of a traveling cowboy before settling down in middle age.

Ed had never showed any sign of resenting playing second fiddle to his younger cousin. He'd admitted once that he didn't relish taking risks, or he'd have found a way to buy his own ranch by now. Mason was glad he'd stuck around. He relied on Ed, sometimes more than he realized.

Lines formed along the man's weathered forehead as he weighed his words. "Ever since Rance died, you've been plunging ahead like a stampeding bull. Sometimes I get the feeling you're whipping yourself and the rest of us as hard as you can because you're afraid if you don't keep a tight rein on everything, it'll all fall apart."

"It nearly did," Mason said.

The foreman shook his head. "You gotta ease up. A ranch isn't just a business, it's a way of life. At least wait a year before you sell the horses. Otherwise Paul and Jennifer may decide to pull up stakes, and I don't think that would be good for the Blackstone Bar. Or for any of us on the ranch."

It hadn't occurred to Mason that the young couple might leave. They belonged here.

"I'll think it over," he said.

Ed nodded and moved away. Mason took one more look at Jennifer, who was leading the horse into the barn, and decided he'd wasted enough time for one day. There was work to do.

GINA COULDN'T BRING herself to admit the whole truth to Mrs. Parker—that the marriage had been a sham from the beginning. She did have to confess the obvious fact that they were separating.

"I don't know what went wrong," she admitted, sitting in the cozy front room of the boardinghouse. "He just withdrew since the tornado. Then today he ordered me to pack a suitcase."

The landlady poured them each a cup of Earl Grey tea. "He strikes me as a man who holds his emotions inside."

"That's for sure," Gina admitted. It was strange to be back here. The light was too hazy, the spaces too small, the street noises too loud. In only three weeks, the ranch had become her natural habitat.

"Also, he lost his loved ones a few months ago," the woman pointed out. "Perhaps he married too quickly. I saw in his face that he loves you, Gina. He might be overwhelmed by so many demands, so soon."

"I tried not to make any," she said miserably.

"He's a man who takes others' burdens on his shoulders, whether they ask him to or not." She passed a cup to Gina. "He must have reached his limit."

"You may be right." She emptied a packet of artificial sweetener into her tea. "So what should I do?"

"There's no need to get your job back this instant, is there?" asked Mrs. Parker.

"I've got some savings," she admitted. "Anyway, I'm not ready to go to work."

"Then don't. Give yourself a week or so to think."

"I—I guess I will."

At dinner, Gina could hardly eat. That night, she tried

to talk herself into going out for coffee and to hear a country band, but she couldn't muster the energy.

She wondered how the twins were doing, and whether they were restless without her. Did Mason miss her? What had he told the others on the ranch about her departure?

In her room, she watched late-night television, scarcely noticing what program was on. For want of anything else to do, she resumed work on the sweater for Mason. It had gone faster than she'd expected, and the last piece was almost finished.

The front, back and sleeves would have to be sewn together, and the whole sweater lightly steamed and ironed. She supposed she could send it to him for Christmas.

At a few minutes before midnight, Gina was still awake, half dozing in her nightgown. She glanced toward the bedside table where her antique-style clock used to sit, and realized she'd forgotten to pack it this morning. It was still in the guest room at the Blackstone Bar.

On her watch, the hands neared midnight. One little tick, and she made the transition from her twenties to her thirties.

"Happy birthday, Gina," she said to the empty room.

THAT NIGHT, Mason tossed and turned half the night. The babies were edgy, too.

Sitting in their room at 2:00 a.m., feeding Lily, he could hardly bear the loneliness. Gina's essence permeated the air, the babies' blankets and his heart.

How long would it take before everything in the house no longer reminded him of his wife? How long before this sharp pain wore down to a dull ache?

The gut-wrenching loss of his brother hadn't faded, that was for sure. Mason had been determined not to yield to his grief, just as he was determined now not to break down and admit how much he needed his wife.

He recalled what Ed had said that afternoon. *"You're afraid if you don't keep a tight rein on everything, it'll all fall apart."*

Sorrow couldn't be buried in a grave. It had to run its course. He supposed he could start, tomorrow morning, by visiting the rose garden his mother had loved and where Rance and Amy had said their wedding vows.

He hadn't been up there in months.

ON THE MORNING of her thirtieth birthday, Gina awoke with the vague understanding that she needed to take charge of her life. But how?

She tried on three outfits and chose an A-line dress. It suited her more adult image, a dress that meant business but didn't mind mixing in a little pleasure. Still, she had no idea why she chose to wear it.

Before putting it on, she washed her hair, blow-dried it and clipped it with gold barrettes. On impulse, she stuck the pieces of Mason's sweater into her purse before she went down to breakfast.

While the other residents ate their bacon and eggs, Gina nibbled at her toast and longed for her husband.

He would come marching through the boardinghouse to the dining room. In front of everyone, he'd stand there and declare that he hadn't known how much he loved her until she was gone.

Then he would sweep her into his arms and out of the house. Like a groom, he would carry his bride across the threshold, except in reverse.

It was, after all, her lifelong fantasy. The princess in the tower would be rescued by the man she loved....

"You can take my car," Mrs. Parker said.

Gina snapped out of her daydream. "Excuse me?" The

three other boarders, she saw, had left for work, and only the two of them were at the table.

"You're dressed up and you brought your purse downstairs," said her landlady. "I already know you're not planning to apply for work today, so I figured you're going to the ranch."

"I am?" Gina said.

The prospect stirred fear in the pit of her stomach. Mason had already rejected her once. Did she really want to force him to do it again?

Of course, she had an excuse for a visit: the sweater. It might be more plausible if she waited to give it to him until she'd stitched it together, but by then she might lose her nerve.

On this, her thirtieth birthday, Gina intended to get a grip on the future, didn't she? And Mrs. Parker was, once again, willing to play fairy godmother. She'd already provided the gown, and now she was offering the carriage, so to speak.

"I don't know what I'm going to say," Gina admitted.

"You could start with 'I love you,'" advised her landlady.

"What if he orders me to leave?"

"That's the risk you run," she said.

The fairy godmother wasn't going to make it easy for her and neither was the prince, Gina could see. But life on a ranch could be tough. If she expected Mason to accept her as his wife, she needed to show that she was made of stern stuff.

A short time later, she found herself in the car, heading northwest. She'd found Horseshoe Bend on a map, which lay open on the seat beside her.

As she drove past ranches, through the window drifted the familiar scents of native plants and cattle. She saw a few broken trees and fallen fences, reminders of last weekend's storm.

The closer she got, the more butterflies surged in her stomach. Soon they turned into sparrows, and then hawks.

There wasn't much traffic on a Saturday afternoon. Maybe that was why, a few miles short of Horseshoe Bend, Gina noticed the pickup truck headed toward her from the opposite direction.

It was the same blue-green as Mason's. As she passed it, she noted that it, too, had an extended cab and a silvery cover on the bed.

She barely glimpsed the man behind the wheel, but the impact knocked the air out of her lungs. That cowboy hat. Those powerful shoulders. If he wasn't Mason, the man must be his secret twin brother.

Ahead, Gina spotted a rest area half-hidden among mesquite trees. She pulled into it and stopped, trying to sort out her jumbled impressions.

Mason might conceivably drive into town on a Saturday, but she could think of no reason for him to drive past it. Unless he was heading to Austin…

He wasn't, of course. That was her own wishful thinking getting the better of her.

The driver's Stetson had fooled her. He probably didn't look like Mason at all. She ought to continue on to the Blackstone Bar, as planned.

It took a minute to turn around on the heavily rutted ground. As Gina waited to pull out, a truck stopped on the road, blocking her exit.

Why wouldn't the man let her out? Seeing no alternative, she backed down to let him into the rest area.

The truck bumped off the pavement and nosed toward her. With a jolt, she saw that her mind hadn't been playing tricks, after all. It *was* Mason at the wheel.

Gina's heart thumped wildly. Her hands were so damp

that, after switching off the engine, she had to try twice to get her door open. Then, remembering her weak excuse for coming, she hooked her purse over her shoulder.

Mason stood by the truck, his hat in one hand. In the other, he clutched a bouquet of roses.

"I was bringing you these," he said. "I did promise you fresh flowers every day."

Gingerly, Gina took the bouquet. From the lush red and pink roses floated a sweet, dark scent. "They're beautiful."

"I went to the rose garden this morning." His voice was thick with emotion. "I hadn't been there since Rance died."

"It must have been difficult."

"I thought it would be," he said. "Instead, it made me feel closer to them. Somehow I...knew they wanted to put their arms around me and tell me they're fine."

Gina's vision blurred with unshed tears. She'd received a similar impression once while visiting her parents' graves.

Mason turned the hat brim in his hands. "I missed you so much, I couldn't resist bringing you these flowers. Besides, I wanted to make sure you were all right."

She remembered Mrs. Parker's advice. It was now or never. "I love you," she said.

The words hung in the warm August air. Nearby, a fly buzzed about its business. Across the fields, a tractor started.

"Does that mean you forgive me?" Mason said.

"For what?"

He stared at her in surprise. "For hurting you. I meant the roses as a kind of apology. I realized I owed you that, at the very least."

"I'm lost," she said. "What are you apologizing for?"

His mouth twisted. "For last Sunday. At Saucer Rock."

"You didn't hurt me at Saucer Rock," Gina said.

Mason frowned. "I saw the bruises. All over your back. I behaved like a brute."

"That's why you withdrew?" She couldn't believe the reason was so simple, and so wrongheaded. "That's why you stayed away from me all week?"

"What I did was unforgivable." Yet in his glowing eyes, she saw hope dawning. "I was rough and selfish. You're such a fragile woman, Gina, like a china doll. Sometimes I'm afraid you'll break if I touch you."

"Mason, I didn't even notice the bruises until later," she said. "If you'd hurt me in anger, that *would* be unforgivable. Instead, we both got carried away by our passion. Couldn't you tell I was enjoying it?"

"I thought so at the time," he said. "Then afterward, I didn't trust my own instincts."

"You have wonderful instincts," she said. "You should listen to them more."

"This might be a good time to start." And then he did the one thing that no self-respecting rancher ought to do. He dumped his hat right in the dirt.

That was how he freed his arms to grab her. Gina meant to hold on to the roses but she lost them, too, along with her purse and her self-control.

She threw her arms around Mason and kissed him. He surrounded her, his mouth on hers, his hands gripping her hips, his body molding itself to her smaller shape.

"I wish I could make love to you right now," he whispered close to her ear.

"Where's a tornado when you need one?" she asked.

He started to laugh. Then he choked a little, as if he were crying, too. Startled, Gina discovered she had tears running down her cheeks.

"Maybe we could do it again," Mason said when he had recovered.

"I certainly hope so!"

He chuckled. "I mean, get married. A private cere-mony, just the two of us, saying our vows in the rose garden."

"I'd like that," Gina murmured. "Because this time we'll really mean it. Forever."

A tractor-trailer rattled by on the road, and, self-consciously, the two of them separated. Mason dusted off his hat. Gina did the same to the roses and her purse.

"I guess you borrowed that car," he said. "I'll follow you back to Austin to return it, and pick up whatever you've left behind."

"Thanks," she said. "Maybe we can go out for lunch while we're there. Today's my thirtieth birthday."

"I wish I'd known. I'd have bought you a present." Mason beamed down at her.

"I'm doing things backward this year," Gina told him. "I decided to give *you* a present instead." From her purse, she took out the knitted pieces. They looked a bit odd, she supposed. By itself, a flat sleeve didn't bear much resemblance to the sleeve of a sweater.

"Mind if I ask what it is?" he said.

"It's a sweater." She sighed. "The pieces are done. I just need to sew them together."

"That sounds like what we're doing with our marriage. Stitching together the pieces that are already made." Mason picked up the colorful front and held it against his chest. "Looks like a perfect fit."

"I hope so. I'm looking forward to putting it on you." She gave him a mischievous grin. "And to taking it off you, too."

"The sooner the better." He gathered her close, his grip tightening as if he never meant to let her go.

All in all, Gina decided, this was absolutely the best thirtieth birthday a woman could have.

And it wasn't over yet.

For an exclusive peek at the new Harlequin 12-book continuity,

MAITLAND MATERNITY,

please turn the page....

CHAPTER ONE

DR. ABBY MAITLAND was doing her best not to look as impatient as she felt.

Just down the hall in Maitland Maternity Clinic, patients sat in her waiting room on tasteful, blue-cushioned chairs, chosen to afford optimum comfort to women who were for the most part in an uncomfortable condition. She was booked solid without so much as a ten-minute window of breathing space. She'd come into the clinic running slightly behind and praying that no one would see fit to go into labor this morning.

That was when her mother had waylaid her.

Abby had always had difficulty saying no to her mother, not out of a sense of obligation but out of pure affection. It was hard to say no to a woman who had gone out of her way all her life to make sure that her children were happy and well cared for. Today was no different.

Abby supposed that the request to stand by her mother's side as Megan Kelly Maitland met the press this morning shouldn't have come as a surprise. Abby had been born into this goldfish-bowl existence, where almost every detail of her life, and of her family's, was periodically dissected for newsworthiness. Especially if the media were having a slow week.

These days, with tabloid journalism running rampant

on almost every cable channel and lurid headlines leaping out from every supermarket checkout counter, ''newsworthy'' was usually synonymous with scandalous.

But not in their case, thank God. The Maitlands, with their penchant for charitable donations and with the clinic her mother and late father had cofounded all those years ago, were the press's vanilla ice cream. Comforting, everpresent—but uneventful. The closest they had to a ribbon of contrasting chocolate was her younger brother, Jake, with his mysterious comings and goings and secret lifestyle.

Lucky Jake, Abby thought as she followed her mother and two of her siblings to the rear entrance. He wasn't here to go through this with them.

But wealth, Abby knew, brought certain obligations, and she was far too much her mother's daughter to turn her back on that. Although there were days when she would have loved to be given the opportunity, just to see what it felt like.

Today, for one.

Abby glanced at her watch for the third time in as many minutes. With a bit of luck, this wouldn't take too long. She absolutely hated being late.

''I don't see why you need all of us, Mother,'' she heard herself murmuring despite her good intentions.

Megan Maitland smiled as she gently pushed back a strand of Abby's dark hair that had fallen wantonly into her eyes. The same lock she had been pushing back ever since Abby had had enough hair on her head to run a brush through. A wave of nostalgia whispered through Megan. Her children had gotten so big, so independent.

Her sharp, dark blue eyes swept over her son R.J. and daughter Elly standing beside her. R.J. was the oldest of the seven, and Elly and her twin, Beth, were the youngest, with Abby in the middle. Megan wished all her children could be here today when she made the announcement. It was just a silly little press conference, she knew, and they had all promised to come to the party that was being given in honor of the clinic once the plans were finalized. But she missed her children when they weren't around. Missed the sound of their laughter, their voices.

She was as proud of them as she could be, but there were times when she longed for the old days, when they were young and she could keep them all within the reach of an embrace.

Megan blinked, silently forbidding a tear to emerge. She was becoming a foolish old woman before her time. What would William have said if he could have seen her? He would have teased her out of it, she knew, while secretly agreeing with her.

She missed him most of all.

Her smile, soft and gentle, widened as she answered Abby's question. "For moral support, darling. I need you for moral support."

R.J. shrugged. Megan knew this was eating into his precious time as president of Maitland Maternity Clinic, but he would never say no to her. Her love for him had been reciprocated from the day she and William had adopted him and his younger sister Anna after their father had deserted them. Although rightfully they could have called her Aunt Megan, she had never felt anything but maternal love for William's niece and nephew.

"Don't see why moral support should have to enter into it, Mother," R.J. muttered, looking more somber than usual. "We're just announcing that there's going to be a party celebrating the clinic's twenty-fifth anniversary. Not much moral support required for that."

A tinge of pity stirred within Megan. R.J. didn't smile nearly enough. In this past year he seemed to have become even more work oriented than ever.

Elly, her youngest, whom Megan had appointed hospital administrator, despite her tender age of twenty-five, grinned at her serious oldest brother.

"Oh, I don't know." She cheerfully disagreed. "I think facing the press requires a great deal of moral support." She exchanged glances with Abby, a bit of her childhood adoration for her older sister evident still. "I always get the feeling they're waiting for something juicy to bite into."

"That's because they are." Abby could see the trucks from the various cable channels in and around Austin, Texas, through the window that faced the rear of the clinic. "Though I am surprised that so many of them have turned out. After all, this is just a human-interest story to be buried on page twelve."

R.J. tucked his tie neatly beneath his vest. A glint of humor crossed his lips. "Page twelve? If I have to stand on the back steps of the clinic and grin at those hyenas, it better get us lines on at least page four."

Abby patted his arm affectionately. "Don't grin too hard, R.J. Your face might crack."

Though Abby had always known that R.J. and Anna were really her cousins, there had never been a dividing line between any of the Maitland children. They had all been raised with the same amount of affection, shouldering the same amount of responsibility and parental expectation. As a sister, Abby loved R.J., yet as a doctor she worried about him at times.

He pretended to shrug off her arm. "Let's get this over with."

Abby cocked her head. The noise outside the back doors had grown from a dull din to something of a roar. "Is it my imagination, or are the natives getting more restless?"

Elly frowned. "They do sound louder than usual." She looked at her older sister with a silent question.

Abby in turn glanced at her mother. Whatever it was, they'd find out soon enough. "Ready?"

The tall, regal woman beside Abby squared her shoulders. Wearing a navy-blue suit with white trim at the collar and cuffs, her soft white hair drawn into a French twist, Megan Maitland looked more like their older sister than a woman in her sixty-second year.

"As I'll ever be," Megan acknowledged.

"Then let's get this show on the road," Abby declared.

R.J. pushed open the doors before Abby had a chance to do so. But instead of the forward thrust of raised mikes, invasive cameras and intrusive reporters, they found themselves staring at the backs of heads. To a person, the reporters and camera crews were focusing their attention on something off to the side of the clinic's rear entrance.

Abby glanced at her brother, who seemed as much in the dark as any of them. "What the—?"

She edged forward. Had someone decided to stage a publicity stunt and dramatically go into labor on the clinic's back steps instead of coming inside? Maitland Maternity, established by her parents so that no woman would be forced to have her child without medical help, had somehow turned into the darling of the rich and famous as well as that of the emotionally and financially needy. And among those celebrities were some who had what Abby could only term a bizarre sense of humor.

Because it wasn't in her nature to hang back where either her family or her professional life was concerned, Abby didn't wait for her brother to take charge. Instead, she pushed her way farther through the tight throng, determined to find out what had so firmly captured the media's attention.

The next moment, Abby knew. And it was all she could do to keep her mouth from dropping open.

There was a baby on the back steps. A baby, covered with a blanket and lying in a wicker basket. Looking more closely, she saw that there was actually a piece of paper pinned to the blanket.

Abby looked around, half expecting someone to come forward and announce that this was all a stunt of some sort. Or a thoughtless prank. It had to be one or the other. This was where women came to have their babies, not leave them.

From where she stood, Megan was unable to see for herself what all the commotion was about. "Abby, what's going on?"

"It's a baby." Abby tossed the words over her shoulder to her mother.

It was as if the sound of her voice was the flag coming down at the starting gate at the Indianapolis 500. The single sentence unleashed a deafening roar as all the reporters hurled their questions toward her at once.

Abby recognized Chelsea Markum, the fast-rising report of *Tattle Today TV,* a new explore-all news program. The woman was obviously determined to reach the top of her profession and stay there. That meant being first whenever humanly possible.

Pushing her microphone into her cameraman's hand, she elbowed another reporter out of the way and reached for the baby. Slipping her hands within the basket, she triumphantly picked the baby up.

The mewling sound the infant made was all but swallowed up by the noise surrounding them. But Abby could hear it. It shot straight through to her heart and galvanized her. Her eyes narrowed as she pushed her way closer.

"And there's a note," Chelsea declared to the crowd, ripping it from the blanket.

"What's it say?" someone behind her demanded.

Excitedly, Chelsea read, "'Dear Megan Maitland. This baby is a Maitland. Please take care of him until I can again.'"

Armed with anger and indignation, Abby physically pushed a cameraman aside to reach the innocent infant, who had been turned into a sideshow attraction.

Without a single word, she took the baby from the reporter and turned away.

Like a hailstorm, questions continued to fly at her from all sides—fast, furious and callous. Abby gave no indication that she heard any of them. All she wanted to do was reach the back doors and walk through them.

Suddenly R.J. was on one side of her and Elly on the other, buffering her from the crowd and allowing her to retreat with the baby in her arms. Abby's stony expression dissolved and she smiled her relief. She saw R.J. hang back a second to pick up the basket. He looked decidedly paler to her than he had when they had walked outside.

He saw it, too, she thought. The ghostly whisper of a scandal had finally found its way to the Maitland door.

Armed with her reclaimed microphone, Chelsea shoved it into R.J.'s face. "Is the baby yours?" she demanded.

Abby bit back the urge to tell the woman what she could do with her question and where she could next put her microphone.

"Whose is it?" The question echoed over and over again from all sides. "Which one of the Maitlands is the father?"

A tall, redheaded man with a trace of mustard on his shirtfront pushed a mike at Megan. "C'mon, Mrs. Maitland, we've all got a living to make. Which of your sons is responsible for this baby?"

Megan Maitland lifted her chin regally and faced the

crowd that had been, only minutes earlier, awaiting her arrival with polite smiles and banal good wishes.

"None of them, to the best of my knowledge."

Queen Victoria couldn't have defended the realm better, Abby thought, making eye contact with her mother. But she knew the answer wouldn't satisfy anyone.

"Who are you covering for?"

"Hey, give us a break. We're not all well-off like you."

"You might as well come clean now. It'll all come out eventually."

Megan looked sharply in the direction the last question had come from, but she focused on no one, talking to the crowd in general.

"The truth usually does, if we're lucky," she agreed. "This press conference is at an end."

Turning on her heel, Megan waved Abby and Elly in before her, then followed, leaving R.J. to cover the retreat.

He did, then ushered the women into his office quickly. Caught off guard, his secretary looked startled as they entered. She raised a quizzical eyebrow at Abby before turning toward R.J.

"Don't let anyone in, Dana," he ordered. Dana began to open her mouth. "And I mean *anyone*." With that, he closed the door to his inner office. Only then did he turn to the others. Avoiding the infant, he looked directly at his mother. "Is this someone's idea of a joke?"

There was sweat on his brow, Abby realized. Her glance went from the baby to R.J. But the baby was hardly more than an infant, and no outstanding feature seemed to link them.

Nothing but the slight nervousness her brother was attempting to hide.

Abby dismissed the thought, annoyed with herself that she'd allowed the media circus outside to get to her and dignify the unthinkable with even a silent question. The baby couldn't be his. He would have admitted it long before now, if it were. R.J. was far too upstanding to shirk his responsibilities. That was one of the reasons he was so perfect to head up the clinic.

But he was human, for all that, a small voice whispered in her head, and humans had weaknesses.

There had to be another explanation. Besides, he wasn't the only brother she had, she reminded herself. R.J.'s pale color was probably due to nothing more than the shock of a scandal finally touching the family.

"A dribble glass is a joke," Megan replied quietly, struggling to make sense of the situation. The infant suddenly voiced his displeasure, and her eyes, as well as her heart, were drawn to him. "A baby isn't a joke."

Megan experienced the maternal pull she always felt at the sight of a baby. Forgetting for a moment the note, the accusations and the implications that went along with them, she took the infant from her daughter.

COMING NEXT MONTH

#837 THE BRIDE SAID, "I DID?" by Cathy Gillen Thacker
The Lockharts of Texas
Dani Lockhart didn't remember her marriage to Beau Chamberlain—
and neither did he! They had to get their memories back, and doctor's
orders were to spend every possible moment together. After all, their
baby was going to want to know how its parents had fallen in love!

#838 THE HORSEMAN'S CONVENIENT WIFE by Mindy Neff
Bachelors of Shotgun Ridge
A rugged yet gentle horse whisperer, Stony Stratton could tame the
wildest stallion, but he was no match for the fiery Texan who'd singled
him out as a daddy-to-be. Eden Williams *had* to get pregnant, and
taking the redhead to bed would be Stony's pleasure. There was just one
thing he needed her to do first, and it involved walking down the aisle....

#839 THE GROOM CAME C.O.D. by Mollie Molay
Happily Wedded After
One high-tech mishap and suddenly the whole town thought that
Melinda Carey was engaged to her high-school crush, Ben Howard.
Instead of being furious, Ben suggested that they continue the charade
for a while. But when the townspeople decided to push up the wedding
date and send the "couple" on an intimate honeymoon, how long could
they resist making the pretend situation oh-so-real?

#840 VIRGIN PROMISE by Kara Lennox
She'd always longed to be swept off her feet, and suddenly virginal
Angela Capria got her wish! It was almost as if Vic Steadman knew
exactly what she'd desired. Every touch, caress and whisper told her that
she'd finally found her white knight—now Angela just needed to find
out if Vic was interested in happily-ever-after.

Visit us at www.eHarlequin.com

CNM0700

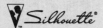

MAITLAND MATERNITY

This was the prequel to the special 12-book series Maitland Maternity, which tells the stories about the world-renowned Maitland Maternity Clinic, owned and operated by the prominent Maitland family of Austin, Texas.

If you enjoyed this book, be sure to read more about the Maitland family and the twenty-fifth anniversary of the clinic!

Maitland Maternity titles are available at your favorite retail outlet in August.

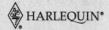

MAITLAND MATERNITY

This was the prequel to the special 12-book series Maitland Maternity, which tells the stories about the world-renowned Maitland Maternity Clinic, owned and operated by the prominent Maitland family of Austin, Texas.

If you enjoyed this book, be sure to read more about the Maitland family and the twenty-fifth anniversary of the clinic.

Maitland Maternity titles are available at your favorite retail outlet in August.

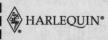
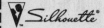

Visit us at www.eHarlequin.com   HARMMUS